I06154

Duran Kimball

The Amanuensis

A series of reading, Writing and dictation lessons - In accordance with the principles of Lindsley's takigrafy. Fourth Edition

Duran Kimball

The Amanuensis
A series of reading, Writing and dictation lessons - In accordance with the principles of Lindsley's takigrafy. Fourth Edition

ISBN/EAN: 9783337423414

Printed in Europe, USA, Canada, Australia, Japan

Cover: Foto ©Andreas Hilbeck / pixelio.de

More available books at **www.hansebooks.com**

THE
AMANUENSIS.

A Series of Reading, Writing and Dictation Lessons, Carefully Arranged with Reference to a Grouping of Words Illustrative of Principles, for the Purpose of Easily and Quickly Teaching a Correct, Rapid and Legible Style of Writing for Amanuensis and Reporting Purposes.

IN ACCORDANCE WITH THE PRINCIPLES

—OF—

LINDSLEY'S TAKIGRAFY.

COMPILED AND PUBLISHED BY D. KIMBALL.

CHICAGO.

FOURTH EDITION,

1889.

INTRODUCTION.

The method of teaching Takigrafy for amanuensis and reporting purposes which is contained in the following pages is believed to be new and superior, and that it will effect a great saving of time and labor on the part of both teacher and pupil. The Lessons contain quite a complete vocabulary of the words and * frases in common use;—many of the words are primitives from which the derivatives may be easily formed, thus greatly increasing the actual working vocabulary of the writer.

These words are classified and arranged in gronps. Each group illustrates a principle of writing or contraction by giving the correctly engraved shorthand form for all the common words employing it. The repetition of the words in the drill necessary to master their forms, will at the same time fix the principle of writing or contraction in the pupil's mind.

In the first Lessons the shortest and simplest words are given, from which may be learned the principles of the Simple Style. With the introduction of the longer words are brot in the principles of contraction which sufficiently shorten them.

A pupil is not required to learn a long form for a word to be afterward discarded for a briefer one. No word occurs more than once in the Lessons. When it does occur it is in the form it will be used by the pupil at the end of his course. If more than one principle of writing or contraction applies in a word the word will be found only in the group wherein the last principle employed is illustrated.

The theory of Takigrafy is so simple but little time need be spent upon it. The greater part of a learner's time and work must be put upon the all important writing, reading and dictation drills. This work furnishes these drills in the most complete and practical form. When these Lessons are thoroly mastered, few strange words will, in general work, confront a writer.

* In the following pages there is used a simplified spelling of some of the frequent words by way of protest against the wretched spelling in common use.

The wordsigns are given a few with each Lesson in the connection where they naturally belong, so that they will be the more readily understood and their gradual mastery not feel burdensome to the pupil.

Accompanying each Lesson is a carefully prepared miscellaneous reading, writing and dictation exercise, the sentences of which are composed solely of words occurring in that and previous Lessons. A line of specially contracted frases is given at the beginning of these exercises, and they with about all the common frases belonging in that connection are woven into the exercises, so that the pupil learns them without extra time and effort and has drill upon miscellaneous matter and frase writing in and from the first day and lesson. A new and most important feature in shorthand instruction.

Concise instructions in common type accompany each Lesson until enuf principles of writing are introduced so that instructions may be given in Takigrafy, after which they are given in that form.

Some new and valuable modes of contraction are introduced in these Lessons for the first time.

To the teacher, these Lessons offer these advantages:

The certainty of furnishing pupils with the most comprehensive as well as conveniently and carefully arranged Lessons, containing forms for wordst hat years of experience have proven to be most facile and legible, upon which to study and drill.

Entire relief from the irksome, vexatious and useless drudgery of correcting a pupil's written exercises.

Equally good results with large as with small classes.

To the student these Lessons insure:

A correct and uniform style of writing.

The entire saving of the time and labor put on the preparation of exercises for correction, and the subsequent unlearning of incorrect forms.

With these Lessons all study and drill are put upon correctly formed words as they will be permanently used. Hence time and labor are economized to the fullest extent.

By my own experience as a teacher, and the experience of others, both teachers and pupils, who have used these Lessons in an incomplete form, I am encouraged to believe that in this more complete shape, I am placing before the public a greatly increased facility for the acquisition of this most useful branch of a modern business education. I commend this work to my fellow teachers and students, confident that with it results may be reached never before deemed possible, and with the hope that with this fresh stimulus all will work with more vigor, zeal and unselfishness until the benefits of this wonderful art are everywhere recognized and enjoyed.

Chicago, December 1, 1885. D. KIMBALL.

CONTENTS.

GENERAL DIRECTIONS FOR STUDY AND PRACTICE.

PENS.

1. A good steel pen is the best instrument with which to write Shorthand. Writing can be done with a pen nearly, if not quite, as rapidly as with a pencil, and much more neatly, accurately and legibly, and the reading is not so trying to the eyes. Those who wish to become writers of a really accurate, legible and beautiful style of Shorthand must not fail to do the greater part of their practice with pen and ink.

2. Choose an elastic, fine-pointed pen, such as is best suited to your hand. In this matter tastes will differ. Individual preference shud govern We have found the Falcon an excellent pen for both shorthand amd longhand. We have never found a gold pen that was satisfactory, tho some use and like them.

INK.

3. Shud be free flowing, non-corrosive, of good color when first used, and permanent. We have found the dark purple French "Copier B," or Japan copying, the best for general work, letter writing, copying, etc.

PENCILS.

4. There are times and places when and where it is not practicable to use a pen, and a pencil must be resorted to; some practice with a pencil is therefore necessary. Pencils should be of best quality. It is never economy to work with poor tools. The medium grades, such as Faber's "Stenografie," or, No. 3, Dixon's American Grafite M, are among the best, being neither too hard nor too soft. The leads shud be of good size, strong, uniform in quality, free from hard spots, and make a clean, smooth, black line without wearing too rapidly.

5. A good supply of pencils shud be provided, and if neatly sharpened at both ends the same pencil may be made doubly useful. Don't sharpen the lead to a fine point, or discard a pencil as soon as the point is worn off a little. The whole of the lead may be used if when

it becomes worn too broad in one spot the pencil is slightly turned so as to bring a sharp edge again to the paper.

PAPER.

6. For pen writing shud have a smooth hard finish. For pencil writing the paper may be of a cheaper grade, not calendered. For practice drills, unruled paper cut about the size of foolscap, and put up in blocks of one hundred sheets each, is most convenient.

7. When one begins actual work and it becomes necessary to preserve the writing, and for sake of convenience as well, the two hundred page manilla covered reporting books shud be used. When a book is filled it shud be dated or indexed, numbered and filed for reference, as may be required

8. While it is not necessary to have ruled paper for practice drills or actual work in writing Takigrafy, yet, the writing is likely to be more regular and uniform if the paper used is ruled in the ordinary way, as for longhand.

THE POSITION BEFORE THE DESK.

9. Shud be erect, and with the right side turned toward the desk, so that the right arm may rest on it without constraint; and still the body shud not be turned so far but that the paper may be easily held by the left hand.

HOW TO HOLD THE PEN.

10. In Takigrafy most of the letters are made in an inclined or horizontal direction—the direction in which the hand will most easily and quickly form a letter. To make the letters with the greatest ease, the pen shud be lightly grasped between the first and second fingers and thumb, as shown in the following cut:

THE CORRECT POSITION OF THE HAND AND PEN IN WRITING.

11. The penholder shud point well to the right and the pen be so held that its points will press evenly upon the paper; that position is correct which will admit of making | \ — without changing the position of the pen by rolling it between the fingers.

HOW TO USE THE HAND.

12. The hand shud assume its easiest position on the desk or table—the position it wud naturally take if dropped upon the desk carelessly and without restraint or thot. The knuckle of the forefinger will be directly upward, and the third and fourth fingers slightly curved under the palm, thus forming an elastic support, and steadying the hand in its movement across the paper. The wrist shud be slightly raised so that the hand may move freely.

13. The motion of the fingers shud be limited to keeping the pen in its proper position on the line, extending them at each end and flexing them in the middle as the hand sweeps thro its circular path from one side of the page to the other, and to an almost imperceptible movement employed in the formation of the vowels, hooks, etc.

14. The hand shud be trained to run very lightly over the paper, tracing the light lines very lightly, the pen just touching the paper, so as to form a hair-line, and the shaded letters shud be only enuf heavier to show that they are intended to be shaded.

15. During all practice drills the hand must be constantly watched, its movements closely criticised, errors corrected at once, before bad habits are formed, and it must be kept thoroly and rigidly under control of the will.

16. Care must be taken not to overtax the small muscles of the hand by making them do the work of writing. They are unable to stand a long continued and severe strain. They shud be called upon to do only the slight service indicated above. Serious injury—pen paralysis—is almost sure to result if this is neglected.

THE USE OF THE ARM.

17. The weight of the arm shud rest upon the full muscular part of the forearm near the elbow in such a way as to allow an easy rolling motion, and as a pivot from which the hand may easily sweep the full length of a line across the page without raising the arm to move it along on the desk. Avoid writing with the hand close to the body, the elbow at an acute angle. Such a position is too constrained for easy and rapid movement of the hand. Let the arm be well open, the elbow at an obtuse angle, so that the movement may be free and unobstructed.

18. The propelling force used in writing shud come entirely from the large strong muscles of the arm above the elbow, which can stand the strain of long continued writing with the least fatigue. It is also necessary that the utmost freedom and dash in writing shud be secured, and this can be done only by cultivating this muscular arm movement. It is as necessary in longhand as in shorthand, and shud be persistently drilled upon until mastered. No great measure of success in either long or shorthand can be expected without using this movement. At first, the hand will seem to be unmanageable, but a vigorous exercise of the will directed toward its control and persistent practice will be successful in accomplishing the end desired.

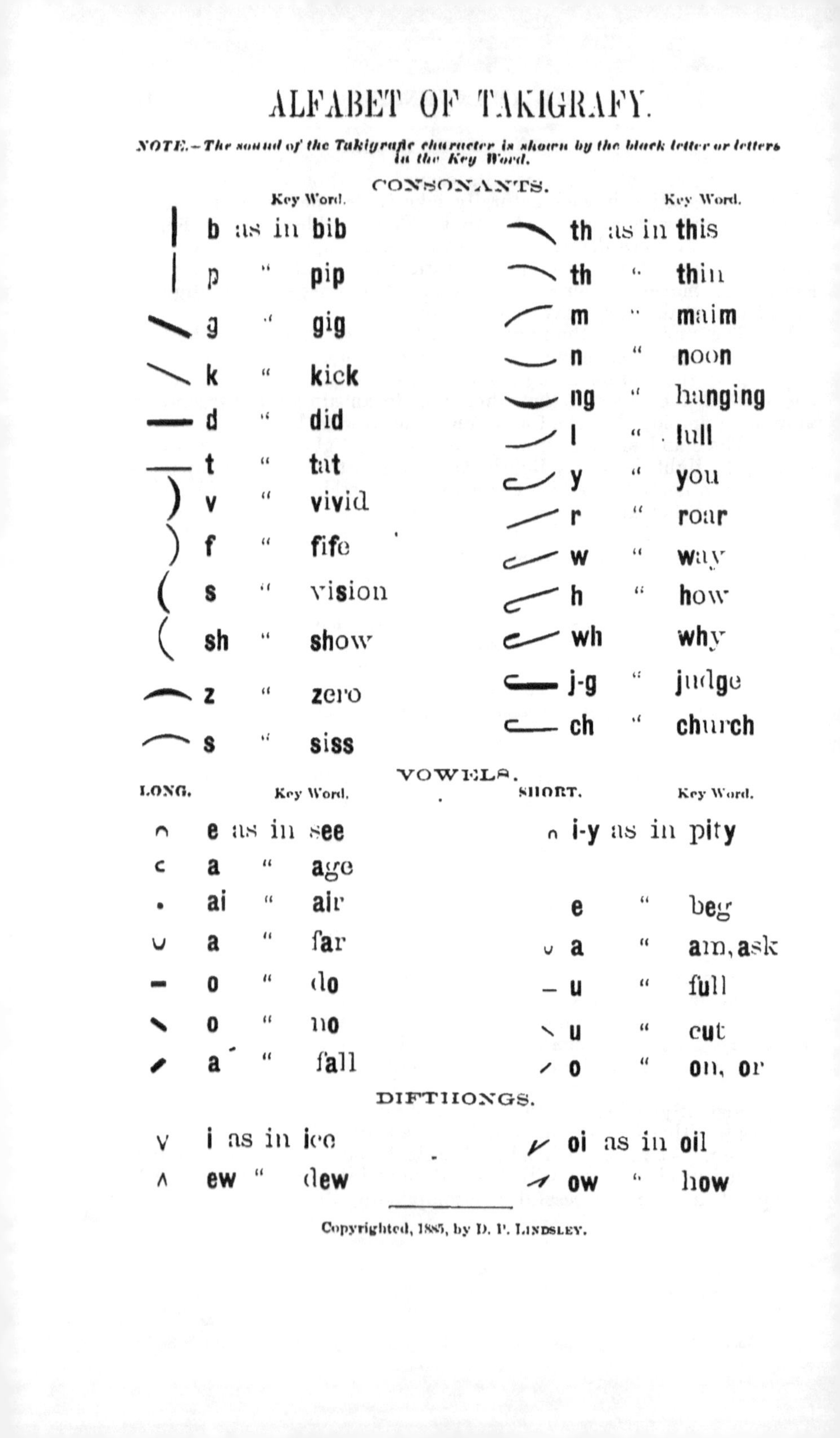

ALFABET OF TAKIGRAFY.

NOTE.—The sound of the Takigrafic character is shown by the black letter or letters in the Key Word.

CONSONANTS.

	Key Word.		Key Word.
b as in	bib	th as in	this
p "	pip	th "	thin
g "	gig	m "	maim
k "	kick	n "	noon
d "	did	ng "	hanging
t "	tat	l "	lull
v "	vivid	y "	you
f "	fife	r "	roar
s "	vision	w "	way
sh "	show	h "	how
z "	zero	wh	why
s "	siss	j-g "	judge
		ch "	church

VOWELS.

LONG.	Key Word.	SHORT.	Key Word.
e as in	see	i-y as in	pity
a "	age		
ai "	air	e "	beg
a "	far	a "	am, ask
o "	do	u "	full
o "	no	u "	cut
a "	fall	o "	on, or

DIFTHONGS.

i as in	ice	oi as in	oil
ew "	dew	ow "	how

HOW TO LEARN THE ALFABET.

19. Read over the Alfabet carefully, noting that most of the letters are in pairs— that is, a letter made of a light line and one made of a shaded line go together; that these paired letters, instead of representing entirely different sounds, represent varieties of the same sound, differing in the stress or emfasis with which the sound is pronounced as the letters differ in shade—the light letter representing the most frequently occurring whispered sound, the shaded letter representing the less frequently occurring spoken sound; that the letters not so paired are made of light lines, and that all the letters are represented by the simplest straight lines and curves, so that a single impulse of the voice is recorded by a single movement of the hand.

20. The letters

are always written downward;

are written from left to right;

are written upward; while the above are written either upward or downward to secure facile joinings and good angles. It will be observed that when written downward the M, L and R are much steeper than when written upward.

21. Carefully analyze the short words in the Alfabet containing the sounds of the letters by pronouncing them so slowly that you are able to separate the sounds from each other. Select the sound represented by the letter you are considering, and speak it many times, until you are thoroly familiar with it.

22. When you have mastered the sounds in this way, take up the letters one by one, in pairs, and in groups of four and six, and write them over and over, hundreds of times, if necessary, to thoroly commit them to memory. Speak the sound as you make the letter, so as to fix and ally together in your mind the sound, the letter representing the sound, and the movement that makes the letter.

Do not draw the letters slowly, but first get their correct form fixed in your mind, then dash them off with the greatest possible rapidity. Spur up your hand constantly to a higher rate of speed, steadily aiming to write each succeeding letter quicker than the one preceding. Do not allow your pen to come to a dead stop on the paper, and in this way destroy the momentum gained in making a letter; but as one letter is finished let the pen immediately, without checking its movement, go on to form the next. Where it is convenient to do so you may join the letters together, and thus save the stroke that wud be wasted in going from one letter to another if the letters were disjoined. Shorthand is a practical application of the strictest principles of economy of time and labor in doing writing, and these principles shud be carefully studied, constantly kept in view, and thoroly applied, in order to attain ease and speed in writing.

23. Drill on the Alfabet shud form part of your daily practice until you can write it thru with ease and accuracy in from fifteen to ten seconds.

24. The horizontal letters, being in the exact direction of the forward movement of the hand, are the most easily and rapidly written. This being the case, it follows that the more nearly the inclined letters approach a horizontal direction the more rapidly and easily they may be written. They shud be made as near the horizontal as possible, and not be liable to be mistaken for horizontal letters. This practice adds greatly to the ease with which joinings are made, to facility in writing generally, and to the beauty of the written page.

25. The double letters BB, PP, GG, KK shud be made one letter above, the other below the line. The letters RR, WR, HR and WHR are wholly above the line.

When a shaded strait consonant is to be joined to a strait light one in the same direction, as BP, GK, DT, JT, begin the letter with a heavy pressure upon the pen, gradually relaxing it as the movement progresses and allowing the elasticity of the pen to form the tapering line needed. The pen shud not be allowed to stop on the paper at the finish, but be raised immediately and carried to the next letter.

When a light strait letter is to be followed by a heavy strait one in the same direction, as PB, KG, TD, CHD, let the pen be moving rapidly when it touches the paper. Gradually increase the pressure to form the tapering line, and finish up the shaded stroke with the pen on the paper.

Where two letters join without an angle, no pause should be made between them. Both should be struck as one letter, and as quickly as possible.

Between strait letters, joinings at acute angles are easiest made, then right, and, lastly, obtuse. Make the joinings at acute angles where possible.

Between curves, the joinings are easiest where they both face the same way, as do FS, SHN; the least facile being the opposing curves, like FN, SHZ, etc.

By a skillful use of the variable letters the careful writer will secure good angles and facile forms in nearly every word.

HOW TO SPELL, WRITE, AND READ TAKIGRAFY.

26. The spelling of words in TAKIGRAFY is very simple. It consists solely in pronouncing them so slowly as to separate their elementary sounds. If you can pronounce a word correctly you cannot help spelling it correctly. For exercises in spelling take up the simple fully written words in the Lessons and spell them as you see them written. The process is so simple that a very little practice will enable you to spell correctly any word you can accurately pronounce.

27. Having, in this simple and easy way, arrived at the sounds in a word, join, in their order, the proper letters representing those sounds, already learned from the Alfabet, and the writing is done according to the principles of the SIMPLE STYLE.

28. The reading consists in simply speaking the sounds as you see them pictured by the letters in the written word, and, if the word is

correctly written, the letters are a sure guide to a correct pronunciation.

29. Thus, it will be seen that the two great difficulties in the way of an easy and rapid acquisition of the English language—the correct spelling and pronunciation of the words—are entirely overcome; that the labor and time necessary to devote to both are reduced to a minimum, and the whole matter put in so simple a form that a child can easily comprehend and master it, and that, too, in a fraction of the time now necessarily devoted to the study of the language in its complicated form—resulting in a correctness of pronunciation of words, a lightening of the burden on the memory, and a great saving of time that can be devoted to other useful studies and pursuits now beyond the student's reach in the limited time that can be given to school studies.

30. It is the simplest, easiest, and quickest way that a foreigner can correctly and thoroly master the language.

HOW TO USE THE LESSONS.

31. At the time the Lessons are being drilled upon, the theory upon which the art is founded shud also be carefully studied.

These Lessons are so arranged that wherever you open the book you have a Lesson, complete in itself, on the left-hand page, showing the application of one or more principles of writing or contraction, or both, and on the right-hand page the practical application of those words, in a miscellaneous exercise, which is also to be read and written from dictation.

32. Make a note of all questions and difficulties you encounter, and refer them to your teacher for explanation. Don't guess at anything. "Be sure you are right, then go ahead."

33. First read over carefully all the words in the Lessons. In case of any doubt as to what the word is, consult your teacher or Key at once, so as not to waste time in unprofitable guessing.

34. The words in the Lessons are formed with great care and accuracy. The form of each word shud be studied minutely and carefully until every part of it is fully understood and a perfect picture of it impressed upon your mind; then, after writing it a few times slowly, until the movement of the hand in making it is also understood, commence in earnest by rushing your hand thru the word form with all possible speed, hundreds of times, if necessary, to a complete mastery of it. You will know when that point is reached, for your hand will glide rapidly thru the form with freedom and ease, and without hesitation or conscious mental effort.

35. Do not allow yourself to form the bad habit of drawing the words, or writing them slowly after a few trials, as above, but accustom yourself, from the first, to writing the words with the greatest possible rapidity. Get upon the upper plain of swift movement as soon as possible, and keep there. Keep constantly in view the fact that you must not only write, but write swiftly, to make a success of shorthand for amanuensis or reporting purposes. Crowd your practice constantly toward a higher rate of speed. At the same time watch your hand

closely, criticise its movements and control them by effort of your will, constantly striving to hold it down to making small, neat and accurate characters. Compare your practice writing with the forms in the Lessons and the writing of good writers, note the differences, and the next time you practice on them correct the defect. Learn to be a critic of your own work, and exercise the office with a severe and unrelenting vigor. Nothing is gained, on the contrary, much is often lost, by making your characters too large. It is a waste of power and movement. What is needed in writing shorthand is power converted into speed, resulting in a fine, nervous, condensed energy, finding its expression in a delicate, swift, and exact movement of the hand that shall execute the characters with the greatest possible rapidity and accuracy.

36. A trouble with most learners is an over carefulness—too much of an effort toward accuracy at the expense of speed. They need to cultivate and increase their dash in writing rather than restrain it.

37. Cultivate a complete confidence in yourself, and in your ability to do whatever you undertake, and work to succeed. Do not be discouraged at trifling failures, or at any failure. Learn why you failed, remedy the difficulty, persevere, and you cannot fail to win success.

38. A speed of fifty words per minute shud be gained in private drill by the student on each lesson before writing it from dictation.

39. It will be noticed that no lines are used, either in the Lessons or miscellaneous exercises, they not being necessary to legibility—but it is better, for the sake of regularity, as in longhand, that the writing shud be done with reference to a line, real or imaginary. Let the first perpendicular or inclined consonant of the word rest upon the line, the other letters, before or after it, falling into their proper positions with reference to this controlling letter. The following illustration will show the practice in this regard:

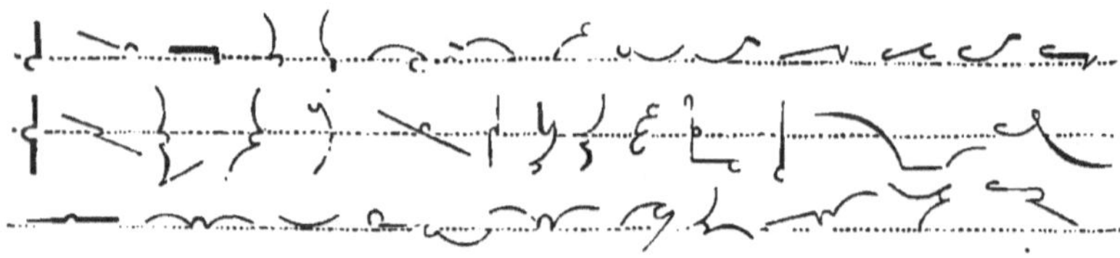

DICTATION.

40. All dictation shud, as far as possible, be governed by a metronome, so that the actual speed of writing may be known, and so that the dictation may be steady and regular. The dictation shud always be a few words per minute faster than the student can easily write, so that there may be a constant incentive to more rapid work. To accommodate the dictation of the drills to those in the same class who write at different rates of speed, each word shud be repeated three times, the fastest writers writing it as many times as spoken, while the slower write it twice, or even once. This repetition of each word also serves to fix it more firmly in the writer's mind. There is little

impression made in hearing or writing a word once and then going to another. Such rapid changes in drilling are confusing, not helpful.

41. In most cases only the root form of words cud be given in these Lessons without making them too voluminous. The dictation shud include the derivative words as well, the writer adding the various terminations, N, D, ING, NESS, FUL, LY, etc., and in that way making the student familiar with the full vocabulary contemplated by the Lessons.

42. From the necessities of the case, the words in these Lessons are very fully written and vocalized, so that they may serve for reading as well as writing lessons, and be easily understood by beginners. When, thru practice, the writer becomes so familiar with the consonant outlines of words that they can be read without vowels, most of the vowels, except the initial and final ones, as well as some of the consonants of lesser importance, may be gradually dropped from the more frequently occurring words, as the writer finds it safe to do so, or it becomes necessary to do so to gain greater speed. It is not intended that the disjoined vowels, except initial ones, shall be written, they are used as an aid in reading.

43. Make frequent reviews, always aiming and working industriously and energetically for greater speed. Your main reliance for an increase of speed must be upon a rapid manipulation, which can only be gained thru such perfect familiarity with the word-forms that they can be struck without a particle of hesitation; all of which is the result of much and diligent practice, rather than by attempting to gain speed by further shortening of words.

44. Settle upon the word-forms you will use, and stick to them. Don't change. Constant changes in the word-forms used in writing are fatal to a high rate of speed. No one can write rapidly while constantly experimenting with and changing the word-forms used.

45. The writing and reading exercise which accompanies each Lesson shud be drilled upon in connection with that Lesson until so thoroly mastered that it can be well written at least one hundred and twenty-five words to the minute. When a sufficient number of the Lessons have been mastered, so that it can be done without bringing in unfamiliar words, other miscellaneous matter may be dictated each day, using the simple language of a First or Second Reader at first, and gradually going on to that which is more difficult. If a proper selection is made of the miscellaneous matter to be written, the speed can easily be raised to one hundred words a minute, and steadily increased during all subsequent instruction. It is well, also, to read the miscellaneous matter three times over, increasing the speed each time it is re-read ten to twenty words per minute. Then the teacher shud write the same matter upon the black-board, so that the pupils may compare the word-forms, frases, etc.

46. In writing, if you are pushed beyond your speed and omit a word or part of a sentence, write a word or frase badly, or find that you have mistaken a word and written a wrong one, or made any other error, take advantage of the first pause the speaker makes, go back, and make the correction while it is fresh in your mind. If you find a speaker too fast for you, your better way is to write complete sentences rather than parts of sentences. By following this practice you will

have complete work that makes sense as far as you go; otherwise, you will have a jumble of words from which you will probably not be able to make any sense.

47. The student shud faithfully read, or, what is better, transcribe into longhand, or on a writing machine, all the miscellaneous matter written. This is the only check upon and cure for careless and slovenly habits in writing. When commencing to write out their notes, it is best for beginners to read thru each sentence, and see that it is in good shape, and reads smoothly, before beginning to transcribe. This will save many mistakes, erasures, or re-writings. If, in your reading, you come to a word or frase that you cannot read readily at first, write all before it, leave a space, go on and complete the sentence. With the matter written in that way on both sides of an omitted word or frase, it will, in most cases, come out clearly.

Another aid to beginners, to whom the shorthand letters are still strange and not suggestive, is to write the words, substituting the ordinary script letters for those written in shorthand. The more familiar appearance of the common letters will often suggest the word at once.

USE YOUR DICTIONARY.

48. You shud become thoroly familar with the spelling and meaning of all the words in the Lessons. A good report cannot be made, or a letter intelligently written by a person who does not know the spelling, meaning, and application of every word occurring in the report or letter. Consult your dictionary whenever you are not SURE you know how to spell a word. This is your only way to avoid the the unfavorable criticism of those who are sticklers for the ancient practices, of whom your employer may be one. Do your work to suit your employer, however ridiculous it may seem to you. He pays for for the work, and shud have it to suit him.

49. It is also necessary that an amanuensis shud be able to write a plain, smooth, even longhand, for there are many places where a writing machine cannot be used; have a good knowledge of grammar and punctuation, and be possessed of sufficient literary skill to trim up and put in shape hurriedly or otherwise imperfectly dictated matter.

Study the best literary models, so as to make your work as nearly faultless as possible in matters of neatness and taste.

50. Much care and attention has been given in these Lessons to group together under one head all the familiar words employing a certain principle of writing, so that the constant repetition of the words in dictation drills will fix the principle in the mind of the student. This makes the Lessons of peculiar value as dictation drills, much superior to miscellaneous matter. The Lessons shud, therefore, form the greater part of the daily dictation drills, and be constantly reviewed until correct writing becomes a fixed habit, and is done without hesitation or conscious mental effort.

51. Use the art as fast as learned in place of longhand so far as possible, and teach it to others. In this way you can make it of the greatest service to you. To teach it to others is the best way to learn it thoroly yourself.

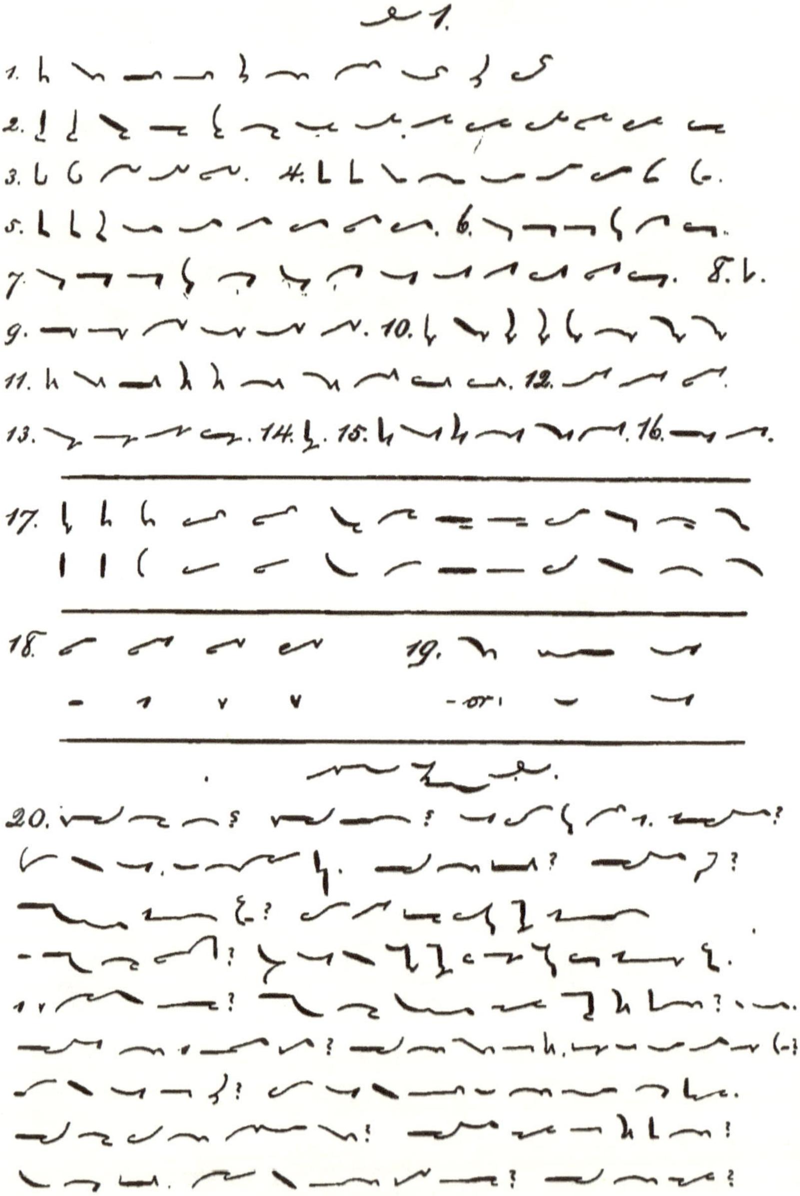

This Lesson teaches the correct way to write words composed of a single consonant followed by a single vowel.

The size, shape, and mode of joining the letters in the Lesson shud be followed as closely as possible. The figures below and in following instructions refer to corresponding figures in the Lessons.

1, 2, 3. These vowels are not shaded. The joinings are made in the simplest manner, as shown in the Lessons. L is written downward before E. It shud be observed that E turns around in the direction the hands of a clock move, far enuf to join easily to the preceding letter, as in the words FEE, KNEE, LEA, and YE.

4. This vowel is shaded. When it will not form a good angle with a preceding letter it must be disjoined, as in the word SHOE. A better joining is secured by writing M downward before this vowel.

5. This vowel is shaded, and admits of being written in the direction of G (6), or B, the direction making the best angle being used.

7. This vowel is shaded, and is written downward, or (8) upward, that direction being used which will form the sharpest angle. The letters  are reversed, thus  when these forms will make better joinings with a preceding or following letter, as in the word THAW.

9, 11, 13, 15. The strokes forming these vowels are made straight, or (10, 12, 14, 16,) curved, whichever shape will form the best angle.

12. EW has its point toward the right, for convenience in writing.

15, 16. The last stroke of OW is shaded, to more clearly distinguish it from EW.

17. Certain words occur so often that they are shortened by omitting part of them. These are shortened by dropping the vowels.

18. These words are shortened by dropping the consonants. The first stroke of I is shaded in the word WHY to distinguish it from HIGH.

19. These three words are shortened irregularly, AND being a letter N made half length and heavy; NOW, the letter N and last stroke of the OW, and THE, a light, straight, short dash, struck in the direction of T or P, and should be joined to the word before or after it.

Note that in Nos. 17, 18 and 19 the fully written shorthand words are given in the upper line. This is so that you may have no difficulty in reading the words. The shortened forms for the words are given in the lower line. It is upon these shortened words in the lower lines that all the practice drill shud be put.

Read and write over, with all possible speed, the Writing and Reading Lesson at the bottom of the page. You will see that some of the simple words which are intimately connected with each other are joined together. As the object of language is to convey ideas, and for convenience in learning, speaking and writing, it is divided into sentences, words, syllables, and letters, and as we join together letters to form syllables, and syllables to form words, so in Takigrafy, we often join two, three, or more words together into what we call frases, care being taken that the words shall join easily, be associated in sense, and spoken connectedly, as the syllables of a word are spoken, with no pause between them. This joining of words in frases adds much to the speed and ease of writing, and does not lessen the legibility.

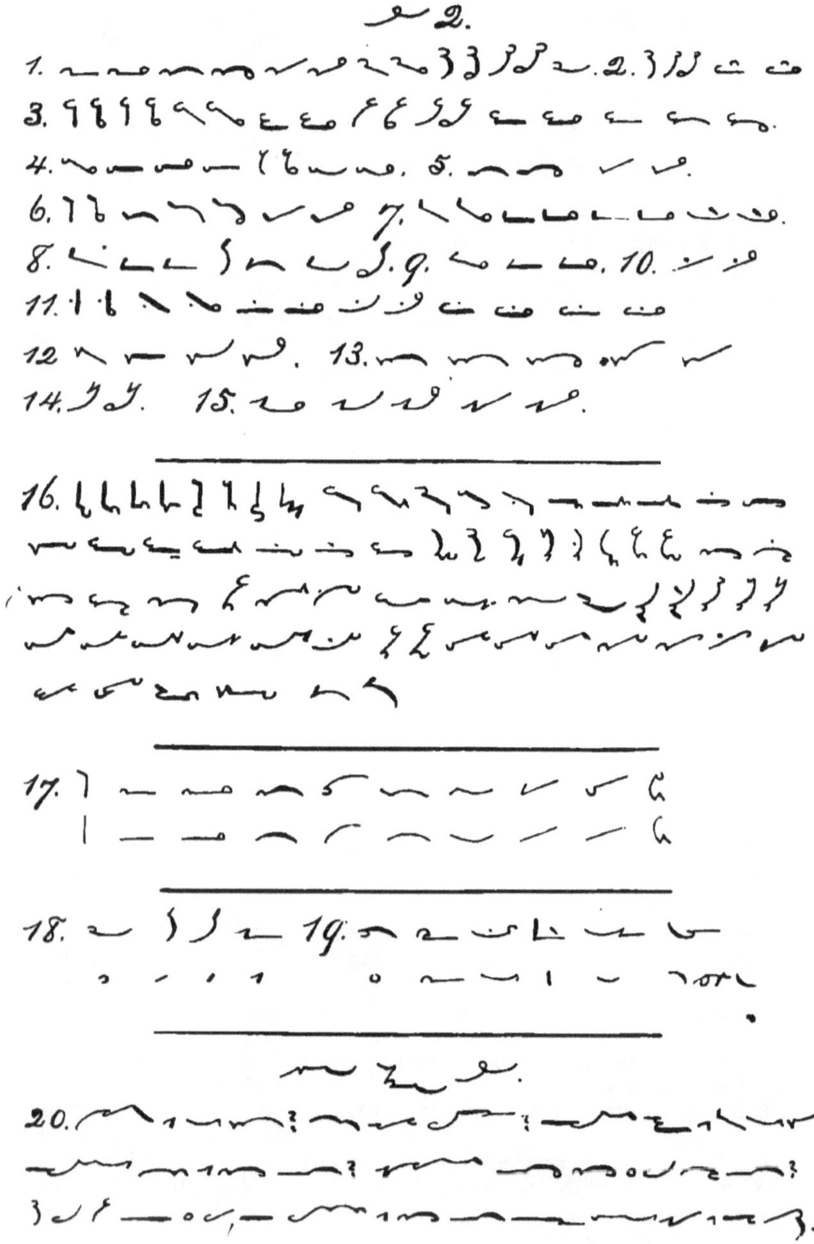
1.
2.
3.
4.
5.
6.
7.
8.
9.
10.
11.
12
13.
14.
15.
16.
17.
18.
19.
20.

INSTRUCTIONS FOR LESSON 2.

This Lesson teaches the correct way to write words composed of a single vowel followed by a single consonant, and how Z and S are added by means of a circle to words ending with a consonant.

Rule.—A vowel must form an angle at its joining with a following consonant.

1, 2. These vowels are distinguished from each other by size. Both may be turned in the direction the hands of a clock move, far enuf to form a good angle with a following letter. L is written downward after these vowels.

3. The manner of writing this vowel is clearly shown in the Lesson. Write M, L and R downward after A. To distinguish A-D from J, and A-T from CH, a slight connecting stroke may be made, as shown in the Lesson, or the A may be disjoined. The same offsetting stroke is usually employed between this vowel and a following Z or S.

4. This vowel is distinguished from AH by its size. Its use will be readily understood from the words in the Lesson.

5, 6, 7, 8. The instructions given in Nos. 4, 5, 6, 7 and 8 of Lesson 1 apply equally to the same vowels in this Lesson.

9. The form and direction of this vowel is the same as No. 8. It differs from that letter in not being shaded.

10. This letter is a heavy dot, and occurs only before R. Its position is shown in the Lesson.

11. This letter should be written near the middle of the consonant, to the left of perpendicular, and inclined and above horizontal consonants when it is to be read before them. It is customary to write the consonant first, the disjoined vowel last.

12, 13, 14, 15. See Nos. 9 to 16 of Lesson 1 for explanation.

16. These words need no special explanation. Vowels join with each other under the same rule as with consonants. The vowel I (short) is sometimes written as a small hook on the under side of another letter, as in the words EDDY, ADDIE, No. 16, line 1, words 17 and 18.

17, 18. These words are shortened, same as those of like numbers in previous Lesson.

19. Of these word-signs, AS is a circle; EACH drops the hook of the CH; ANY is an N with a light backward tick; BUT a halved B; NOT is a half-length N, and THAT a halved TH.

When the circle is added to a shaded consonant or an M with no intervening vowel, the sound is Z. When added to a light consonant without an intervening vowel, the sound is S; except when it it is added to N, L, and R. On the ends of these letters it may be an S or Z, as ELSE or ELLS. Where a vowel comes between a consonant and an added circle, the sound of the circle on the end of a light consonant may change from S to Z, as in the words ITCHES (Z) ETCHES (Z).

This Lesson shud be drilled upon until it can be written at the rate of 200 words a minute.

3.

1.

2.

INSTRUCTIONS FOR LESSON 3

1. In this and following Lessons a line of specially contracted words is given at the beginning. The fully written words are in the upper line, so that they may be easily read. The shortened word to be drilled upon and mastered is in the lower line.

2. This Lesson teaches the correct way to write A (as in babe) between two consonants: It is not shaded, and shud always have its opening directly to the right.

Where I (short) follows N, as in zany, rainy, it may be written as a slight backwards tick, as in any, No. 19, Lesson 2.

This Lesson shud be drilled upon till you can write the words at the rate of 120 to the minute.

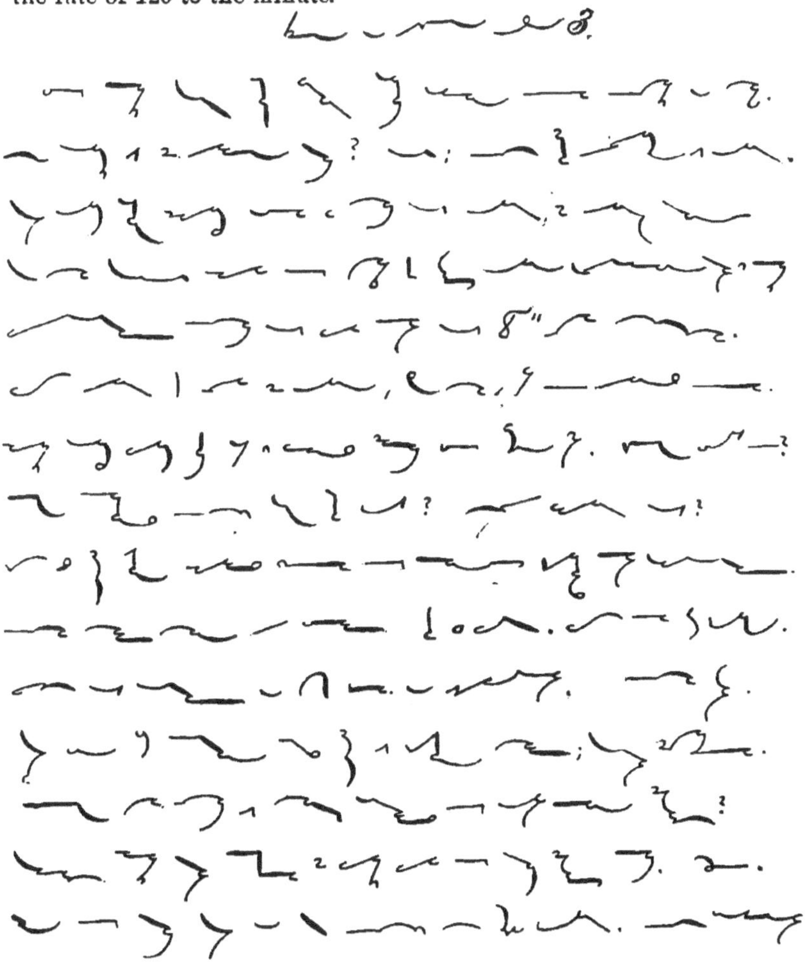

4.

1.

2.
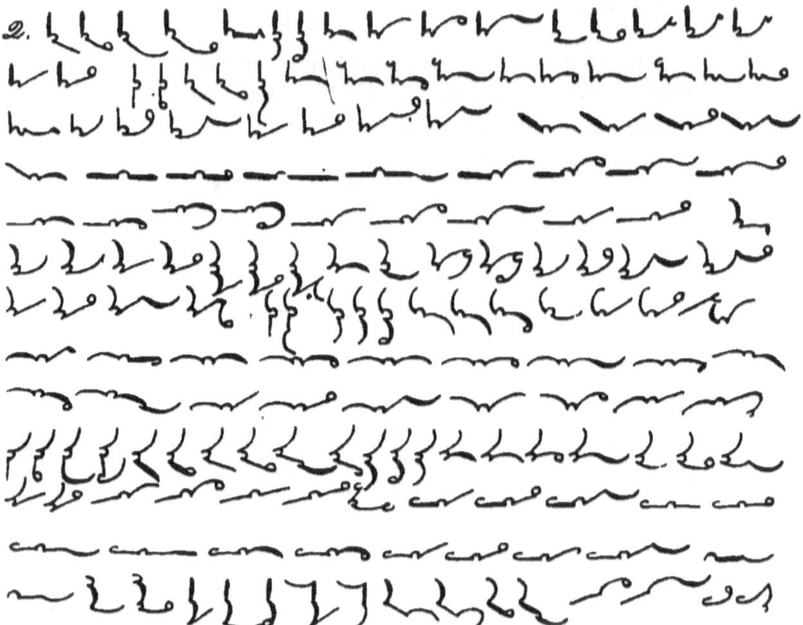

3.
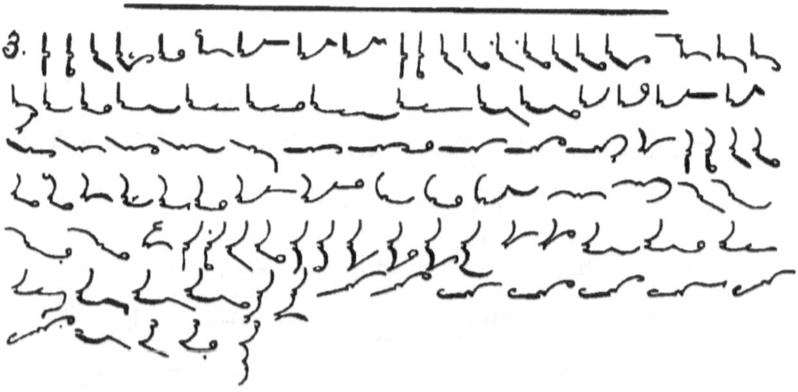

INSTRUCTIONS FOR LESSON 4.

---

1. These words are shortened, same as in Lesson 3. Write the M downward for him.

2. These words show the correct way to write E (as in eve) in its full alfabetic form between consonants.

3. These words show the correct way to write I (as in pin) in its full alfabetic form between consonants.

Do not shade these vowels. Make the distinction between them by the difference in size, as shown in the Lesson. They both turn in the same direction as the hands of the clock move, far enuf to form a good angle with a following letter.

Study and drill upon this Lesson until you can write the words at the rate of 120 per minute.

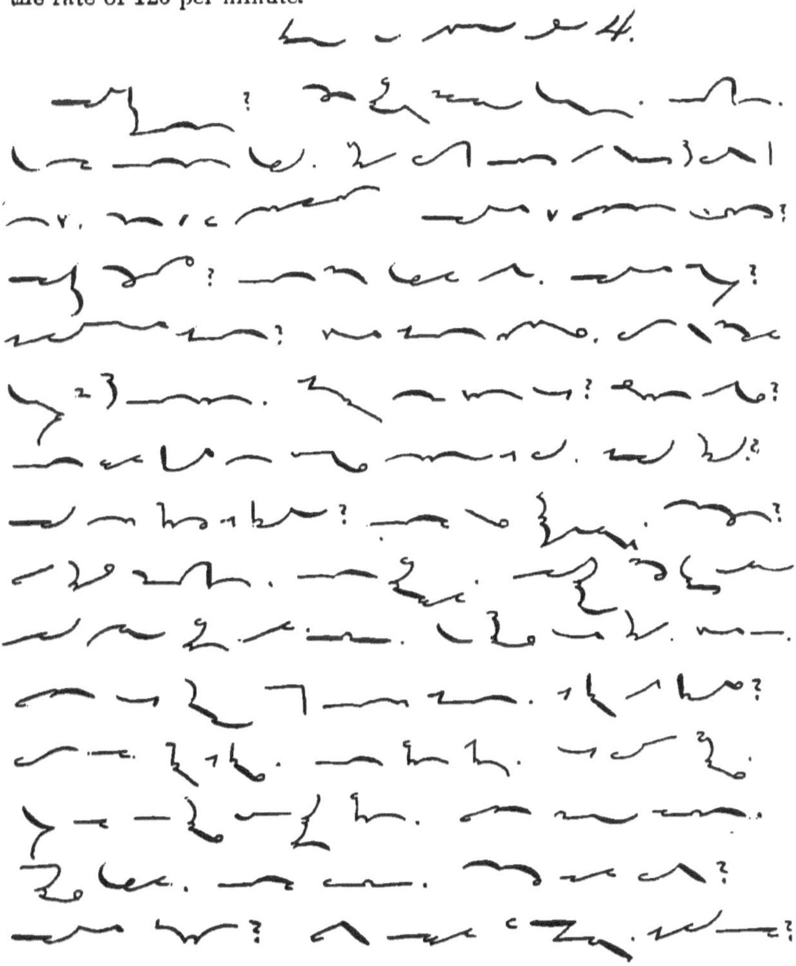

5.

1. 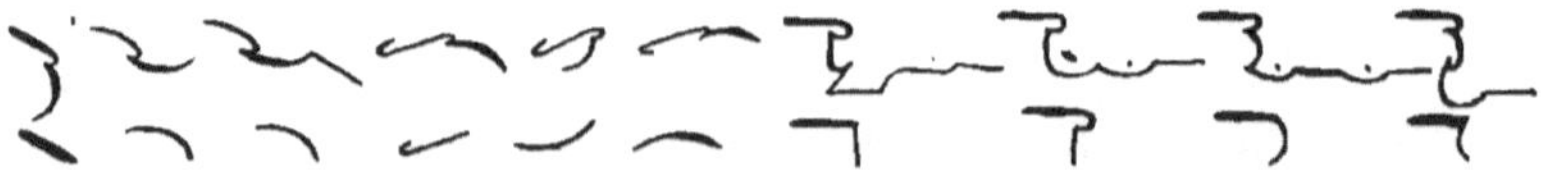

2. 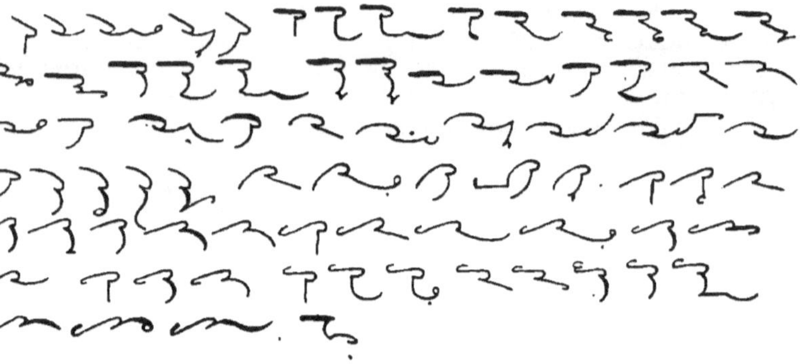

3. 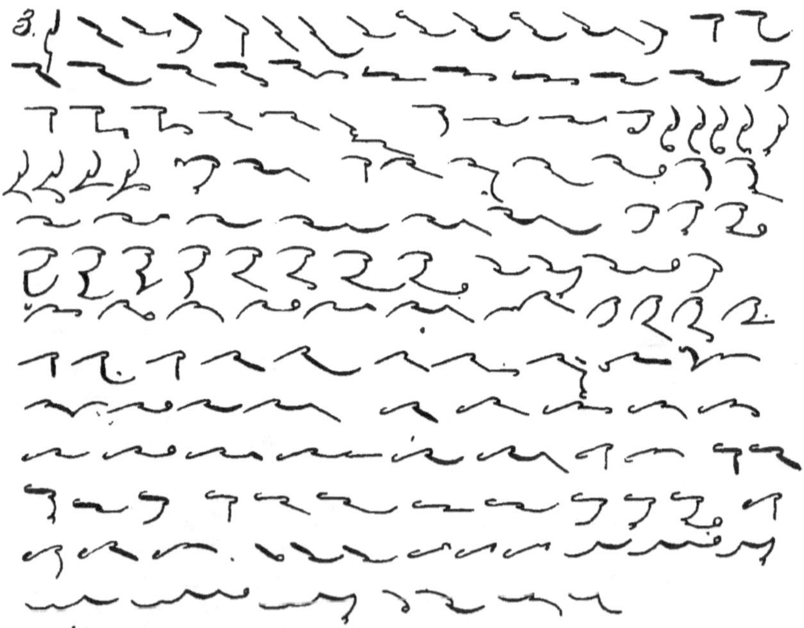

INSTRUCTIONS FOR LESSON 5.

---

2. These words show the correct way to write E (as in deep), as a large hook on the under side of a preceding letter. The Y is written for URE, as in senior, line 3, word 8.

3. These words show the correct way to write I (as in kin) as a small hook on the underside of a preceding letter.

By writing these vowels as hooks in this way, more facile forms are secured, and we are thereby able to express the two sounds with but one stroke of the pen.

Study and drill upon this Lesson until you can write the words 150 per minute.

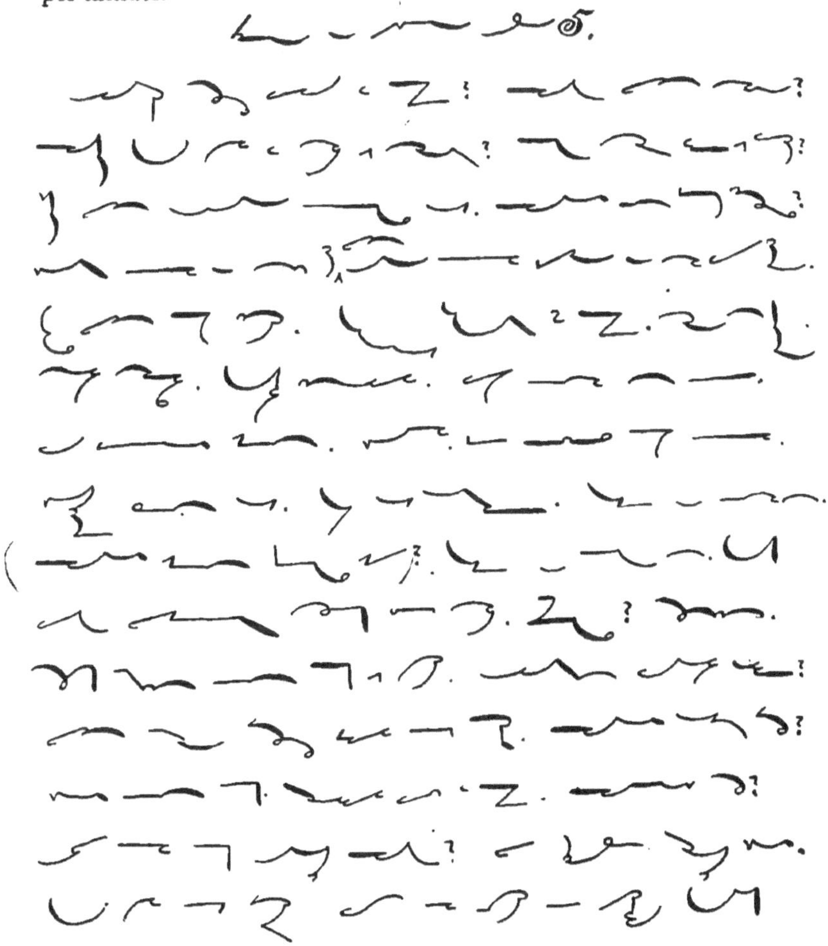

6.

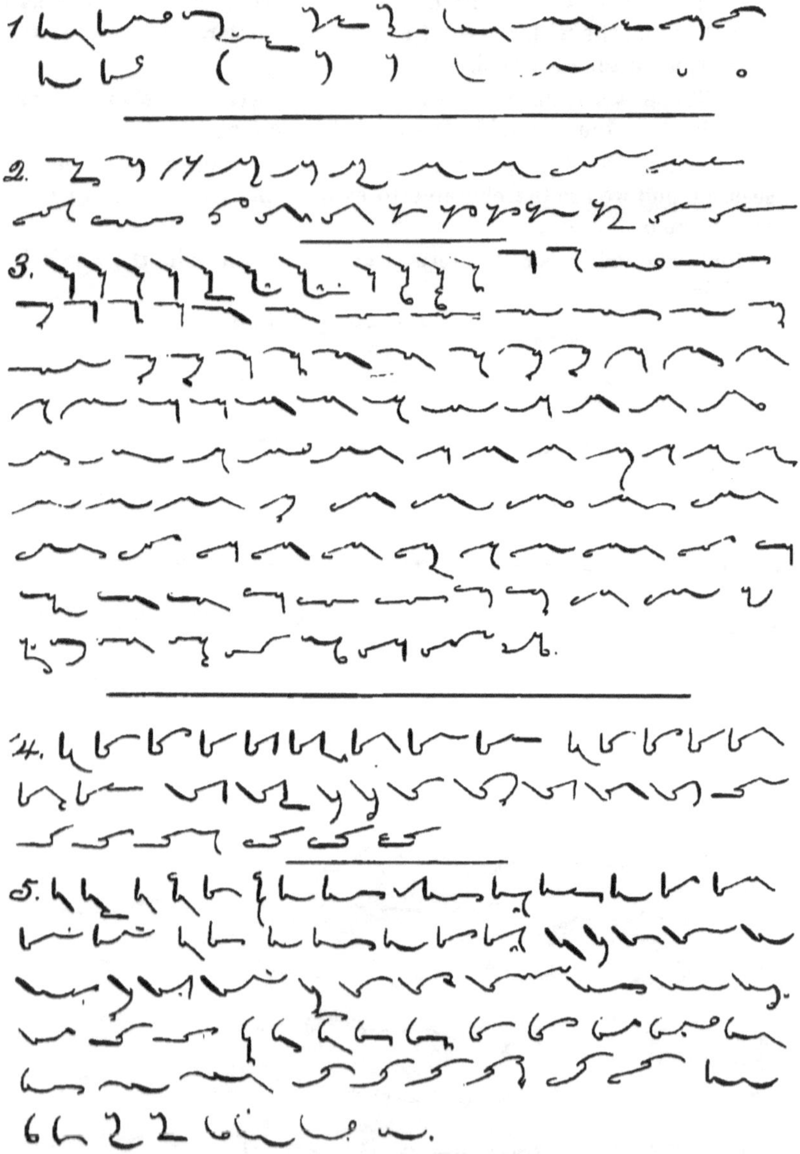

INSTRUCTIONS FOR LESSON 6.

2. These words show the correct way to write A (as in mar) in its full alfabetic form between consonants.
3. These words show the correct way to write A (as in cap) in its full alfabetic form between consonants.
4. These words show the correct way to write A (as in tar) as a large hook on the right or upper side of a preceding letter.
5. These words show the correct way to write A (as in bag) as a small hook on the right or upper side of a preceding letter.

These vowels shud not be shaded, the distinction between them being made by a difference in the size. They turn in the direction opposite to that in which the hands of a clock move, far enuf to form a good angle with a following letter.

Drill upon these words until you can write 120 to the minute.

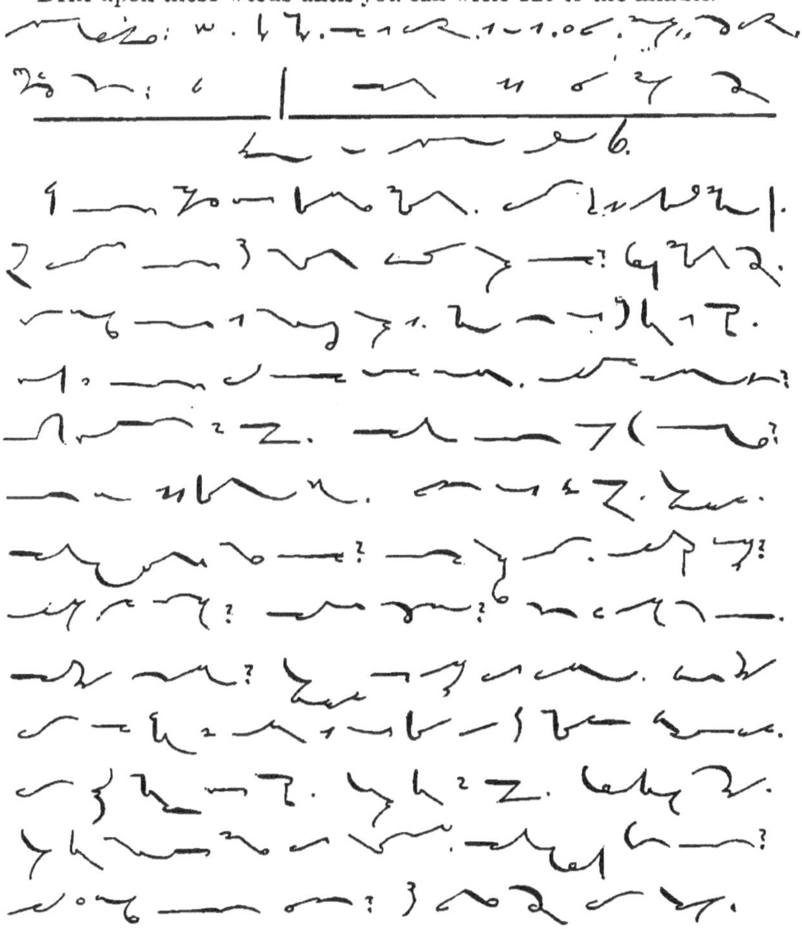

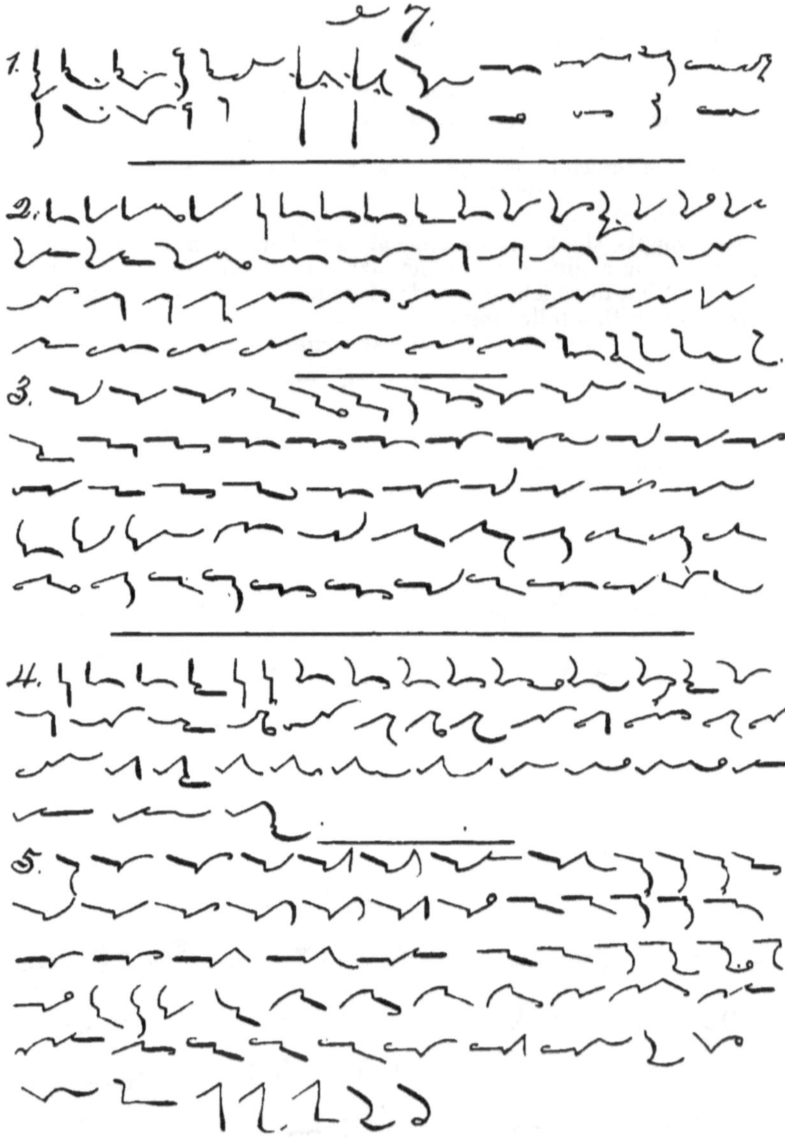

INSTRUCTIONS FOR LESSON 7.

---

2. These words show the correct way to write o (as in bore) in its inclined direction between consonants.

3. These words show the correct way to write o (as in gore) in its perpendicular direction between consonants.

4. These words show the correct way to write u (as in fuss) in its inclined direction between consonants.

5. These words show the correct way to write u (as in gum) in its perpendicular direction between consonants.

That direction for the vowels is used which will make the sharpest angle with a preceding or following letter.

Drill upon these words until you can write them at the rate of 100 to the minute,

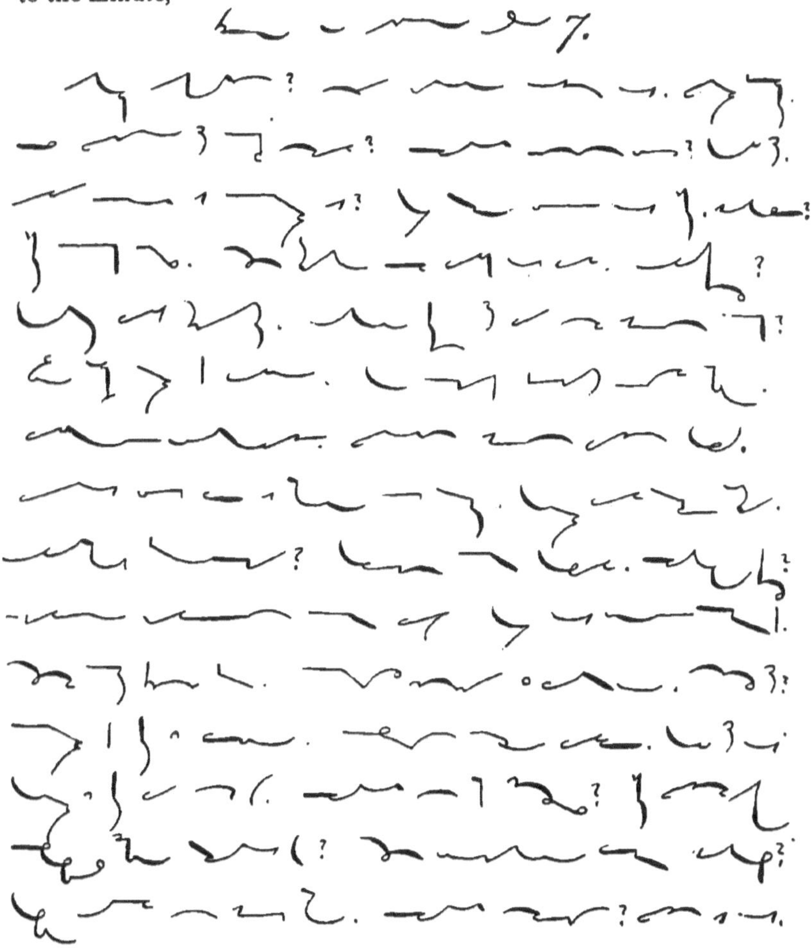

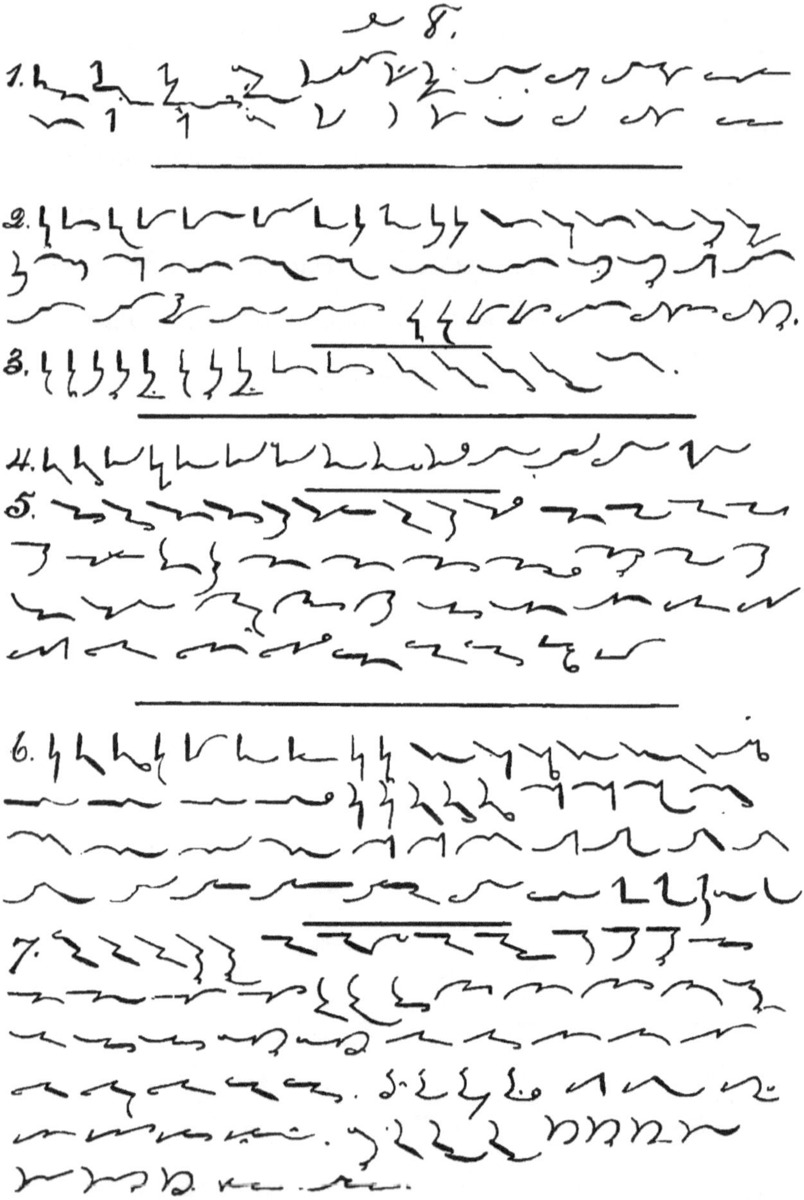

INSTRUCTIONS FOR LESSON 8.

2. These words show the correct way to write oo (as in boom) between consonants.
3. These words show the correct way to write u̧ (as in push) between consonants.
4. These words show the correct way to write A (as in ball) in its upward direction between consonants.
5. These words show the correct way to write A (as in gauze) in its downward direction between consonants.
6. These words show the correct way to write o (as in bog) in its upward direction between consonants.
7. These words show the correct way to write o (as in dog) in its downward direction between consonants.

That direction for the vowels is used which will make the sharpest angle with a preceding or following letter.

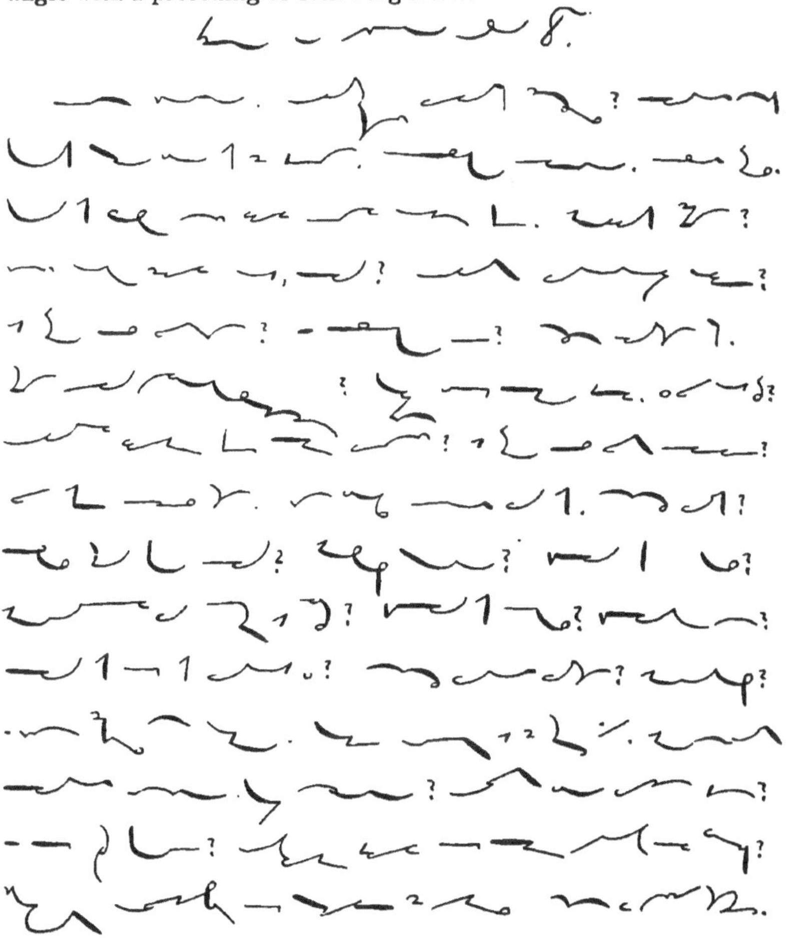

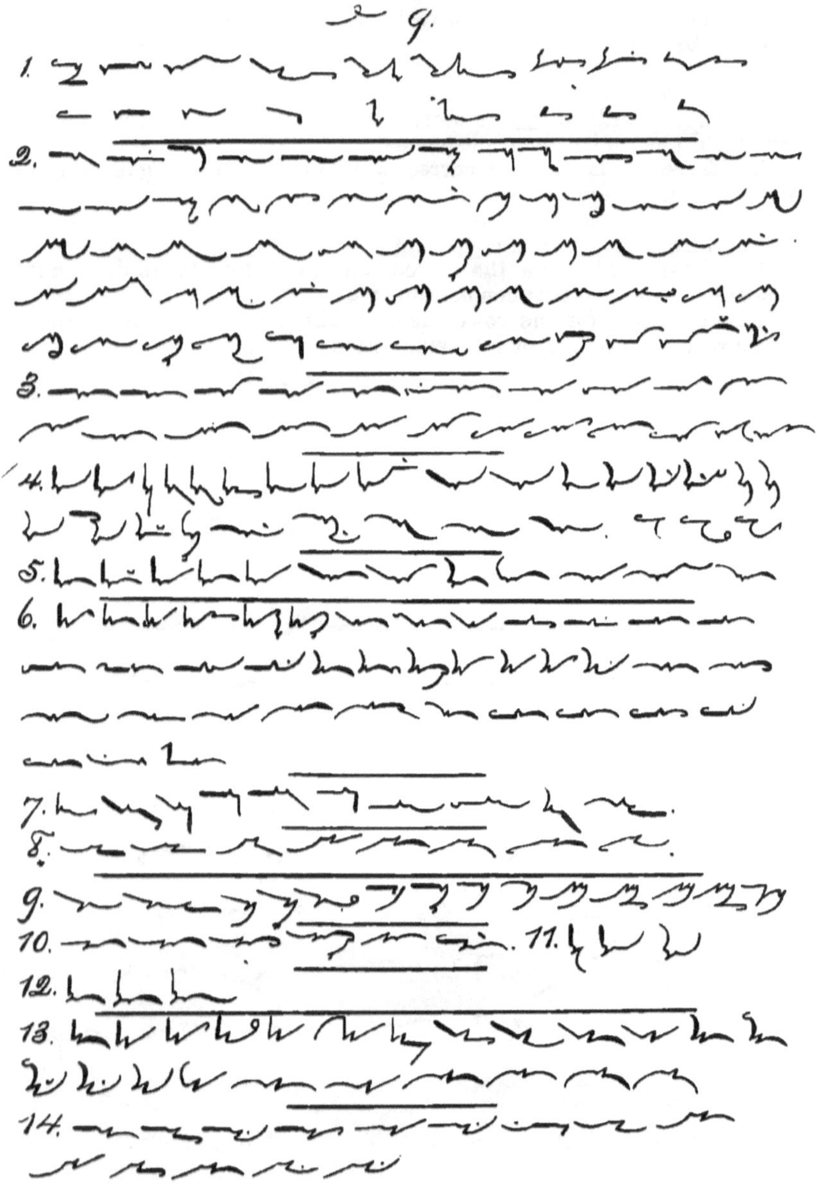

INSTRUCTIONS FOR LESSON 9.

The words in this Lesson show how to write the diamond-pointed vowels -I (as in dike); EW (as in pews); OI (as in toil), and OW (as in fowl) between consonants.

It will be seen that either or both strokes of these vowels may be made strait or curved outward, that form being used which will make the best angle at its joining with a preceding or following letter.

2, 6, 9, 13. In these words both strokes of the vowels are strait.

3, 7, 10. In these words the first stroke of the vowel is strait, the second curved.

4, 11, 14. In these words the first stroke is curved, the second strait.

5, 12. In these words the strokes of the vowels are curved.

Drill upon these words till you can write them 100 to the minute.

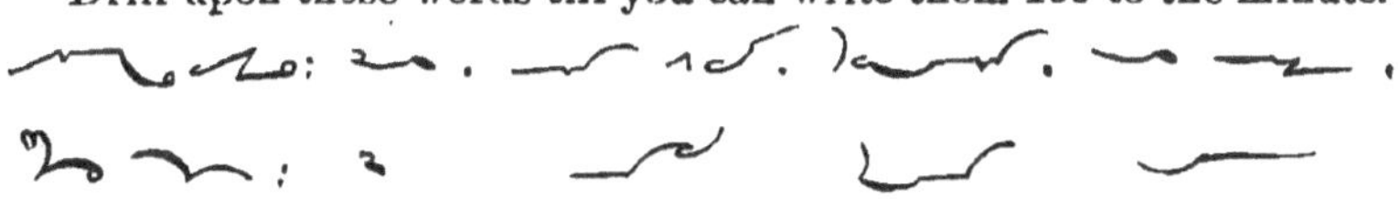

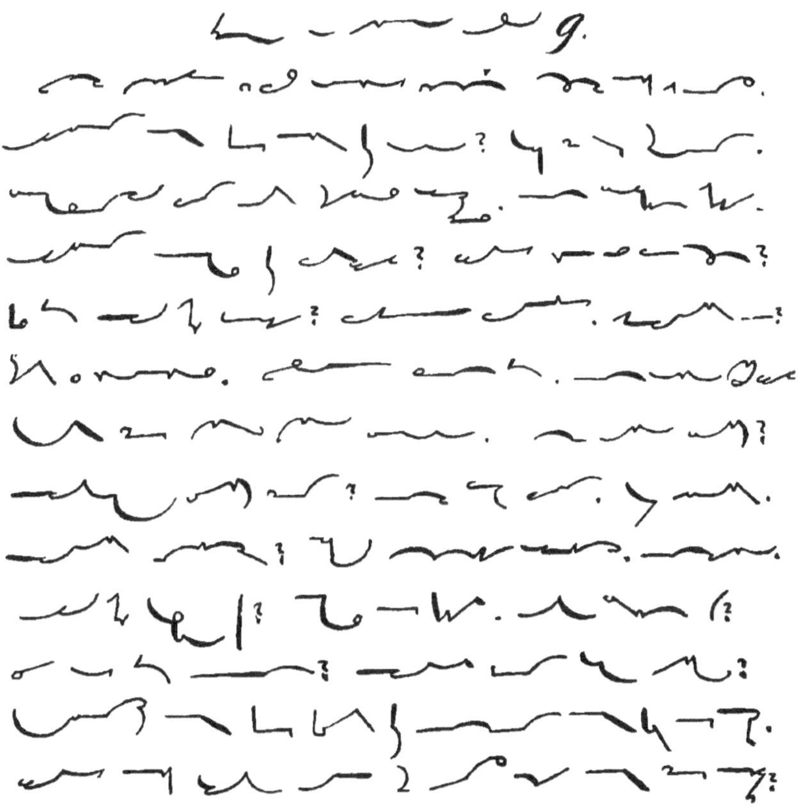

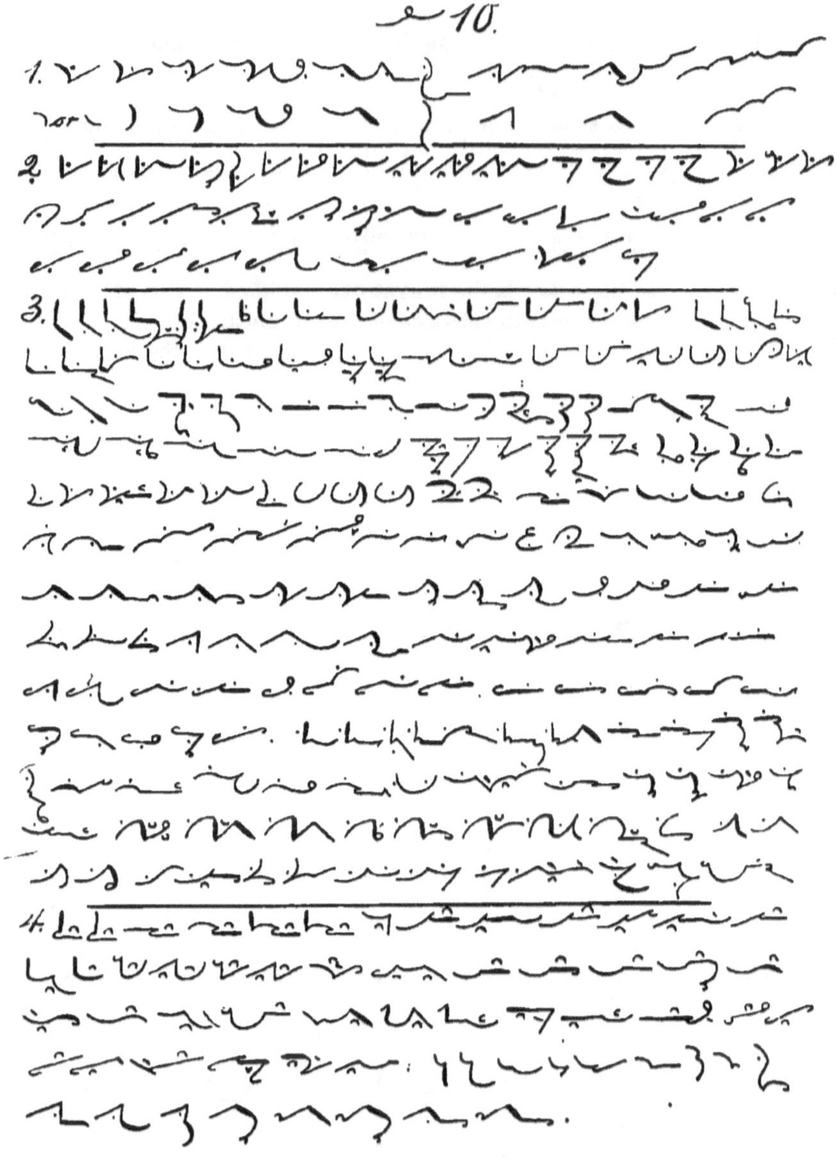

INSTRUCTIONS FOR LESSON 10.

---

2. This Lesson shows the correct way to write the heavy dot vowel AI (as in fair) between consonants. It occurs only before the consonant R, and shud be written beside the consonant which precedes it, as an additional means of distinguishing it from the light dot.

3. This Lesson shows the correct way to write the light dot vowel E (as in ebb) between consonants. Its place is near the middle of the consonant which follows it. It is seldom written except when initial.

4. This Lesson shows the correct way to write E (as in reach) disjoined between consonants. As also some of the compound words, of which THERE is a part, as THEREBY, THEREON, etc.

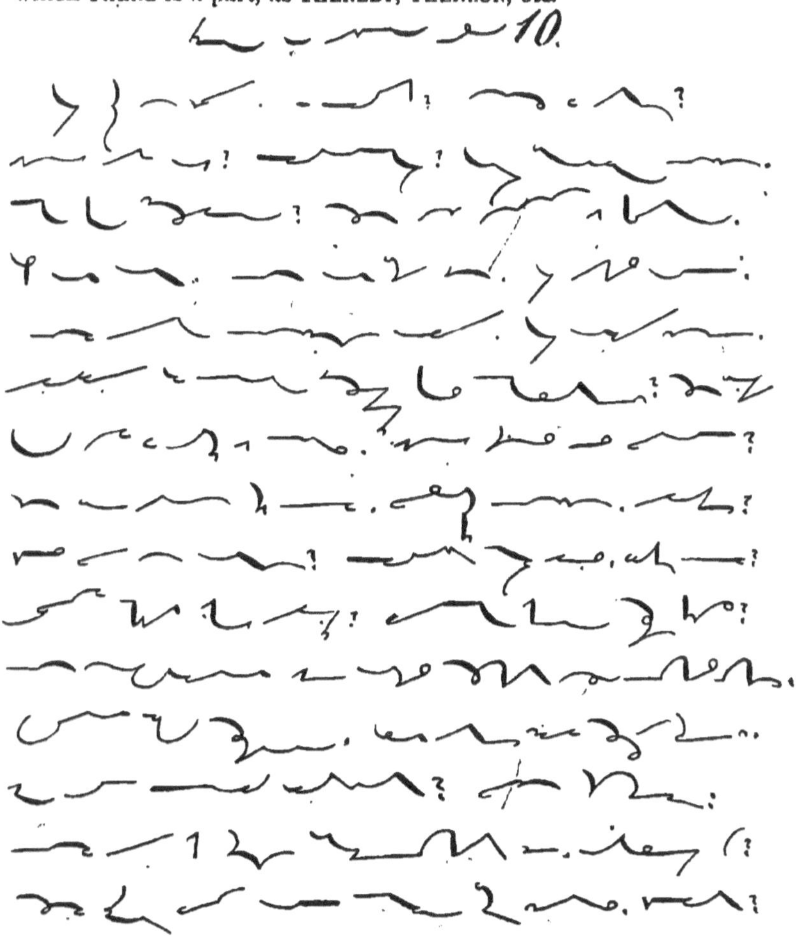

11.

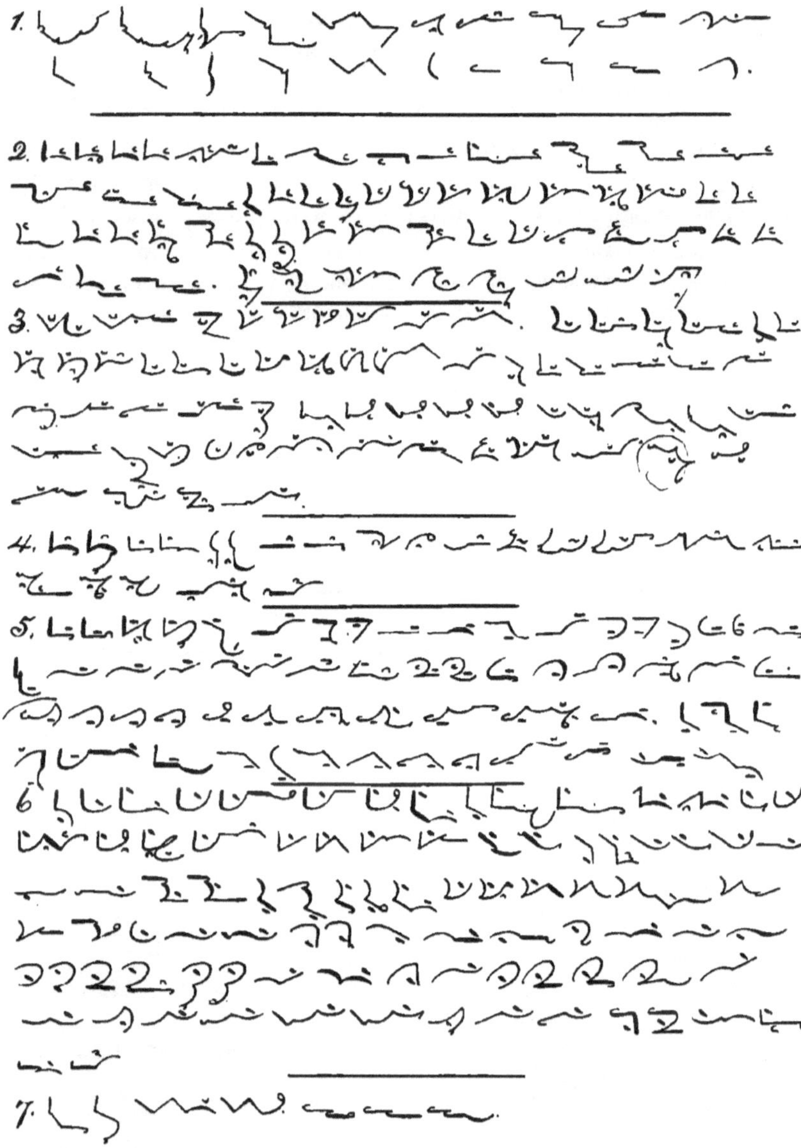

INSTRUCTIONS FOR LESSON 11.

2. This Lesson shows how to write A (a as in base) disjoined between consonants.

3. This Lesson shows how to write AH (a as in far), and A (a as in fan), disjoined between consonants.

4. This Lesson shows how to write I (i as in pit) disjoined between consonants.

5. This Lesson shows how to write OO (oo as in boot) and OO (oo as in book) disjoined between consonants.

6. This Lesson shows how to write O (o as in bone) disjoined between consonants.

Observe that with the exception of the dots in previous Lesson, the disjoined vowel is written as near as may be to the end of the consonant in the syllable to which it belongs. If the vowel is to be read before a consonant it should be written to the left of those that are perpendicular or inclined, and above those that are horizontal, and to the right of perpendicular and inclined consonants, and below horizontal consonants when the vowel is to be read after them.

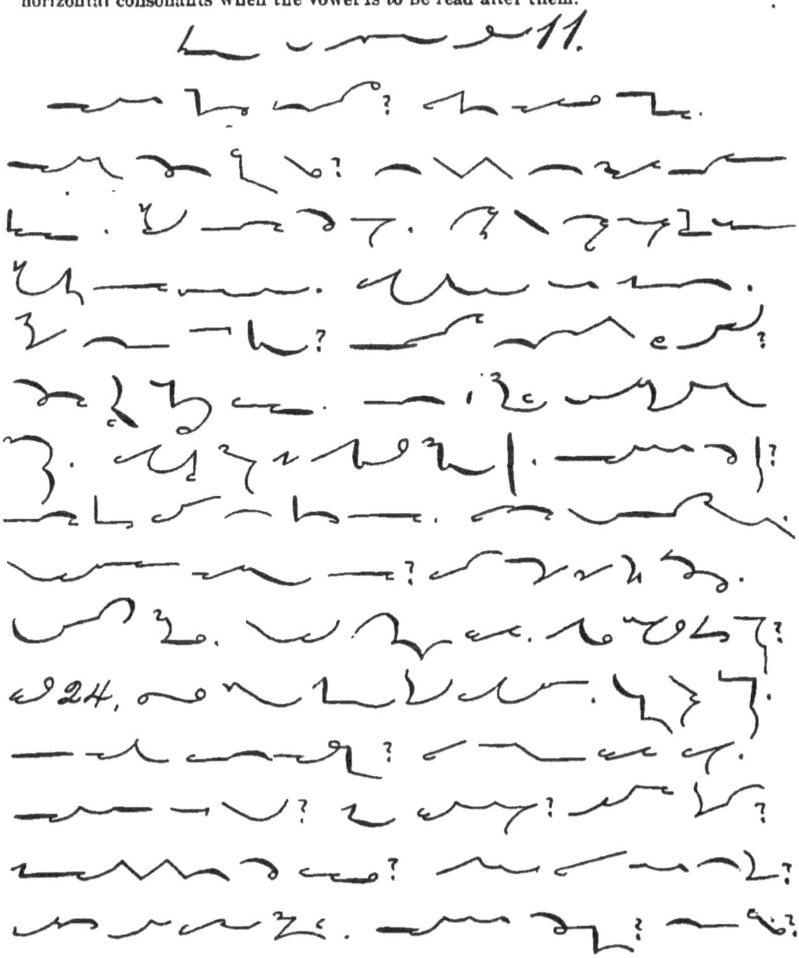

12.

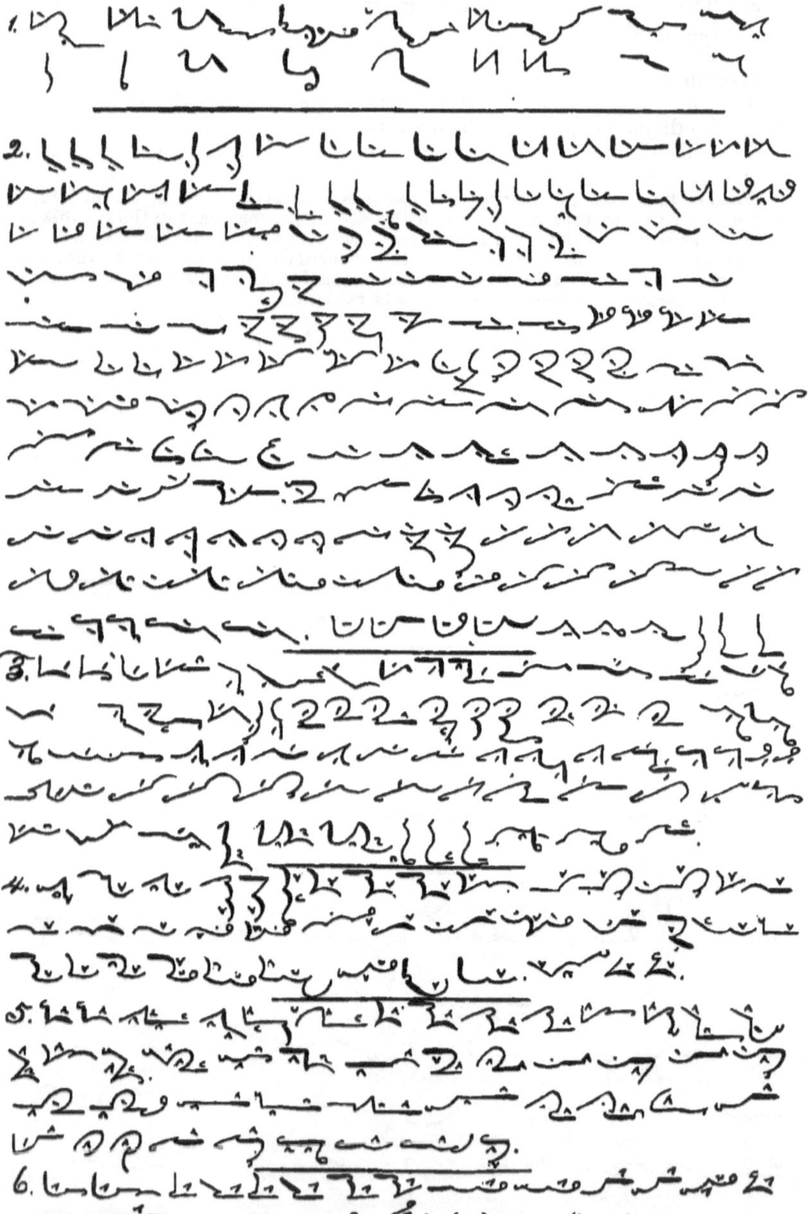

INSTRUCTIONS FOR LESSON 12.

2. This Lesson shows how to write U (u as in bug) disjoined between consonants.

3. This Lesson shows how to write AU (au as in pause) and O (o as in copy) disjoined between consonants.

4. This Lesson shows how to write I (i as in vice) disjoined between consonants.

5. This Lesson shows how to write EW (u as in abuse) disjoined between consonants.

6. This Lesson shows how to write OU (ou as in pout) and OI (oi as in avoid) disjoined between consonants.

Most of these vowels would be joined to the consonants in the word form in the Simple Style, and are put in disjoined here so as to aid the student in reading. They are not to be written in the practice drills.

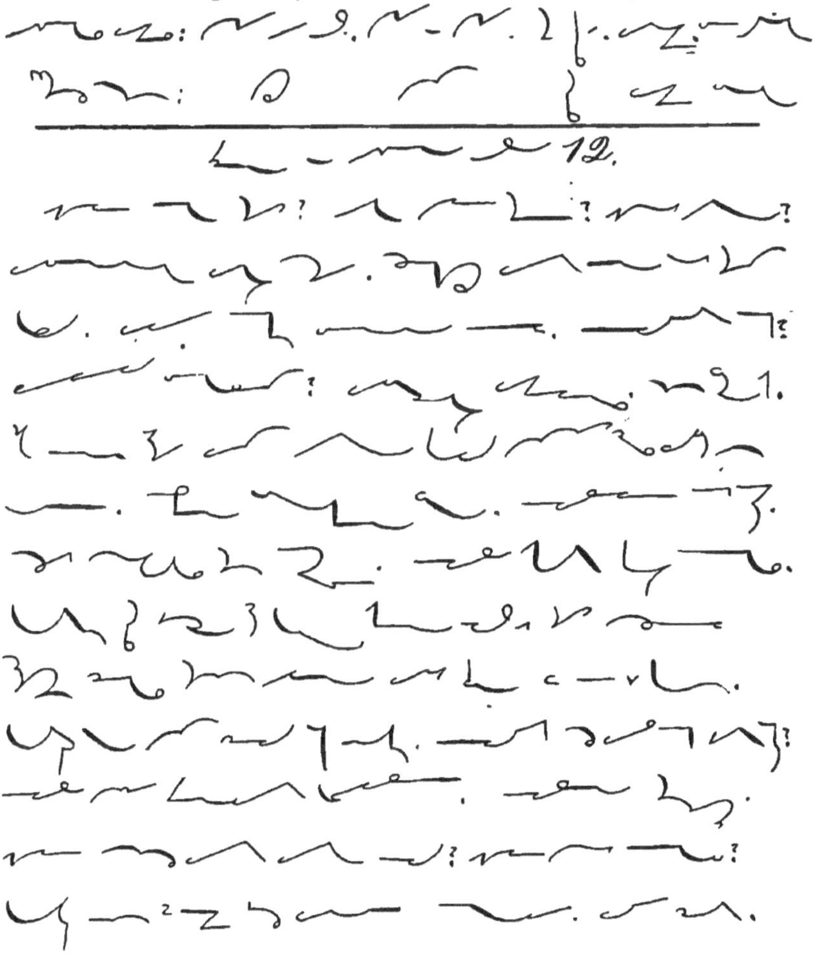

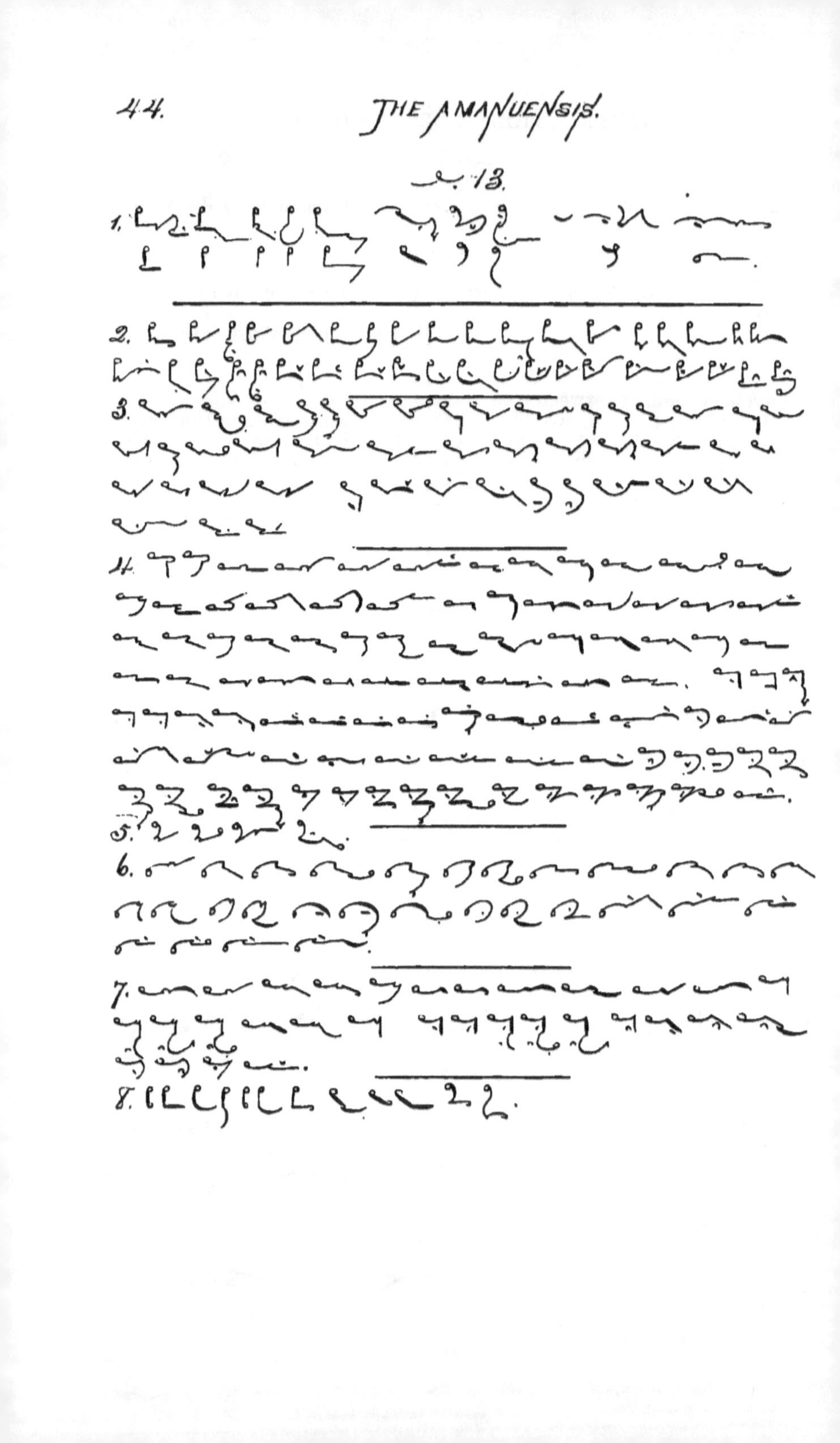

13.

1.

2.

3.

4.

5.

6.

7.

8.

INSTRUCTIONS FOR LESSON 13.

This Lesson introduces the use of the circle at the beginning of words. It has the sound of s.

2. These words begin with SP (as in spear, spell, etc.)
3. These words begin with SK (sc, sk, as in scale, skip, etc.)
4. These words begin with ST (as in steep, steel, etc.)
5. These words begin with SF (sph as in sphere).
6. These words begin with SM (as in smoke, small, etc.)
7. These words begin with SN (as in snow, snap, etc.)
8. These are derivatives formed from the primitive word signs in No. 1 (as subjected, specialty, etc.)

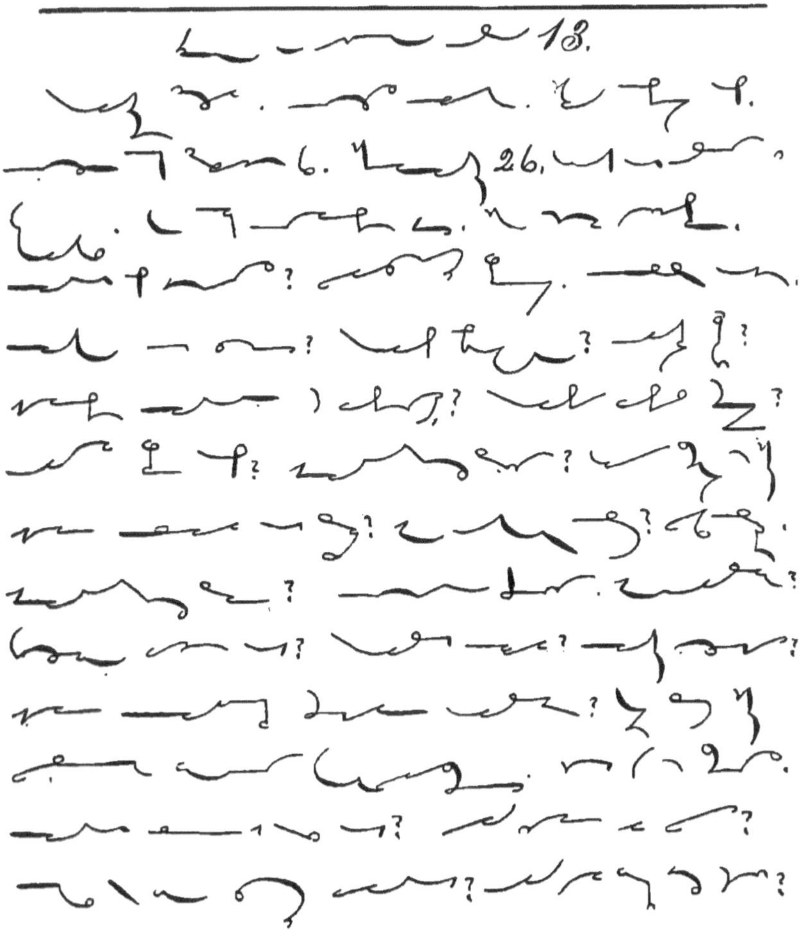

§ 14.

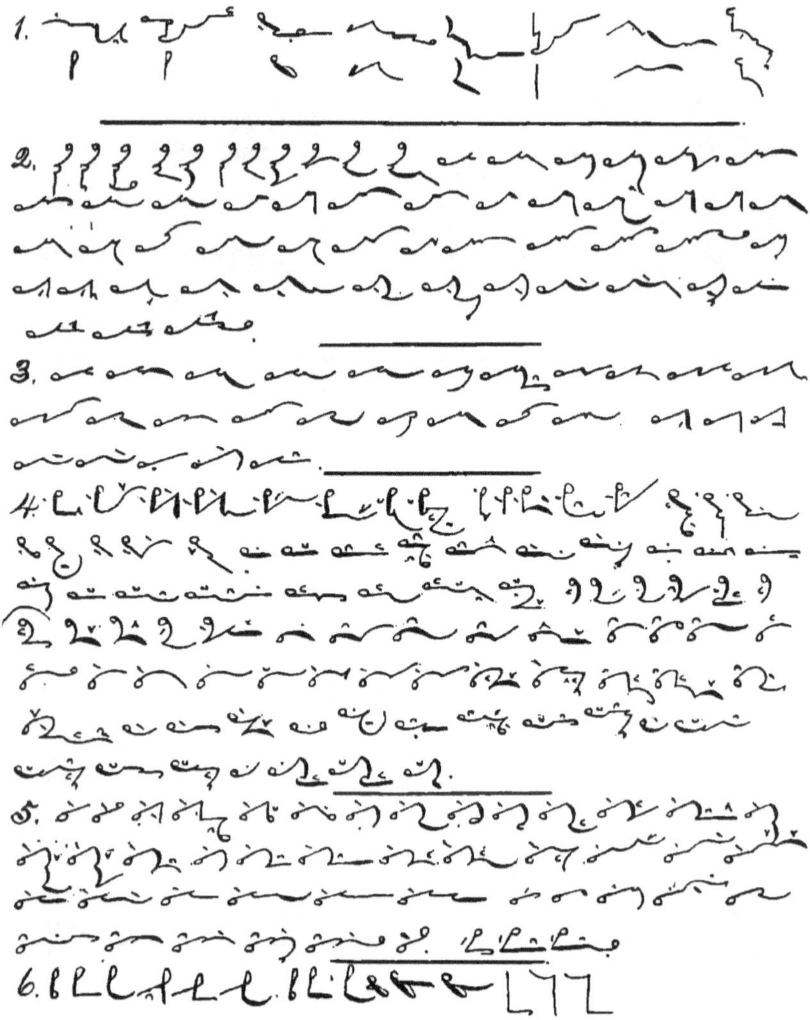

INSTRUCTIONS FOR LESSON 14.

1. The loop in the first three words indicates ST.
2. These words begin with SL (as in sleep, slack, etc.)
3. These words begin with SW (as in sway, swing, etc.)
4. In these words the S does not form a true difthongal sound with the following consonant, as in the previous numbers, but has a vowel between it and the consonant at the beginning of which it is joined. This vowel is written at the left of or above the consonant.
5. These words begin with SR with a vowel between the S and R, which is written to the left of the R, as in sir, serve, etc.

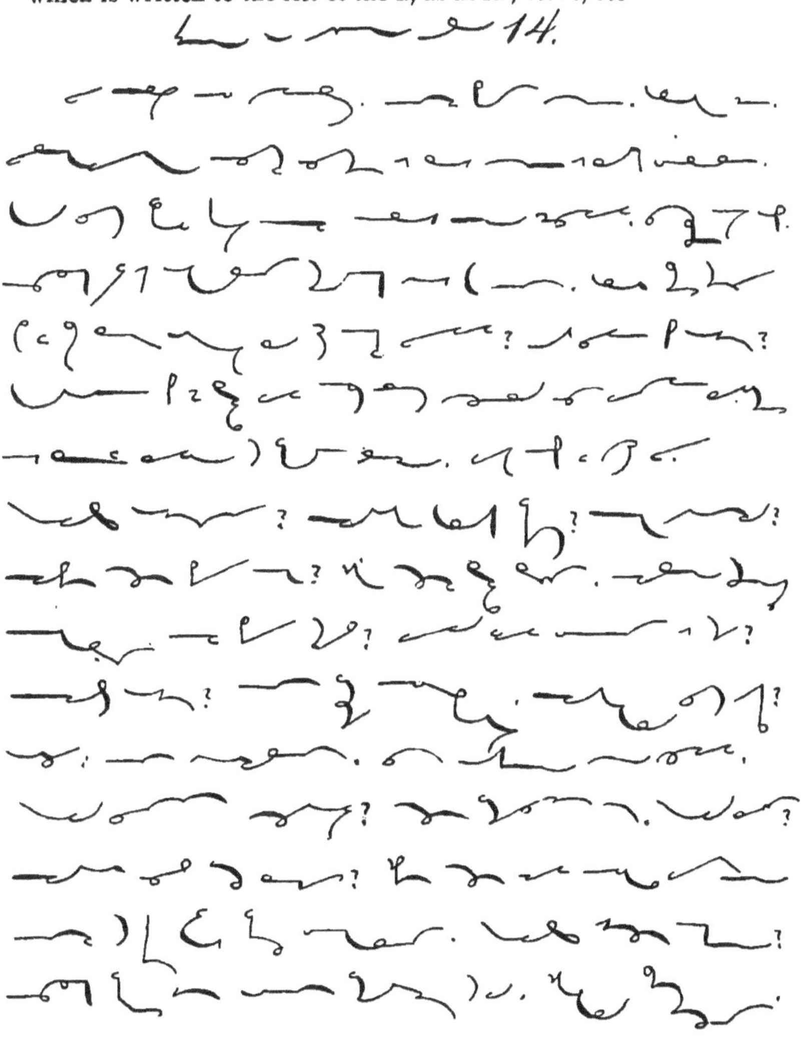

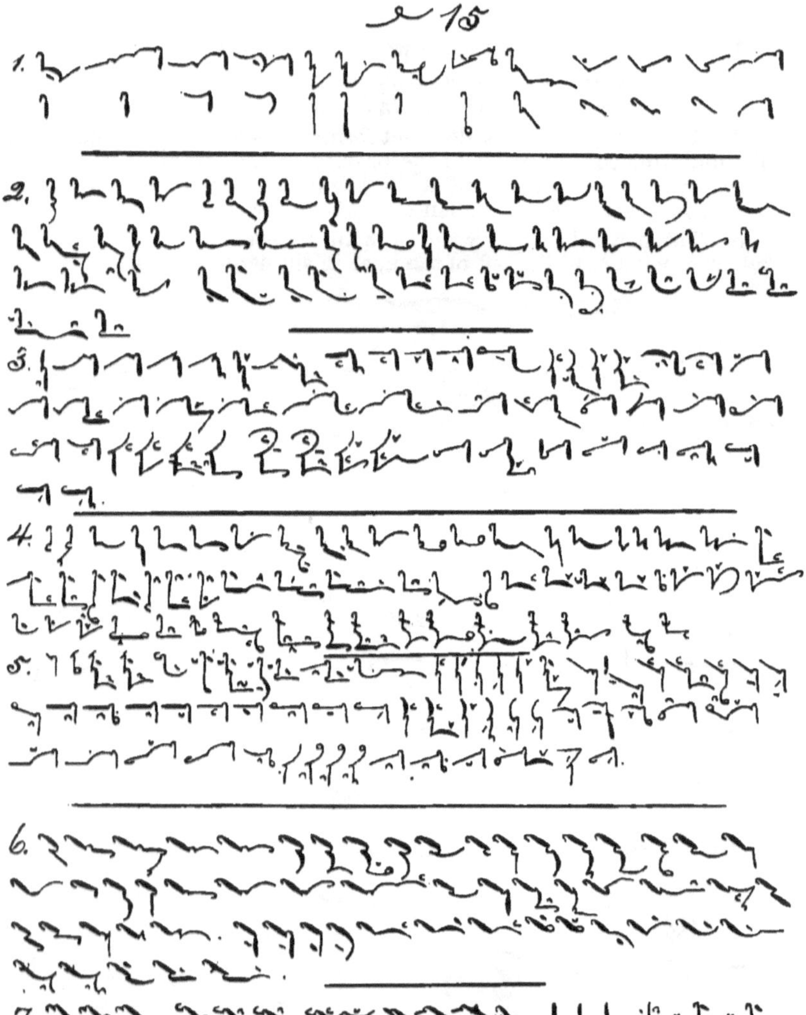
15
1.
2.
3.
4.
5.
6.
7.
8.

INSTRUCTIONS FOR LESSON 15.

A small initial hook is made on the left and under side of strait consonants to indicate the unicn of R with that letter, forming a consonant difthong.

2. These words begin with BR (as in brief, breeze).
3. These words end with BR (ber as in rubber, lumber).
4. These words begin with PR (as in pray, prune).

Generally the use of these hooks is restricted to words where there is no vowel sound between the R and its difthongal partner, but in some very frequently occurring words this practice is not observed, the hooked letter being used in such words as peruse, pertinacious, No. 4, line 3, words 6, 7 and following. In this class of words, in this and following Lessons, the vowel is written thru the hooked letter.

5. These words end with PER (as in upper, caper).
6. These words begin with GR (as in green, grow).
7. These words end with GER (as in eager, meager, etc.)

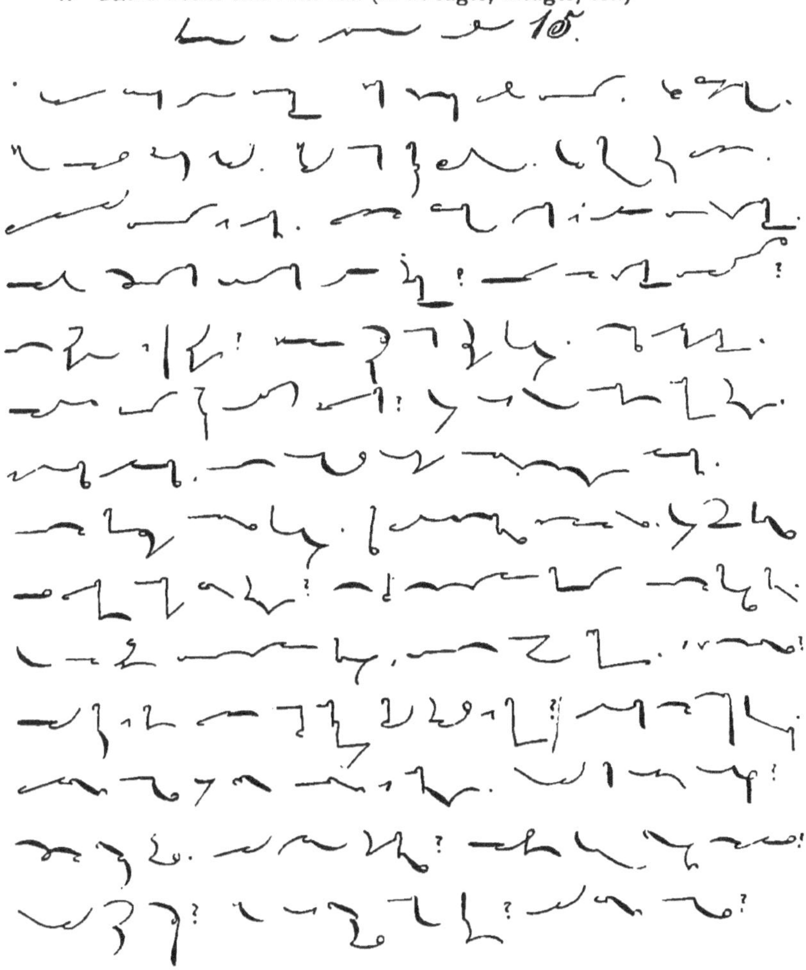

16

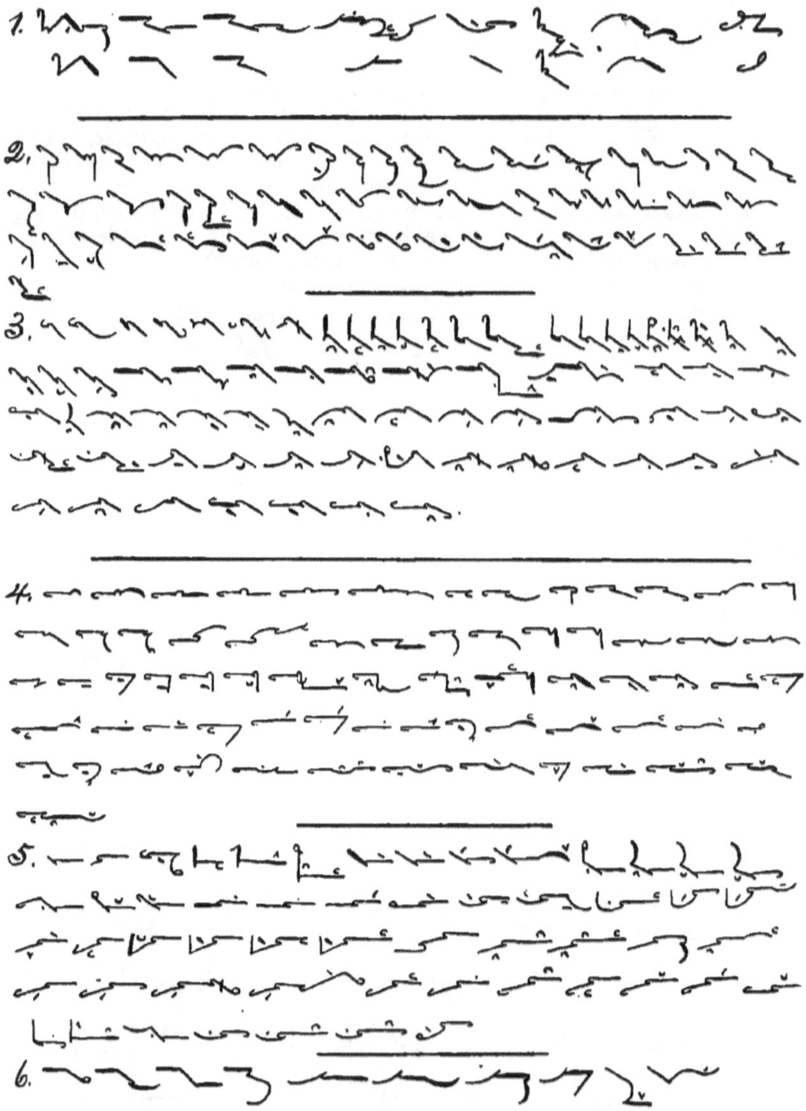

INSTRUCTIONS FOR LESSON 16.

2. These words begin with KR (cr as in creep, crape, etc.)
3. These words end with KR (cur, ker, as in occur, baker, etc.)
4. These words begin with TR (as in tree, try, etc.)
5. These words end with TR (as in utter, victor, etc.)
6. Derivatives from words in No. 1.

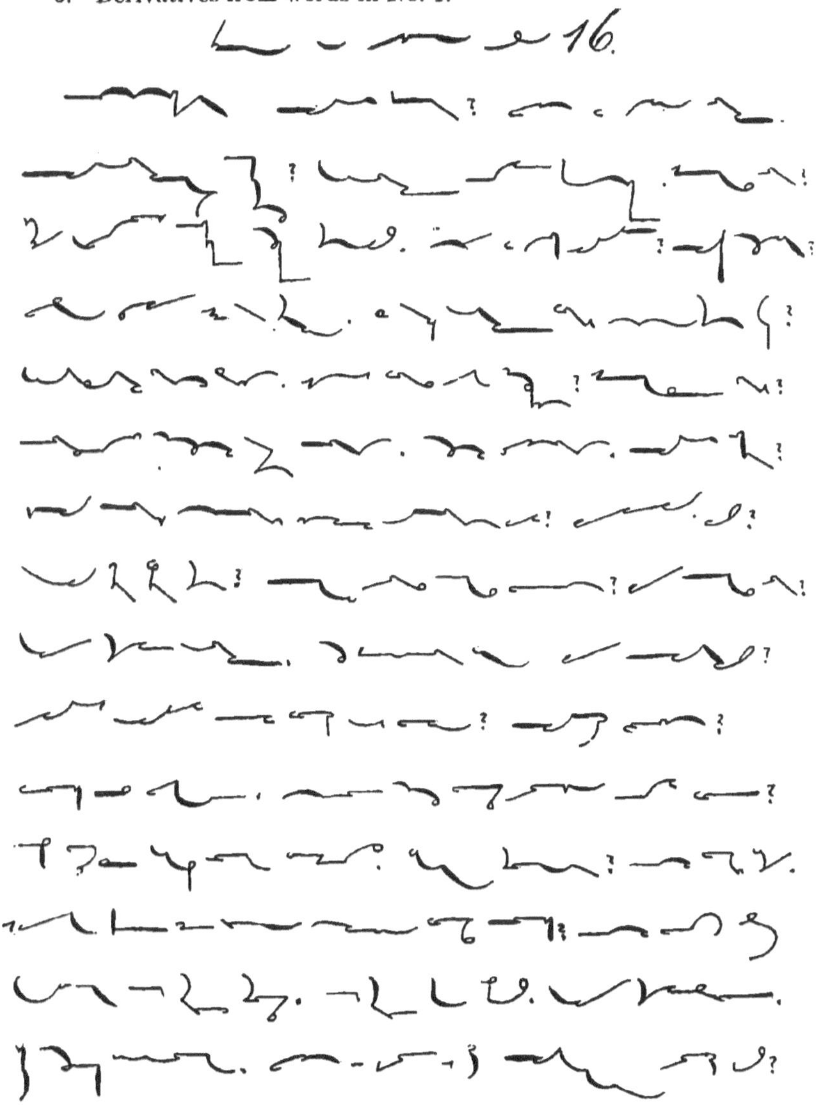

17.

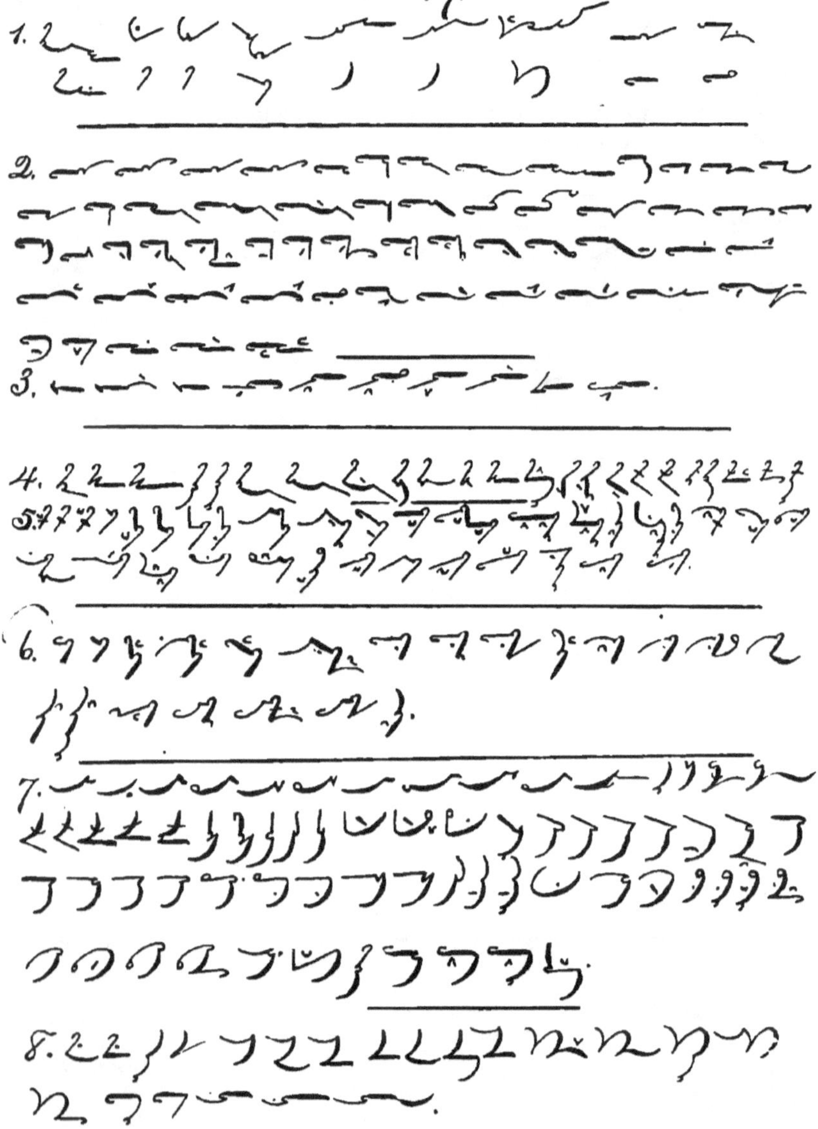

INSTRUCTIONS FOR LESSON 17.

2. These words begin with DR (as in draw, dray, etc.)
3. These words end with DR (as in odor, rudder, etc.)
4. The hook is made on the left of the upper end of R, written downward for SHR (as in shriek, shrine).
5. These word end with SHR (as in usher, pressure, etc.)
6. The compound letter for SHR, explained above, is shaded for ZHR (sure, sier, as in treasure, osier, etc.) It occurs only in the end of words.
7. These words show the letter L shaded to indicate its difthongal union with R, with or without a vowel sound between them (as in layer, solar, etc.)
8. Derivative words formed from primitives in No. 1.

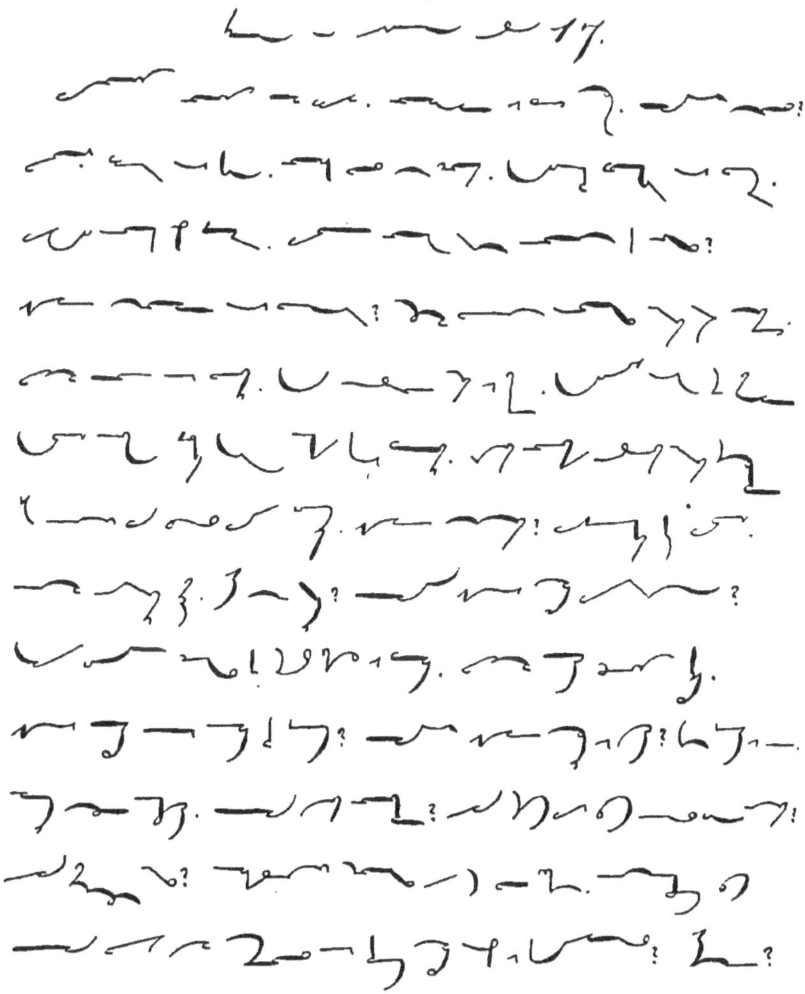

18.

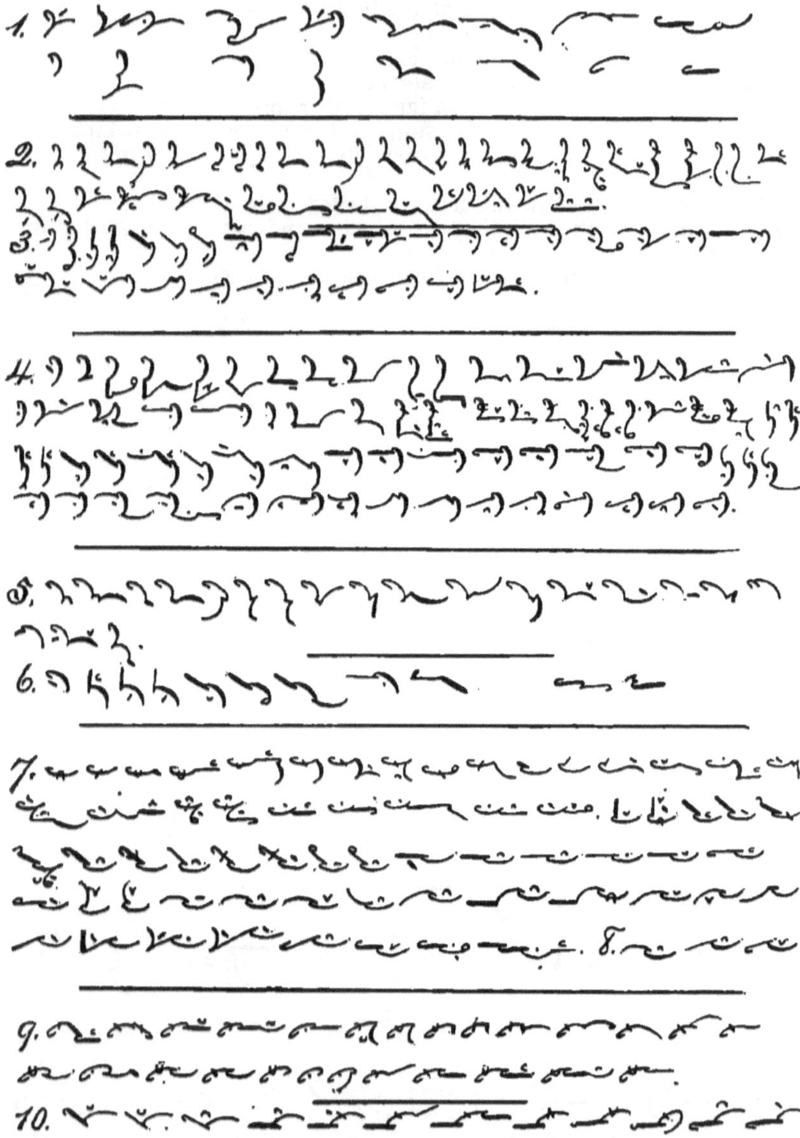

INSTRUCTIONS FOR LESSON 18.

2. These words begin with FR (as in free, fry, etc.)
3. These words end with FR (fer as in offer, wafer, etc.)
4. These words end with VR (ver as in over, sever, etc.)
5. This hooked letter represents THR at the beginning or end of words (as in three, author, etc.)
6. This hooked letter represents THR (as in other, gather, etc.)
7. This hooked letter represents NR, usually with a vowel sound between the N and R (as in near, owner, etc.)
8. This hooked letter represents NGR (as in singer, hanger, etc.)
9. These words begin with MR with a vowel between them (as in merit, morrow, etc.)
10. These words end with MR (as in grammar, farmer, etc.)

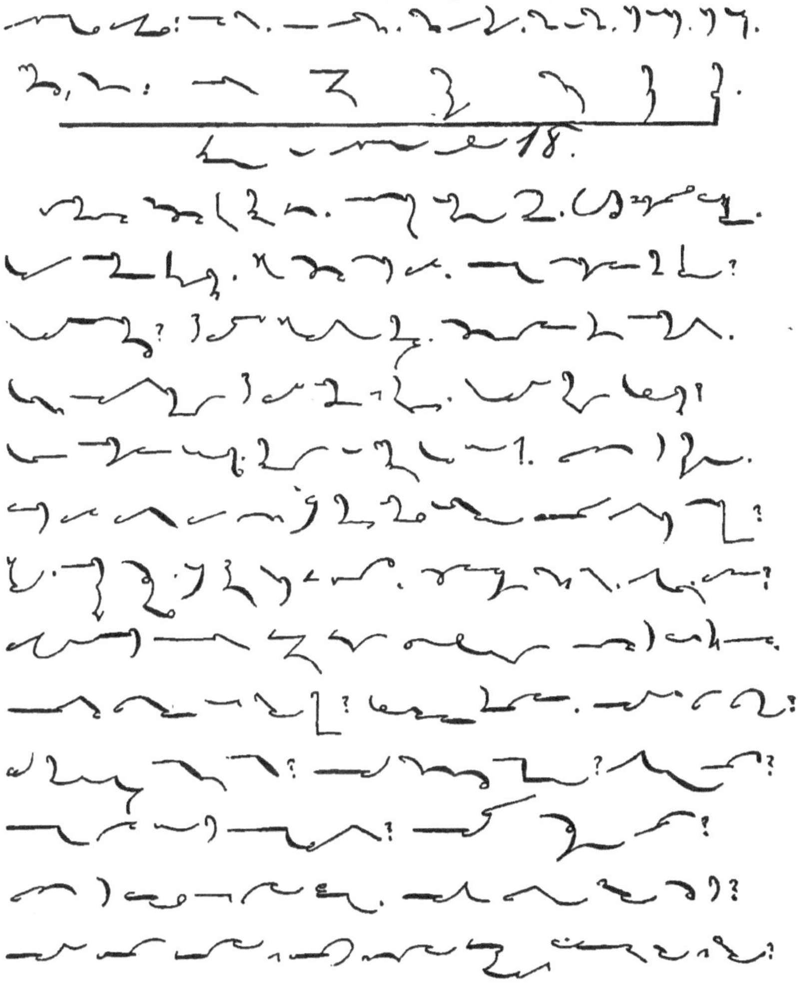

19.

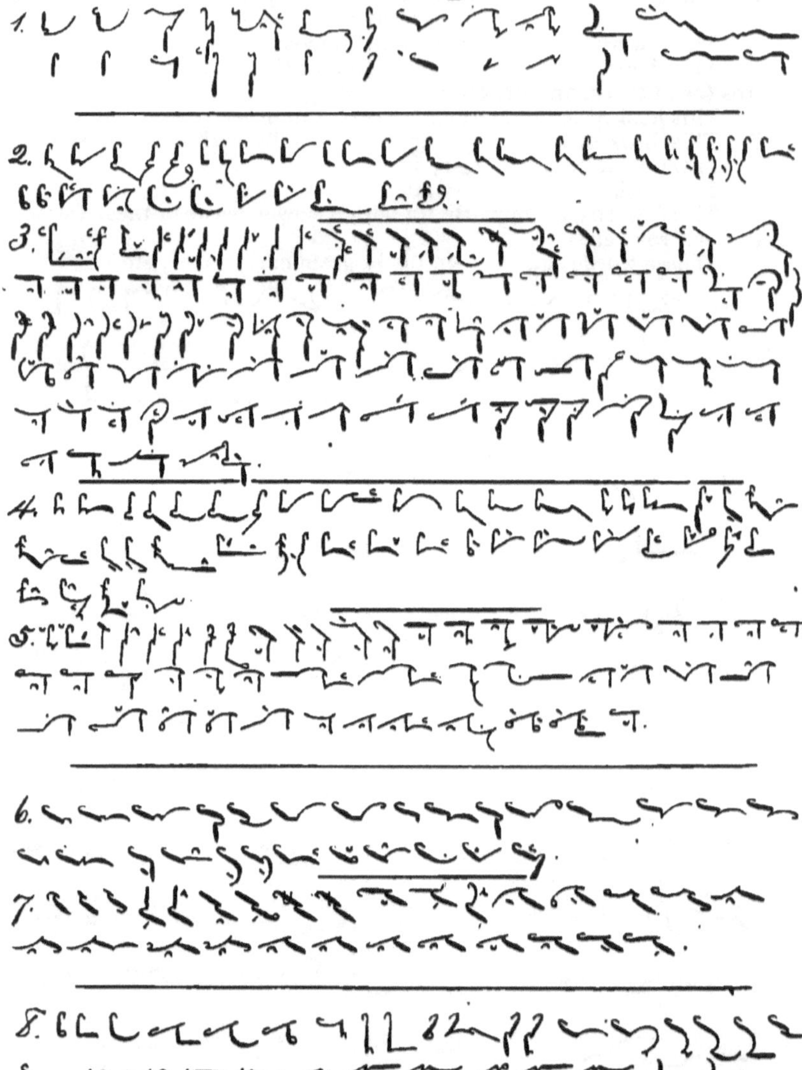

INSTRUCTIONS FOR LESSON 19.

A small hook is made on the right and upper side of strait letters to show their difthongal union with L, as previously explained for R in Lesson 15.

2. These words begin with BL (as in black, blow, etc.)
3. These words end with BLE (as in able, noble, etc.)
4. These words begin with PL (as in plea, plus, etc.)
5. These words end with PLE, PAL, (as in ample, opal, etc.)
6. These words begin with GL (as in glee, glen, etc.)
7. These words end with GLE, GAL, (as in ogle, legal, etc.)
8. Derivatives formed from words in No. 1.

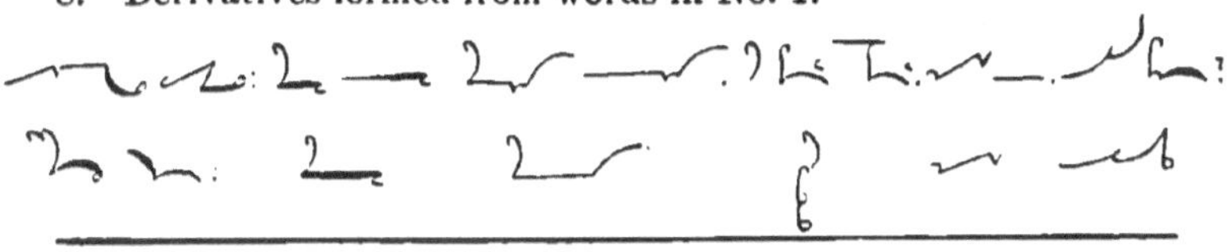

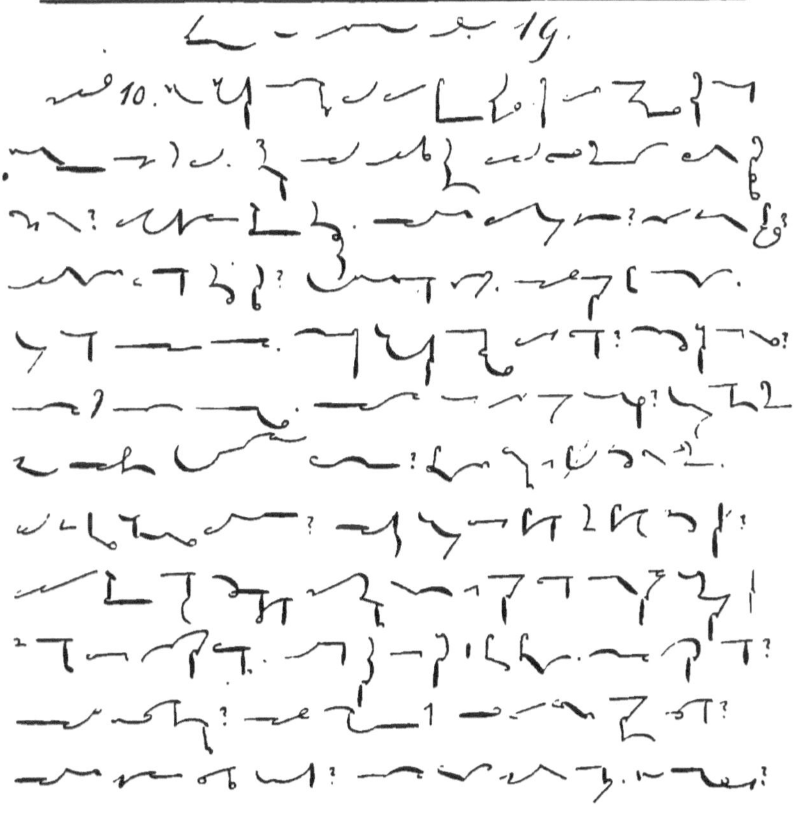

20.

1. 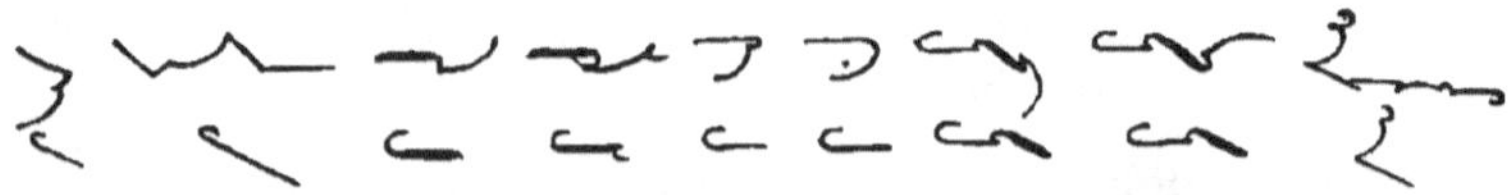

2. 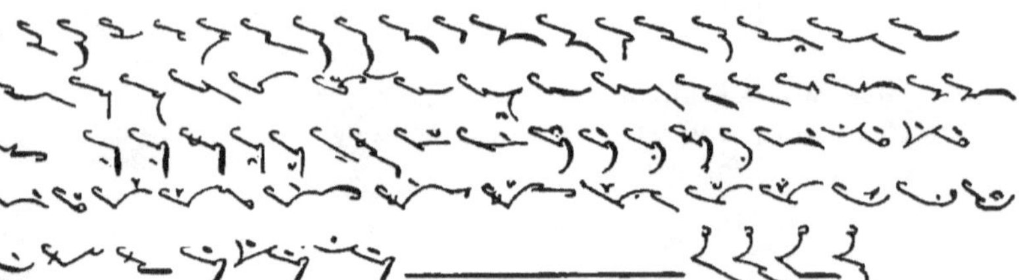

3. 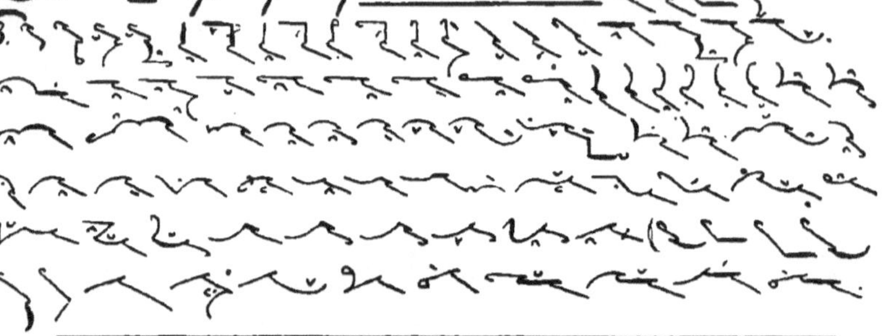

4. 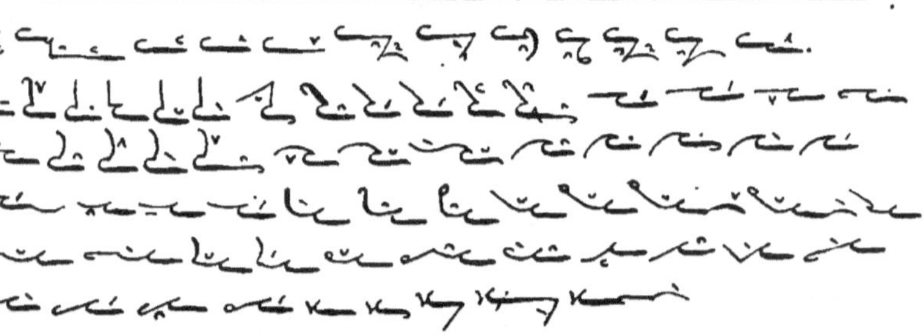

5. 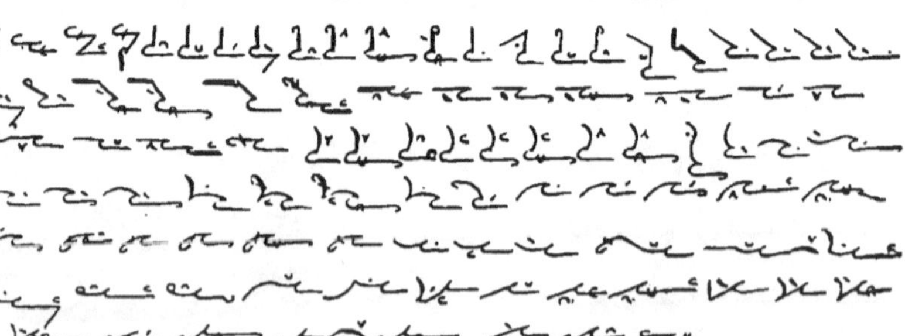

INSTRUCTIONS FOR LESSON 20.

---

2 These words begin with KL (cl as in clean, close, etc.)

3. These words end with KL (cle, kle, as in circle, nickle, etc.)

4. A large hook is made on the upper side of D for DL to distinguish DL from J (as in the words delude, middle.)

5. A large hook is made on the upper side of T for TL, to distinguish TL from CH (as in the words tolerate, metal, etc.)

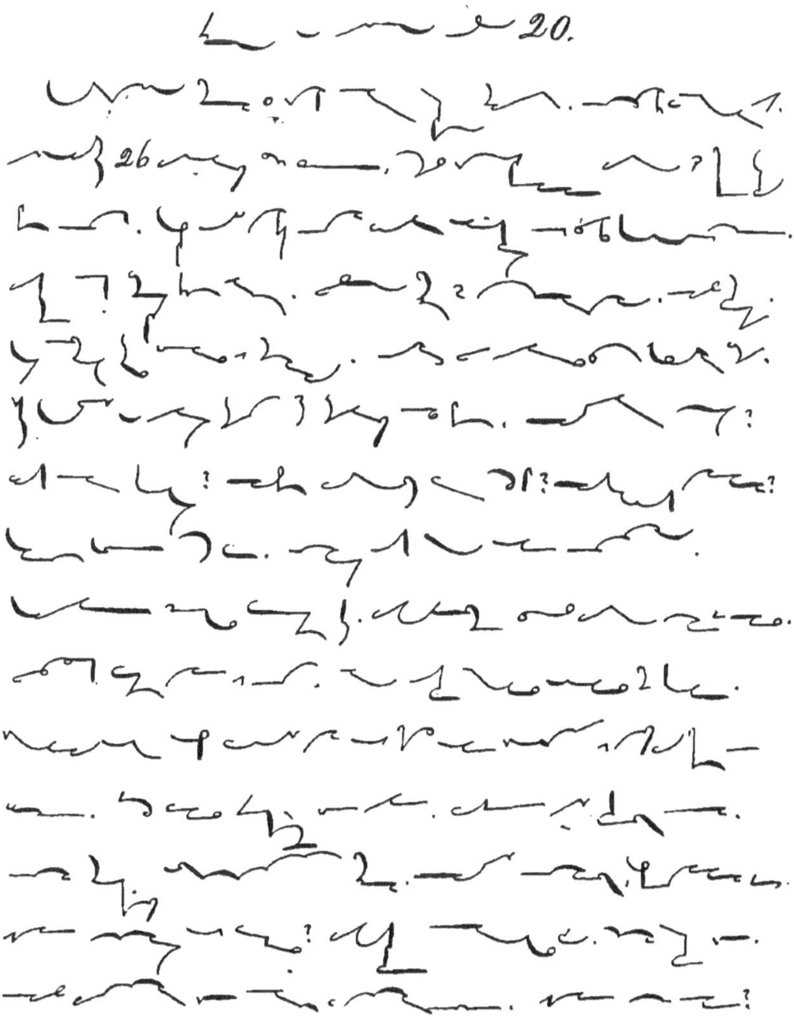

21.

1. 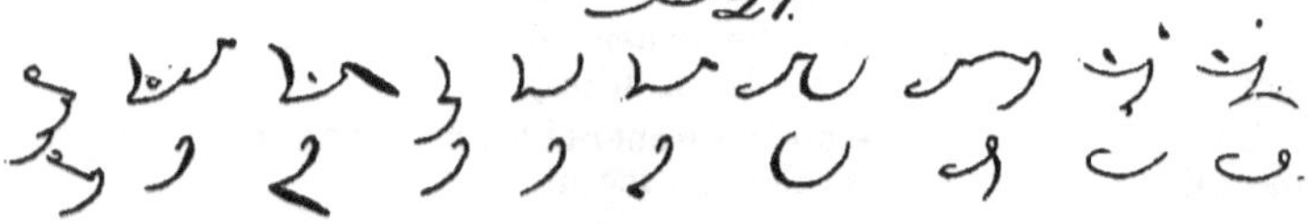

2. 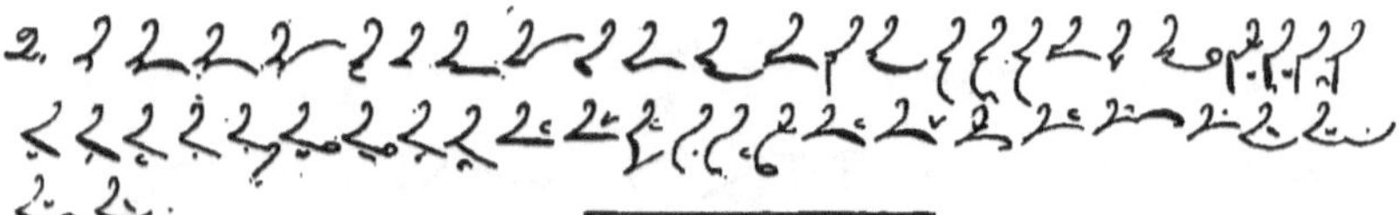

3. 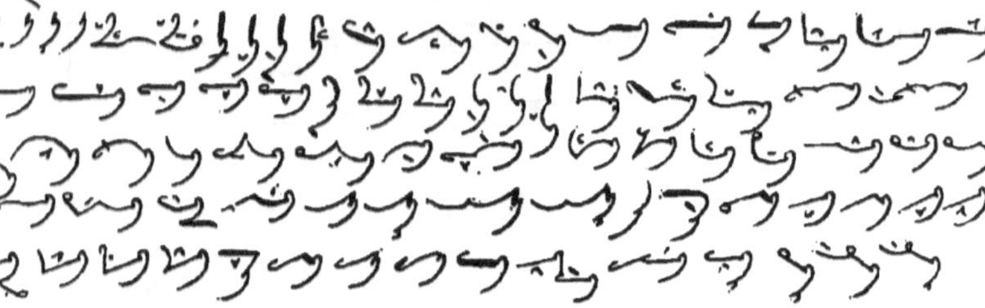

4. 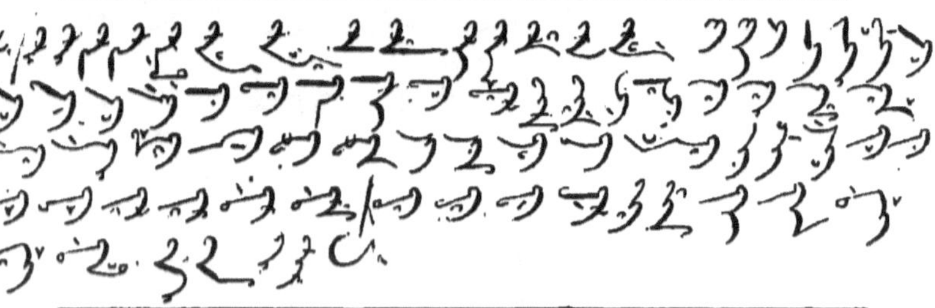

5. 

6. 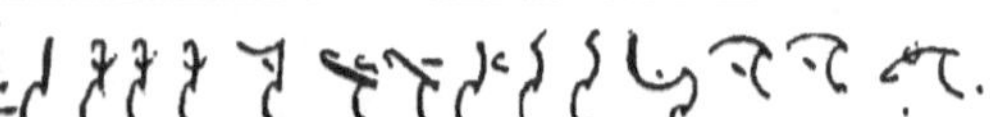

7. 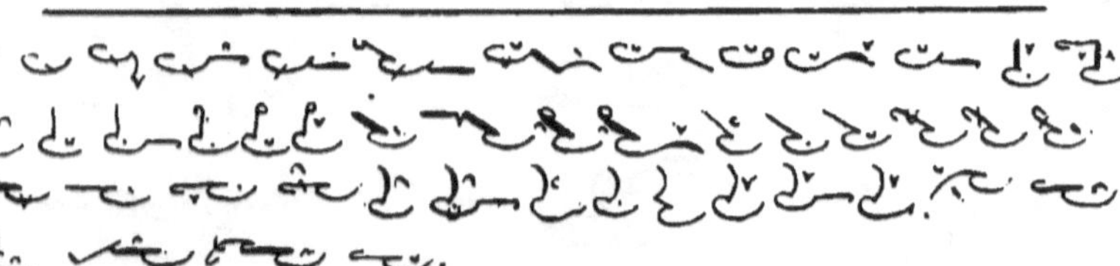

8. 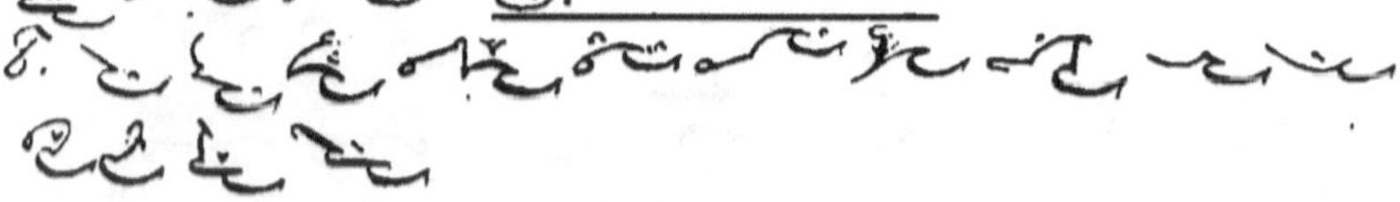

INSTRUCTIONS FOR LESSON 21.

2. A small hook is made upon the upper end of L, written downward, for FL (as in flee, flung, etc.)
3. These words end with FL (fle, ful, as in trifle, awful, etc.)
4. The hooked letter explained above is shaded for VL (as in valley, oval, bevel, etc.)
5. This hooked letter represents ZHL (sial, sual, as in ambrosial, casual, etc.)
6. This hooked letter represents SHL (cial, tial, as in social, partial, etc.)
7. This large hooked letter represents NL (as in null, panel, etc.)
8. This large hooked letter represents the termination INGLY (as in kingly, seemingly, etc.)

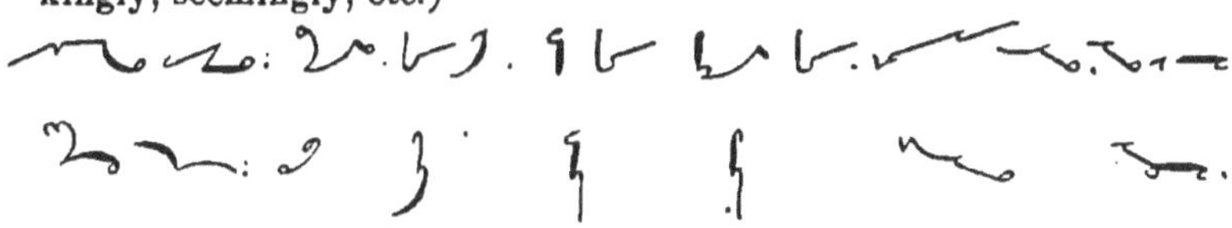

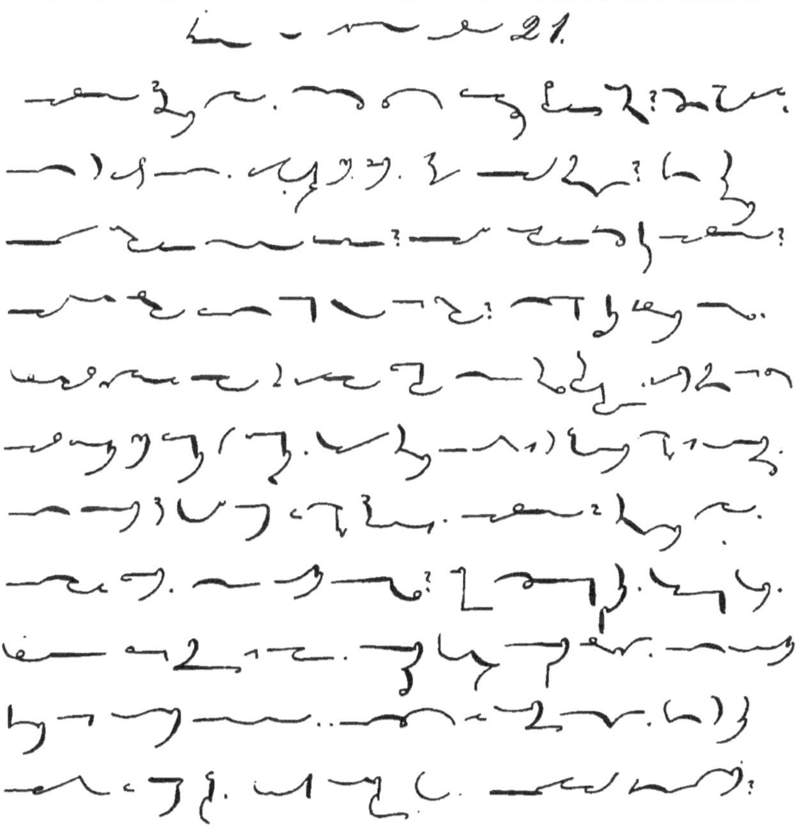

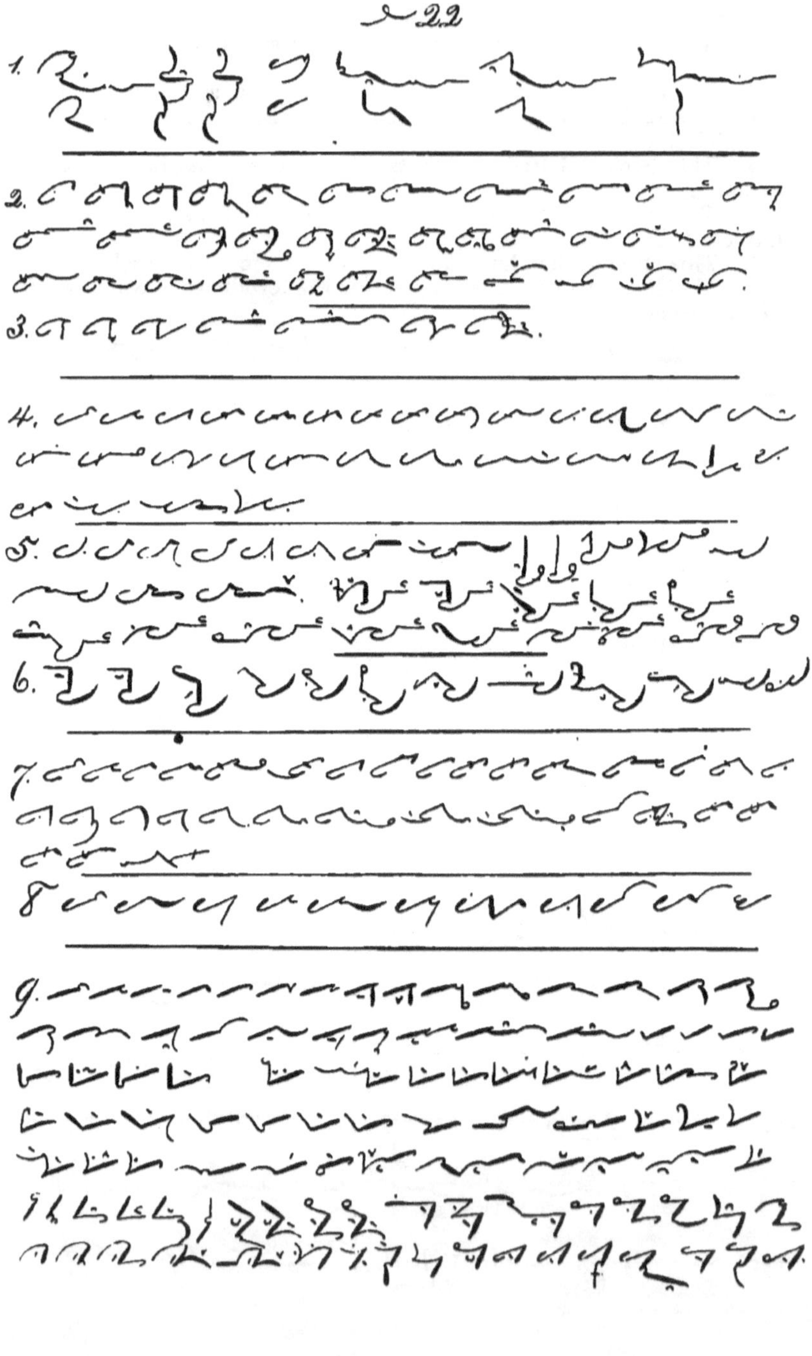
22
1.
2.
3.
4.
5.
6.
7.
8
9.

INSTRUCTIONS FOR LESSON 22.

2. This larged hooked letter represents ML (as in mellow, trammel, etc.)
3. ML in these words stands for the prefix MULTI (as in multiply.)
4. The hook of the W is enlarged for WL (as in wail, well, etc.)
5. The hook of the Y is enlarged for YL (as in yell, emulate, etc.)
6. The large hooked letter for YL is shaded for YLR, ULAR (as in tubular, jocular, etc.)
7. The hook of the H is enlarged for HL (as in heal, whole, etc.)
8. The hook of the WH is enlarged for WHL (as in whale, while, etc.)
9. The letter R is shaded for RL in such words as rule, pearl, sterile, etc.

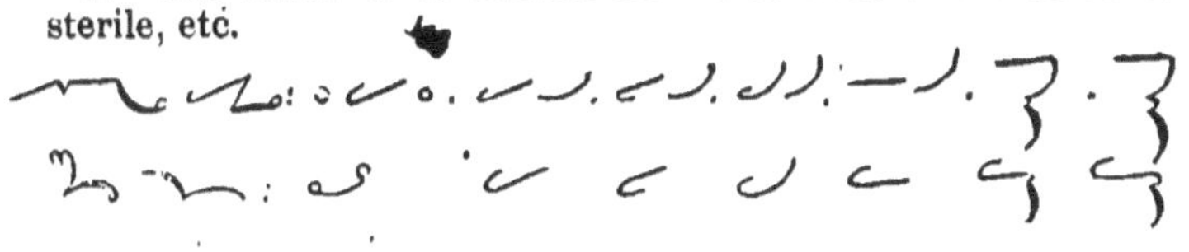

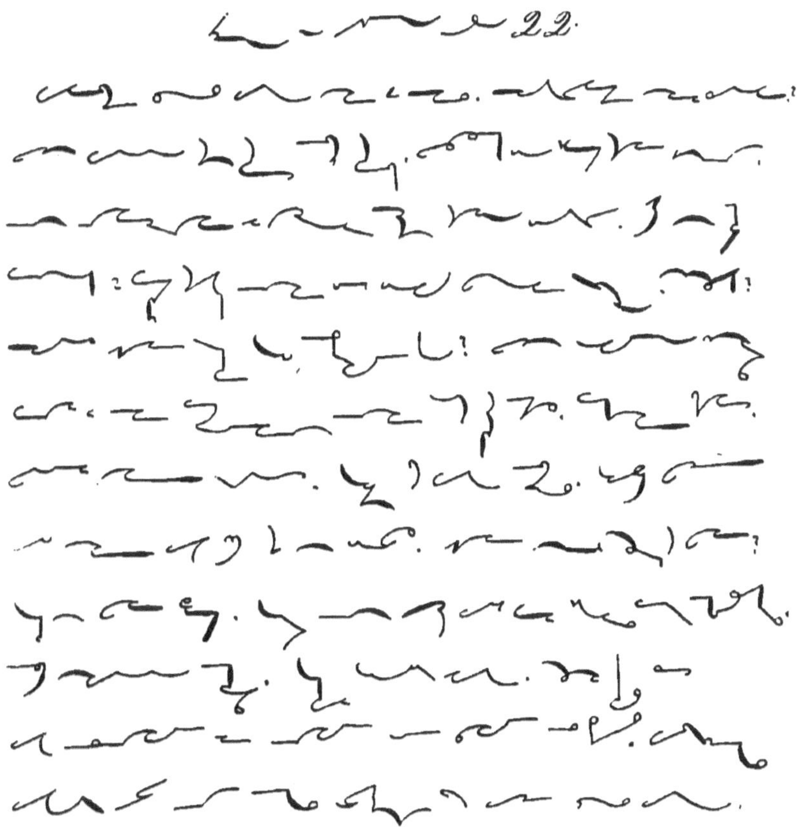

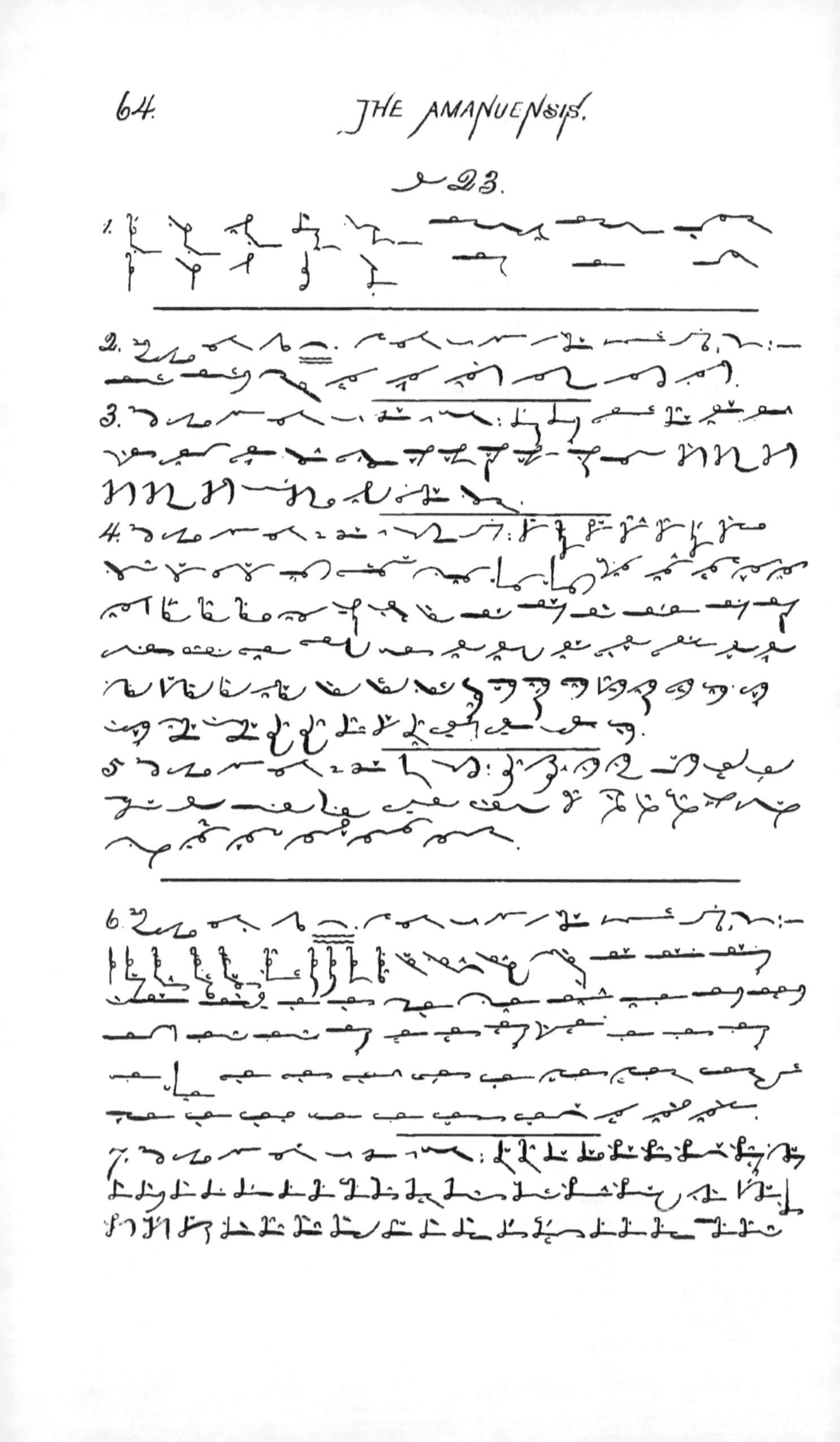

23.

1.

2.

3.

4.

5.

6.

7.

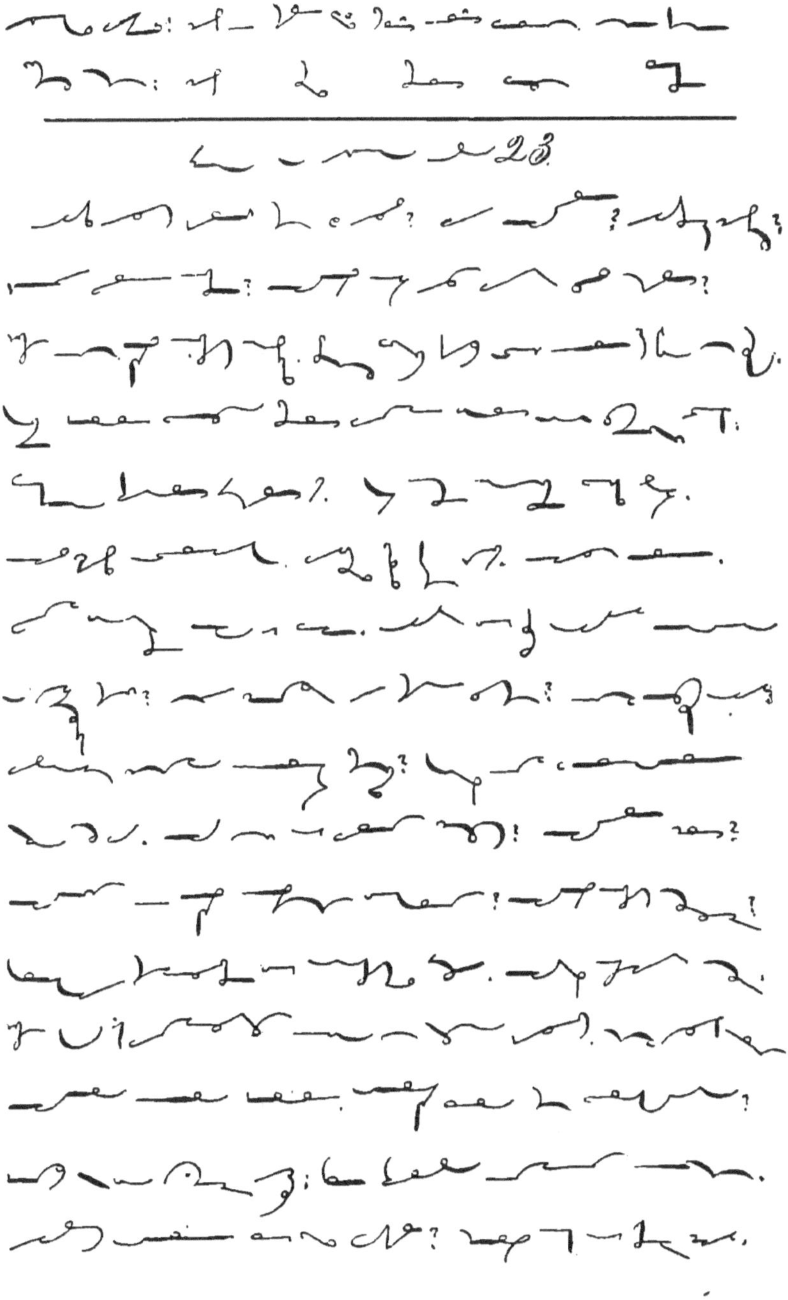

24.

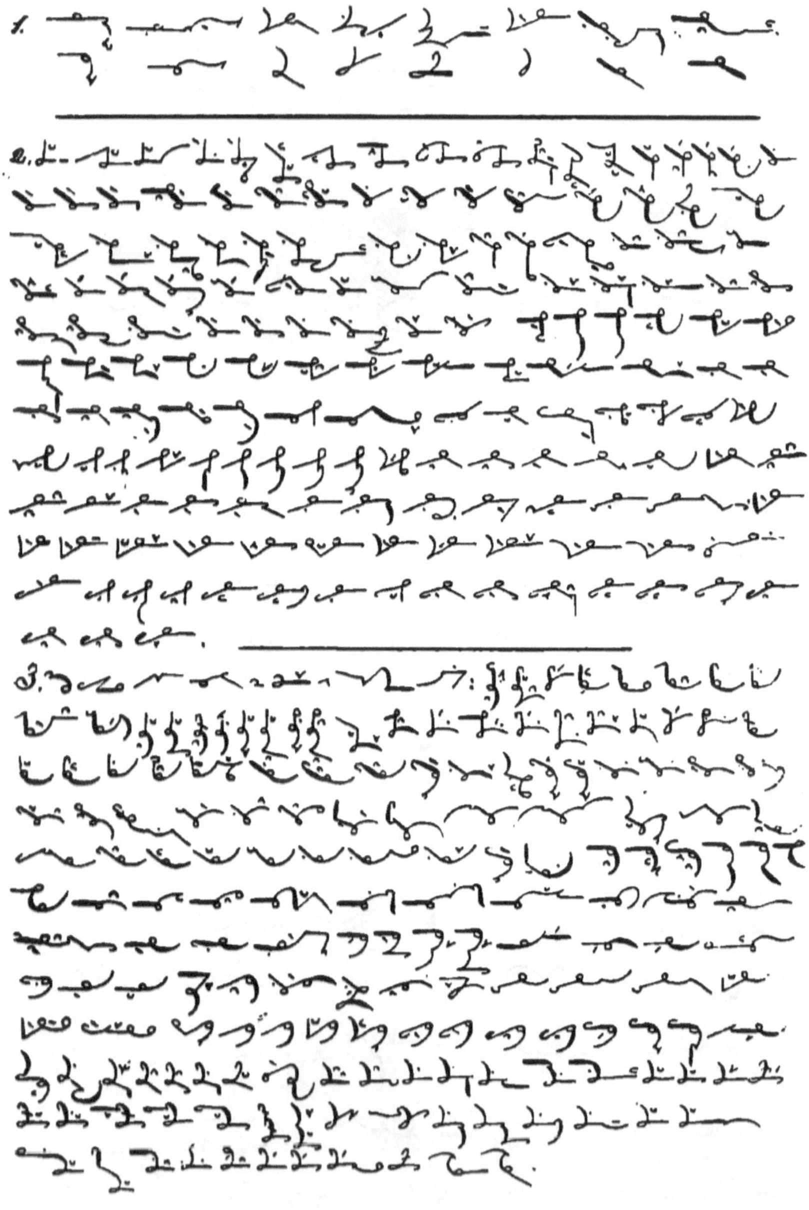

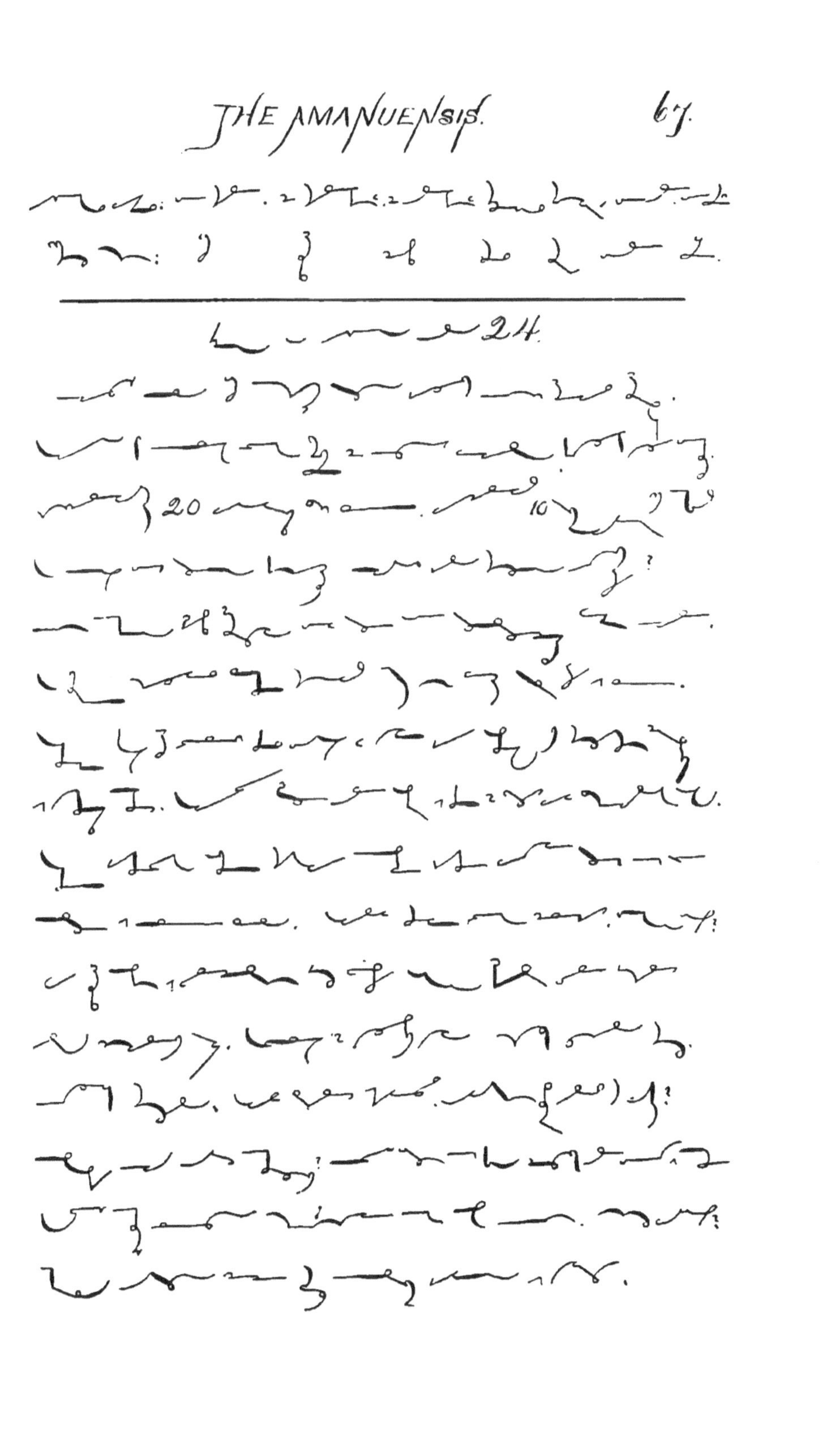

24

25

1.
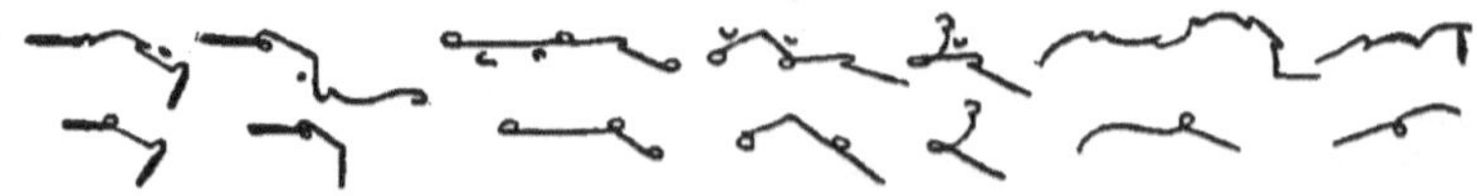

2.
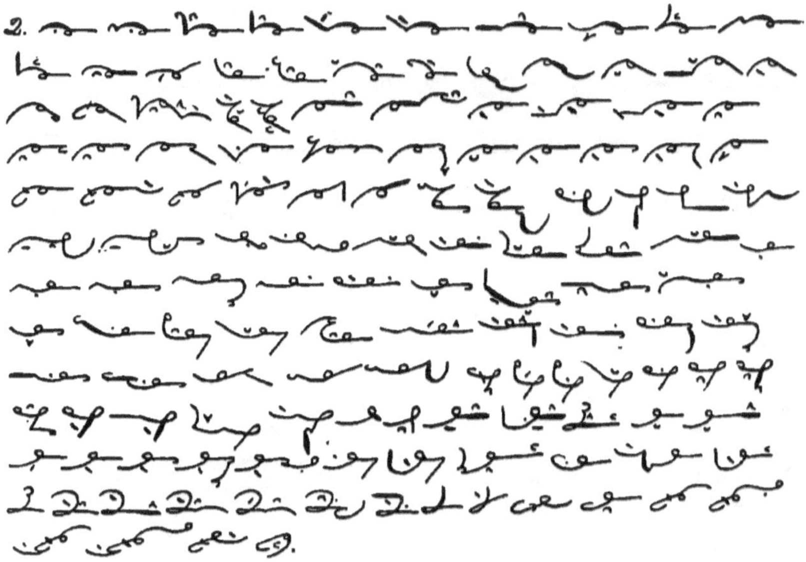

3.
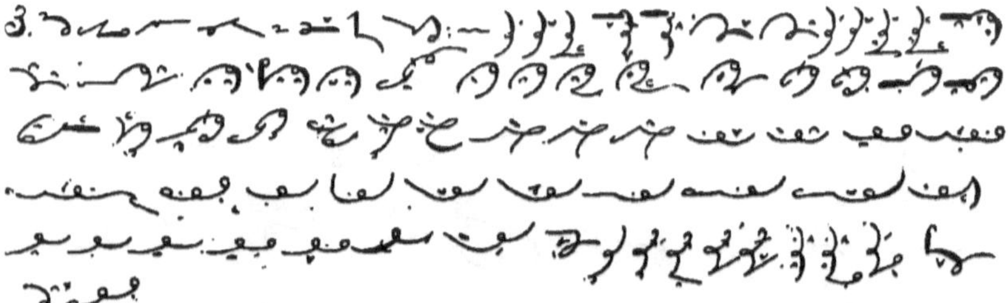

4.
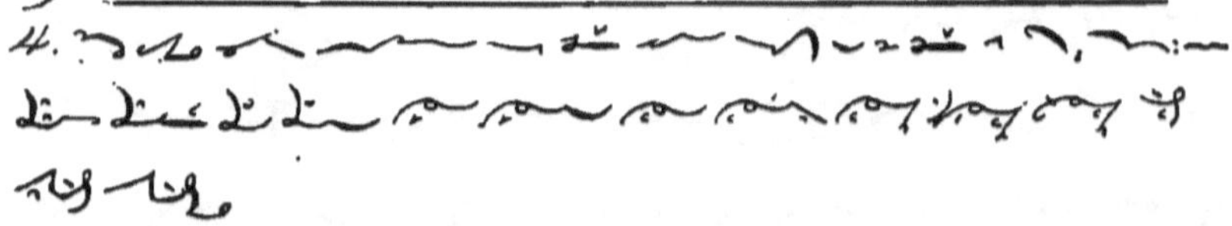

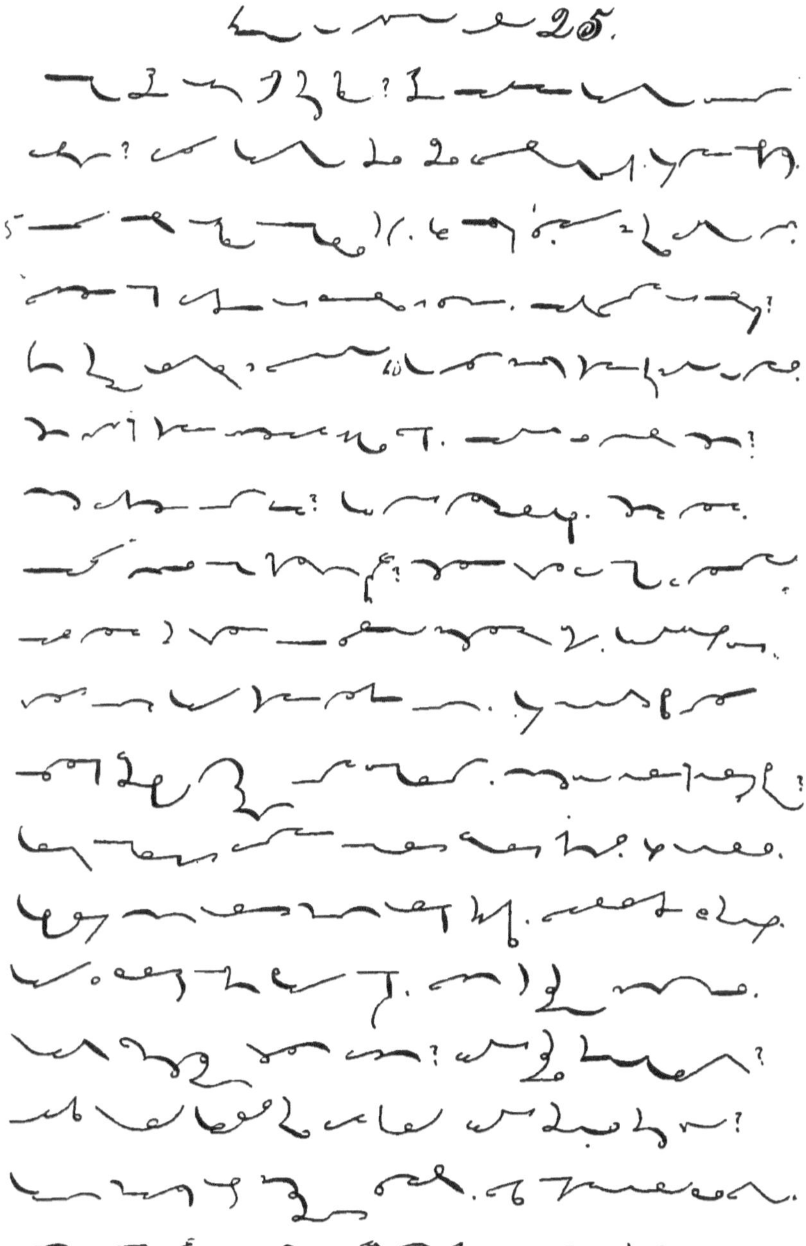

26.

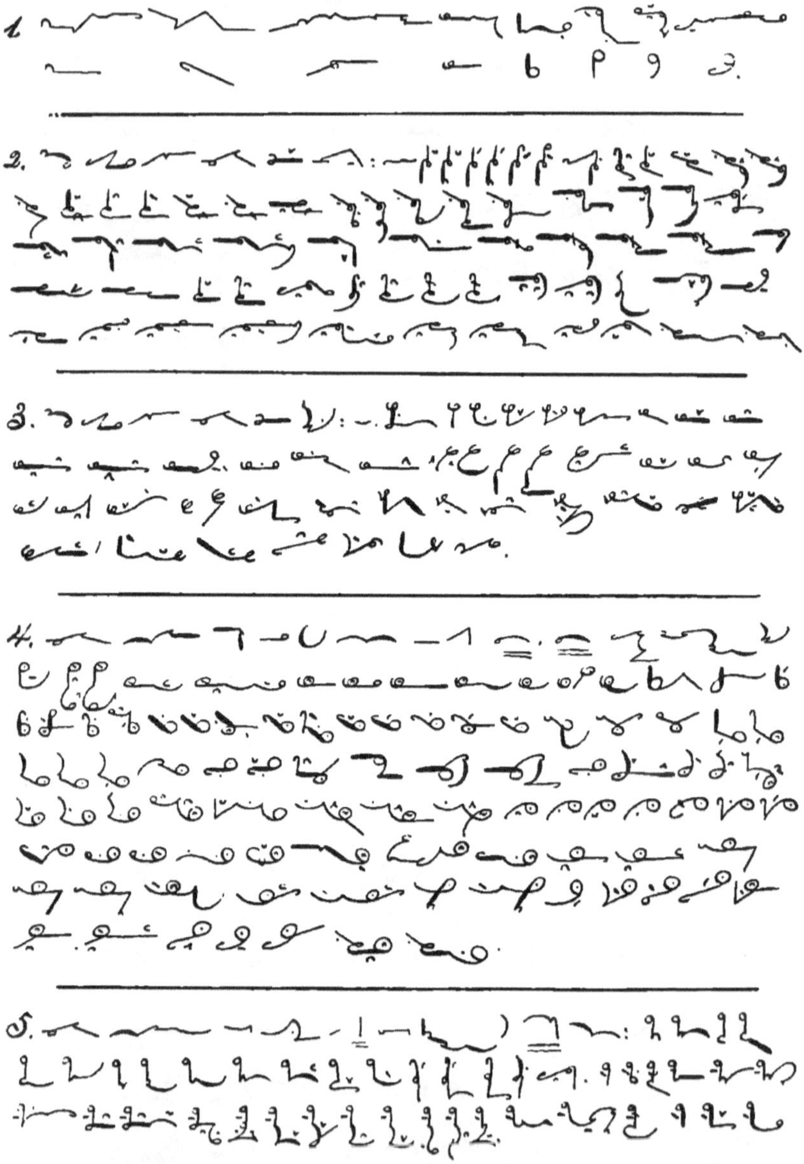

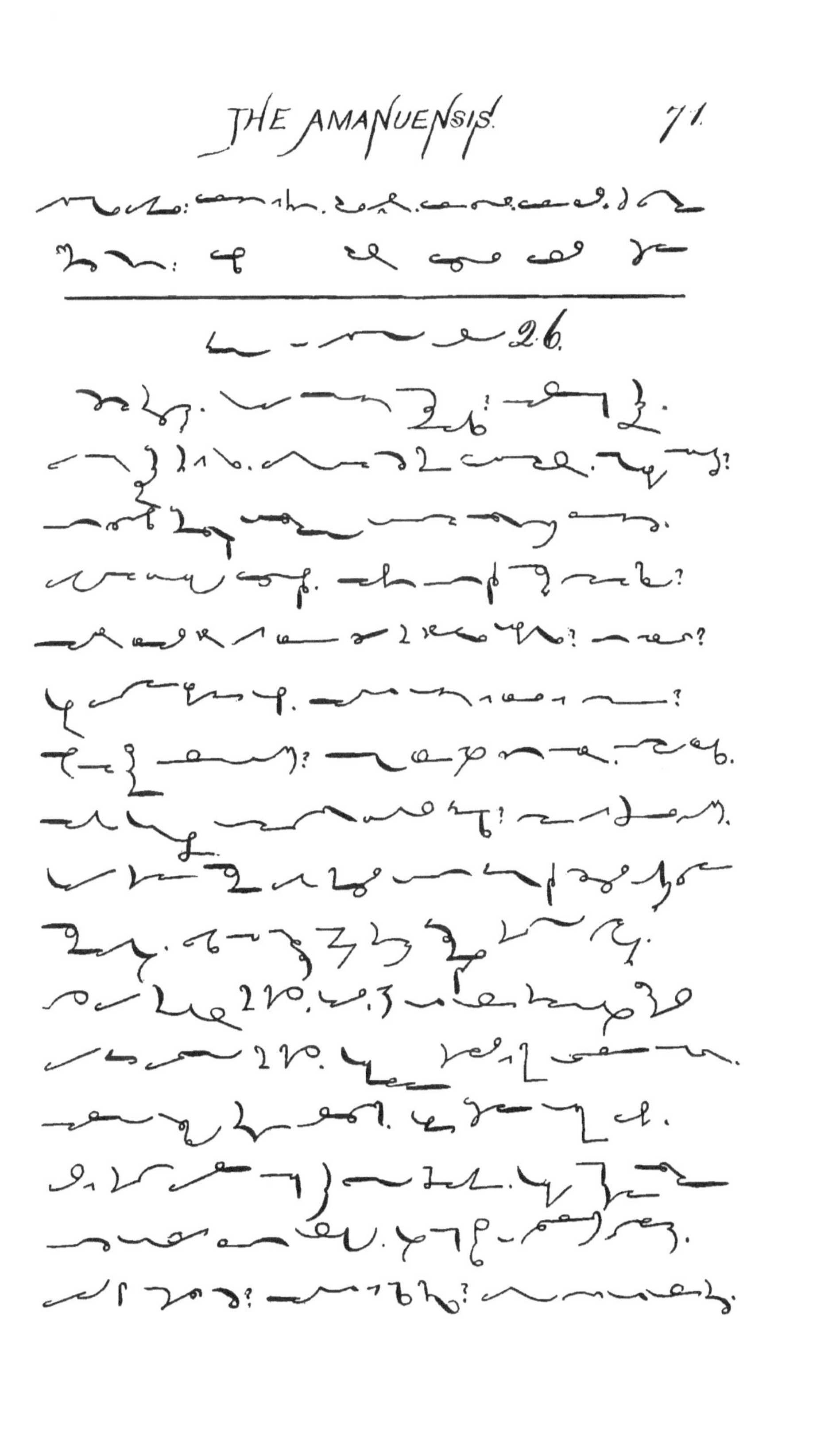

26

27

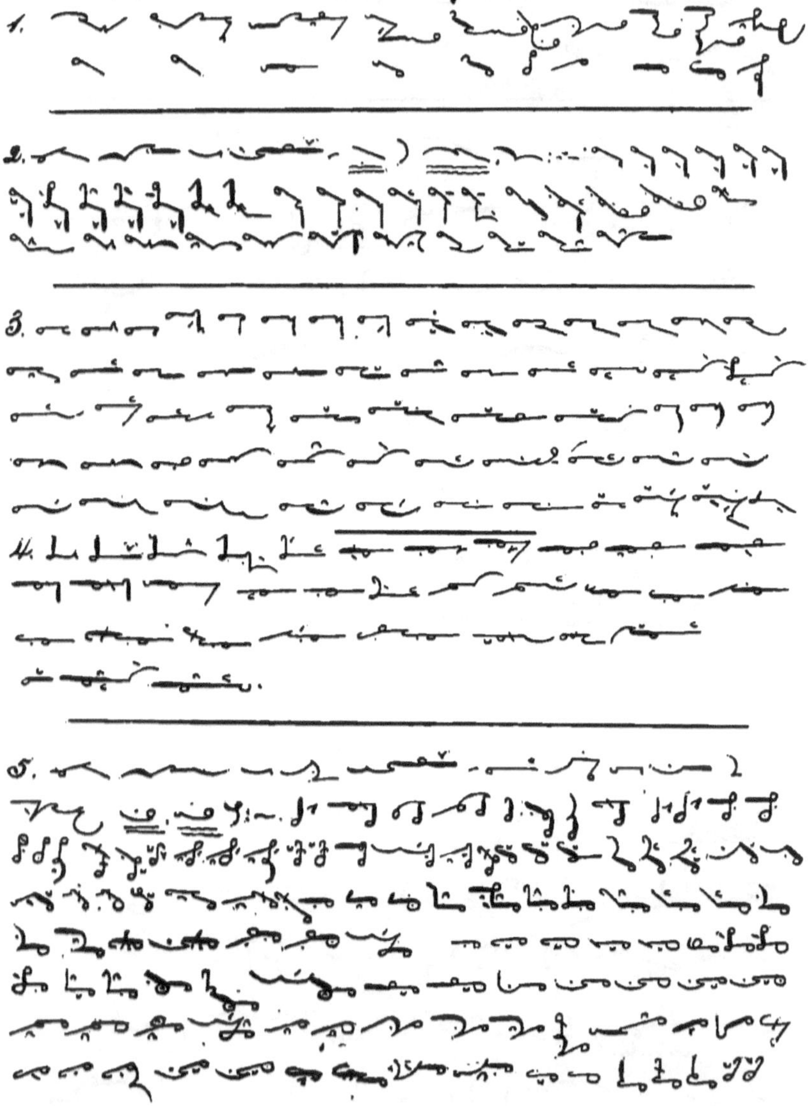

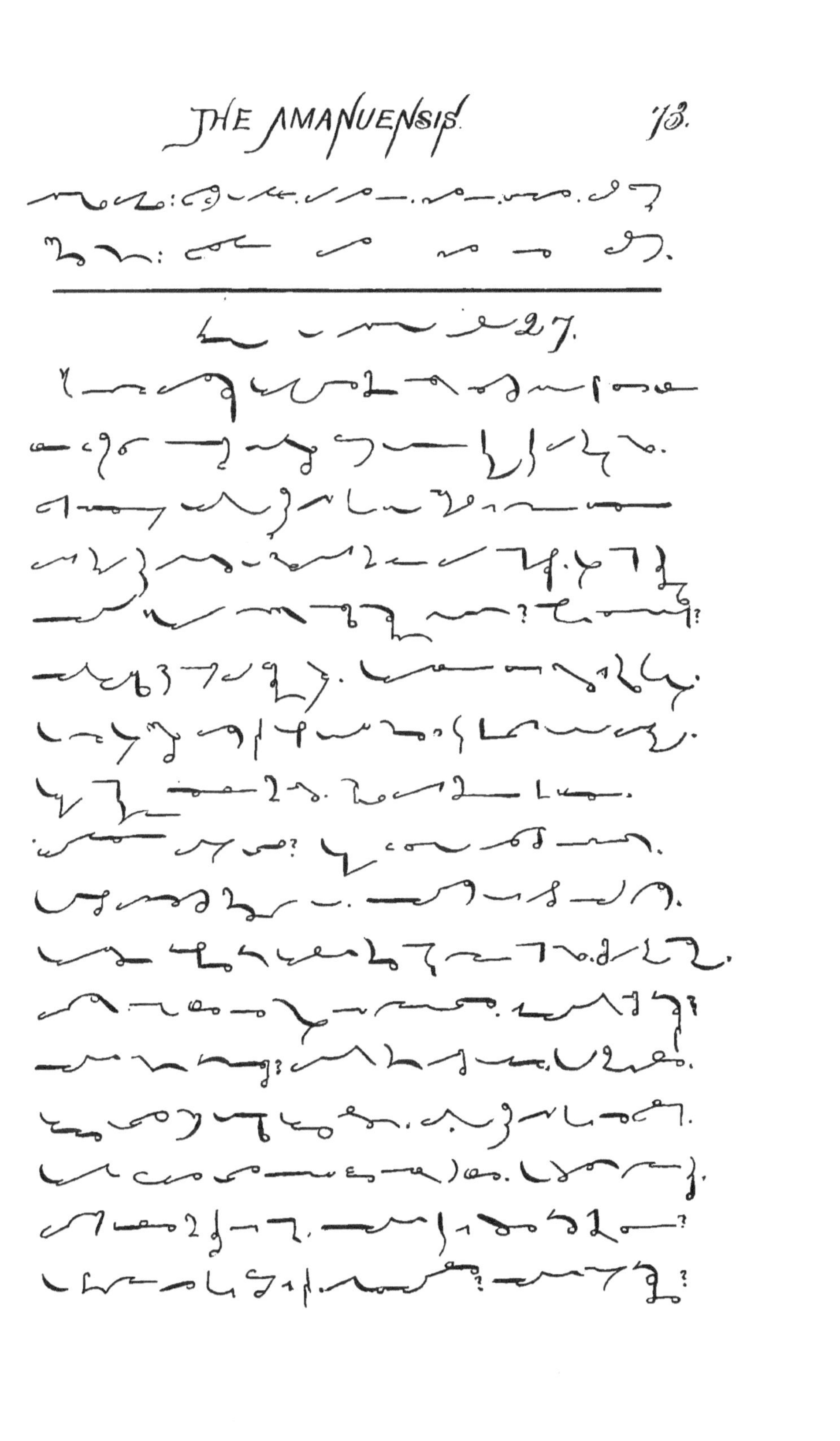

27.

28.

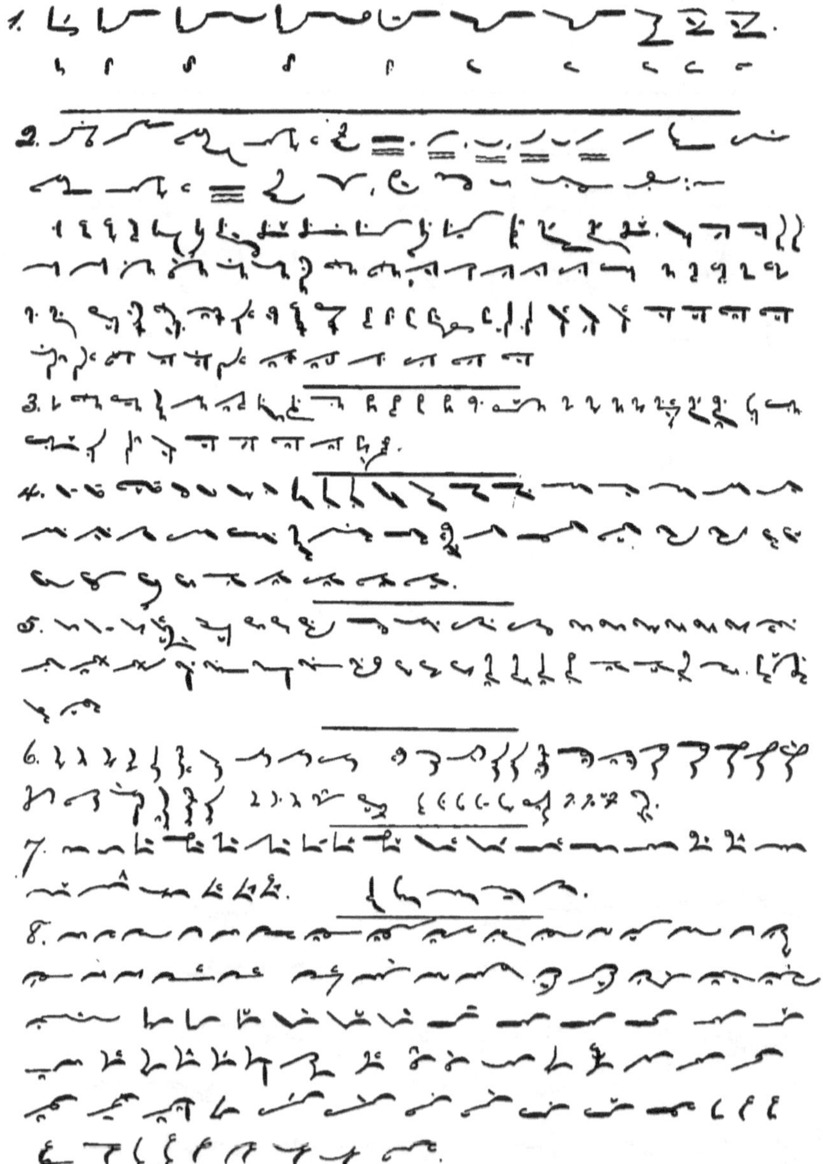

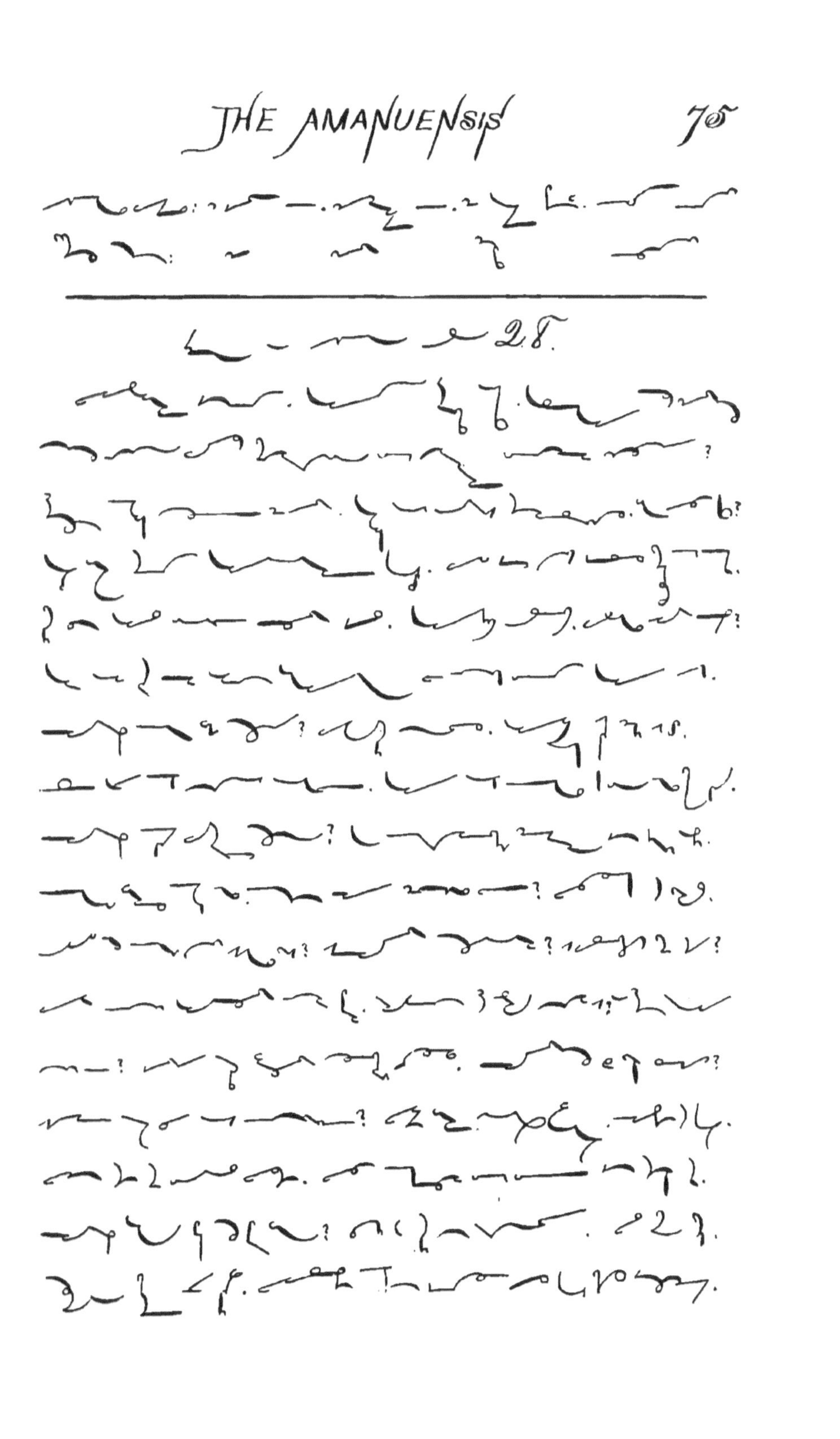

28.

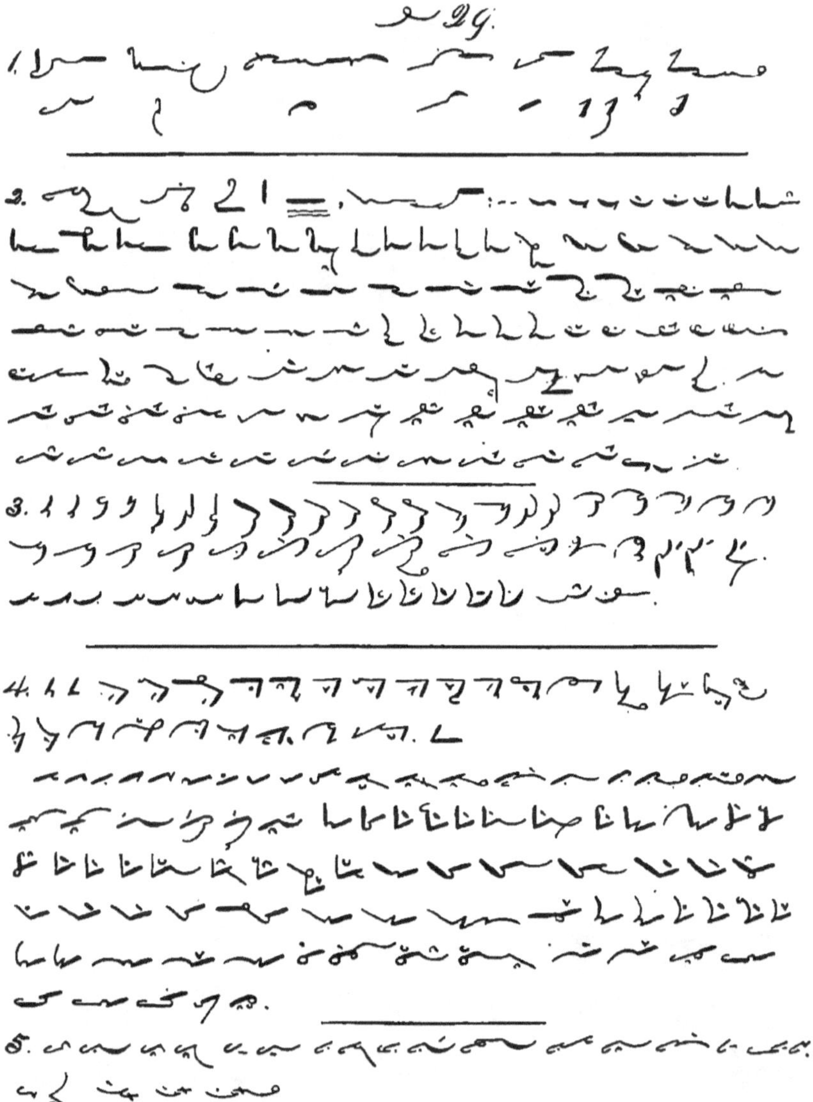

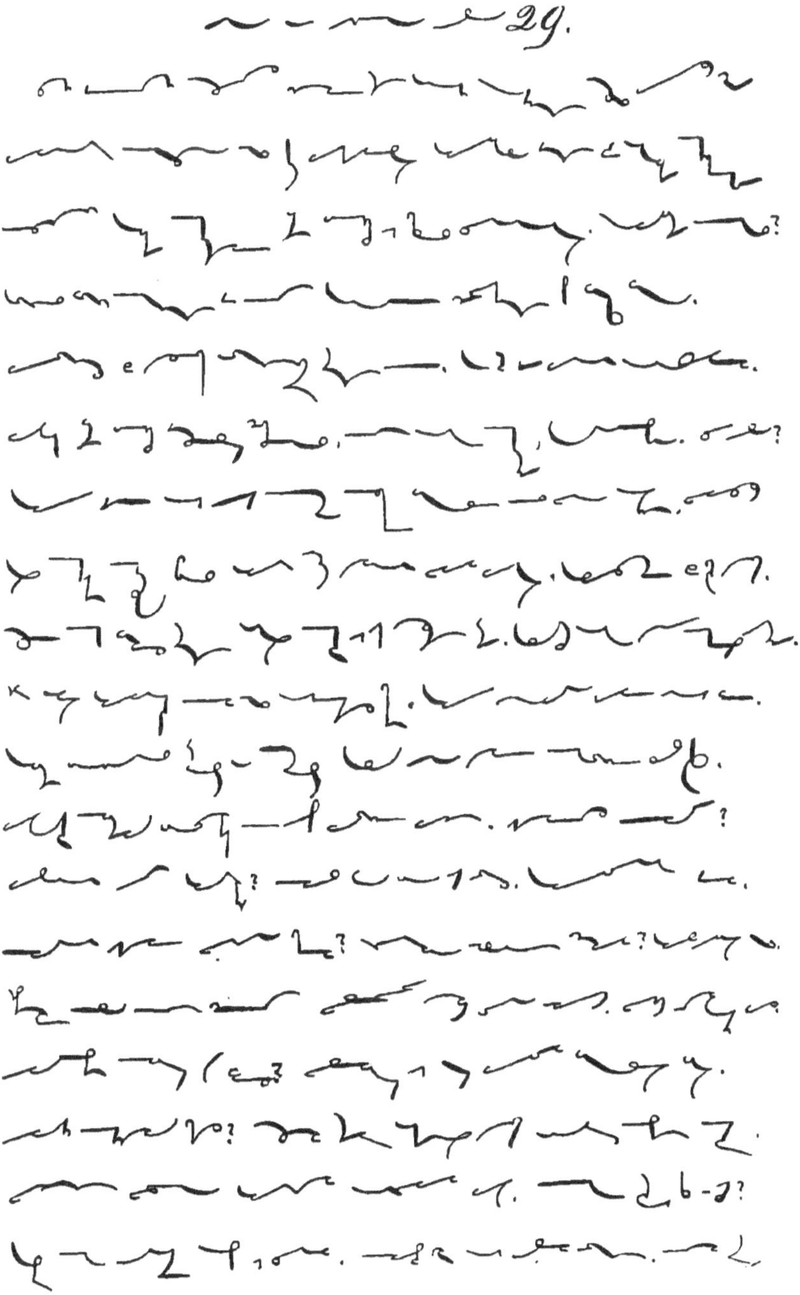

30.

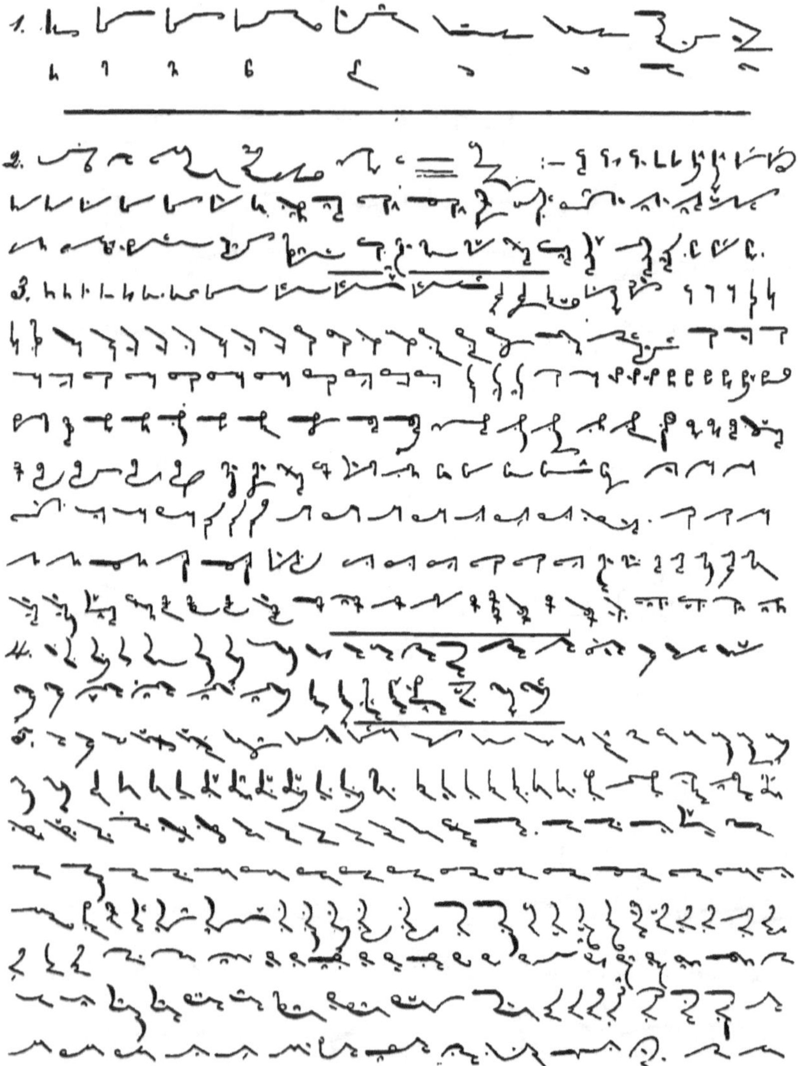

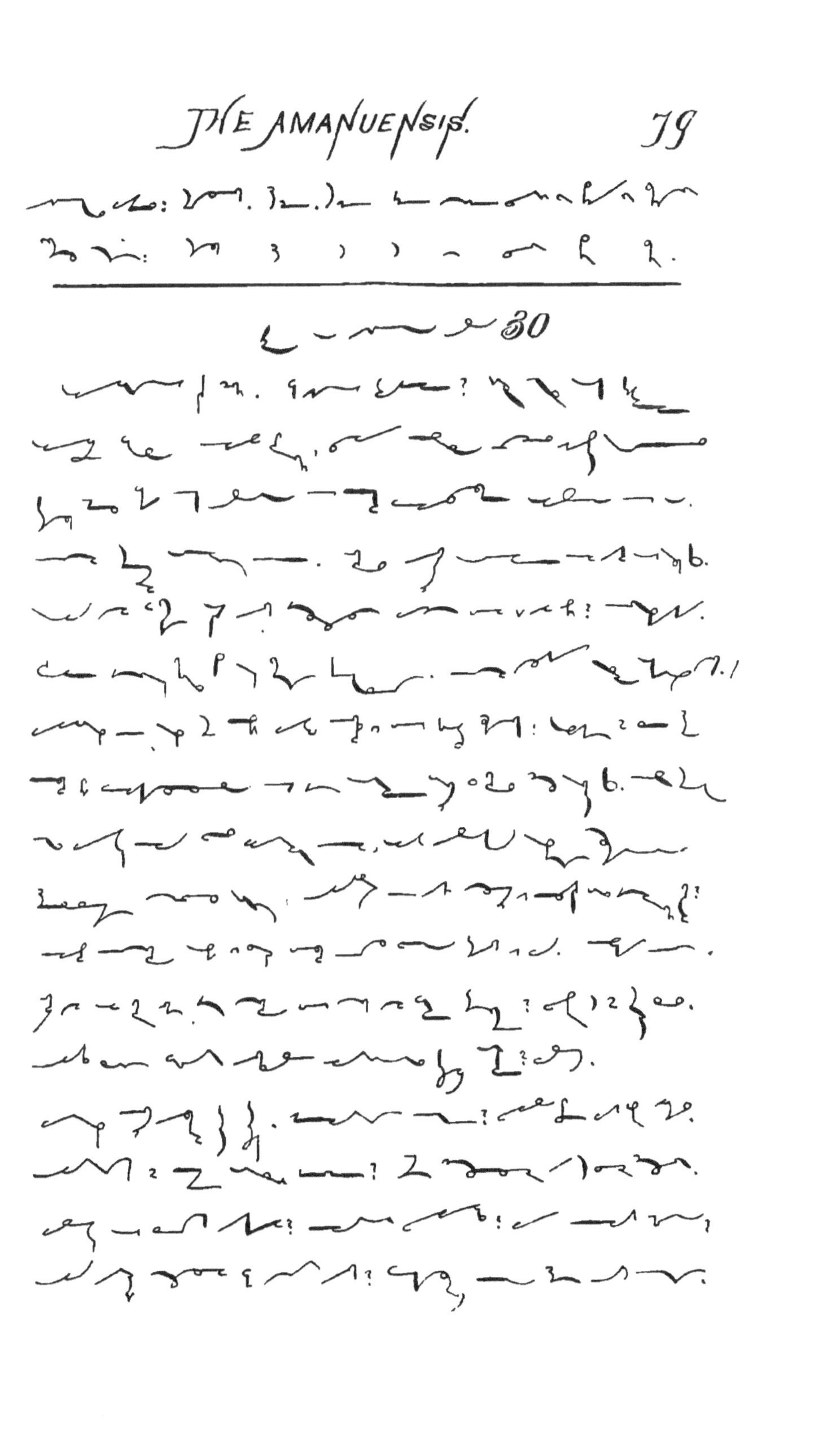

30

31.

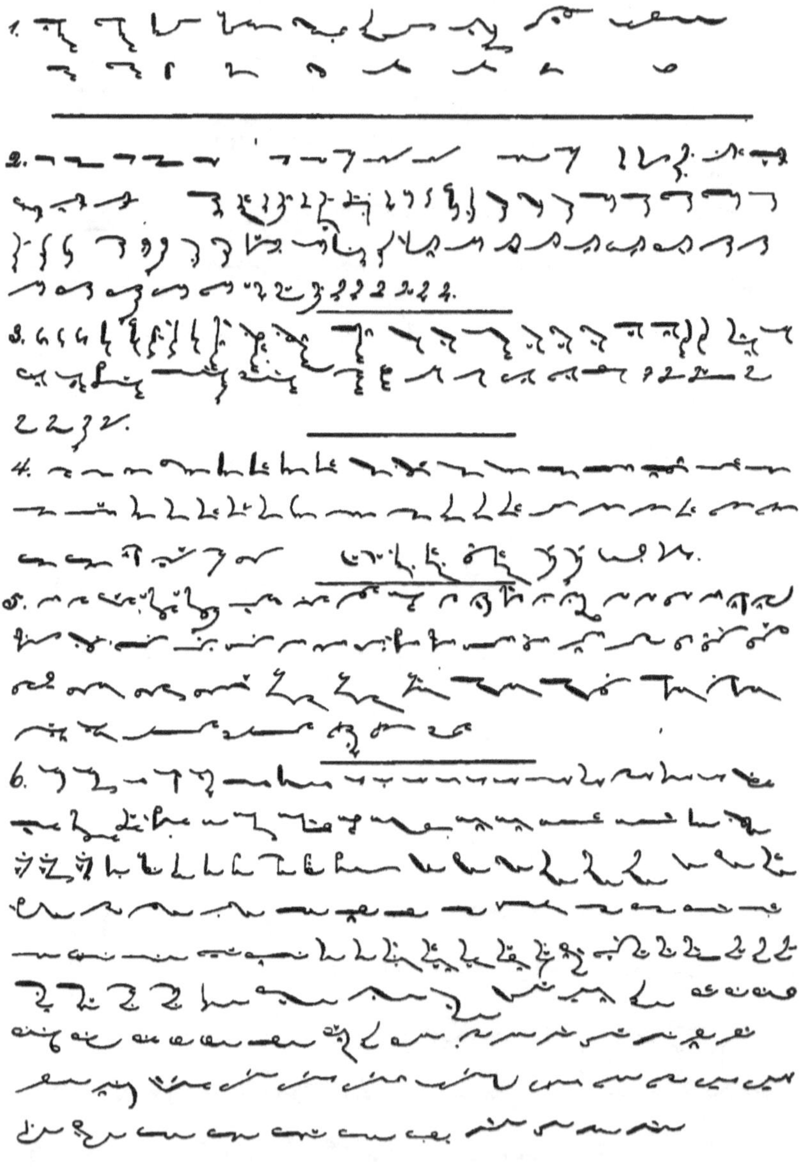

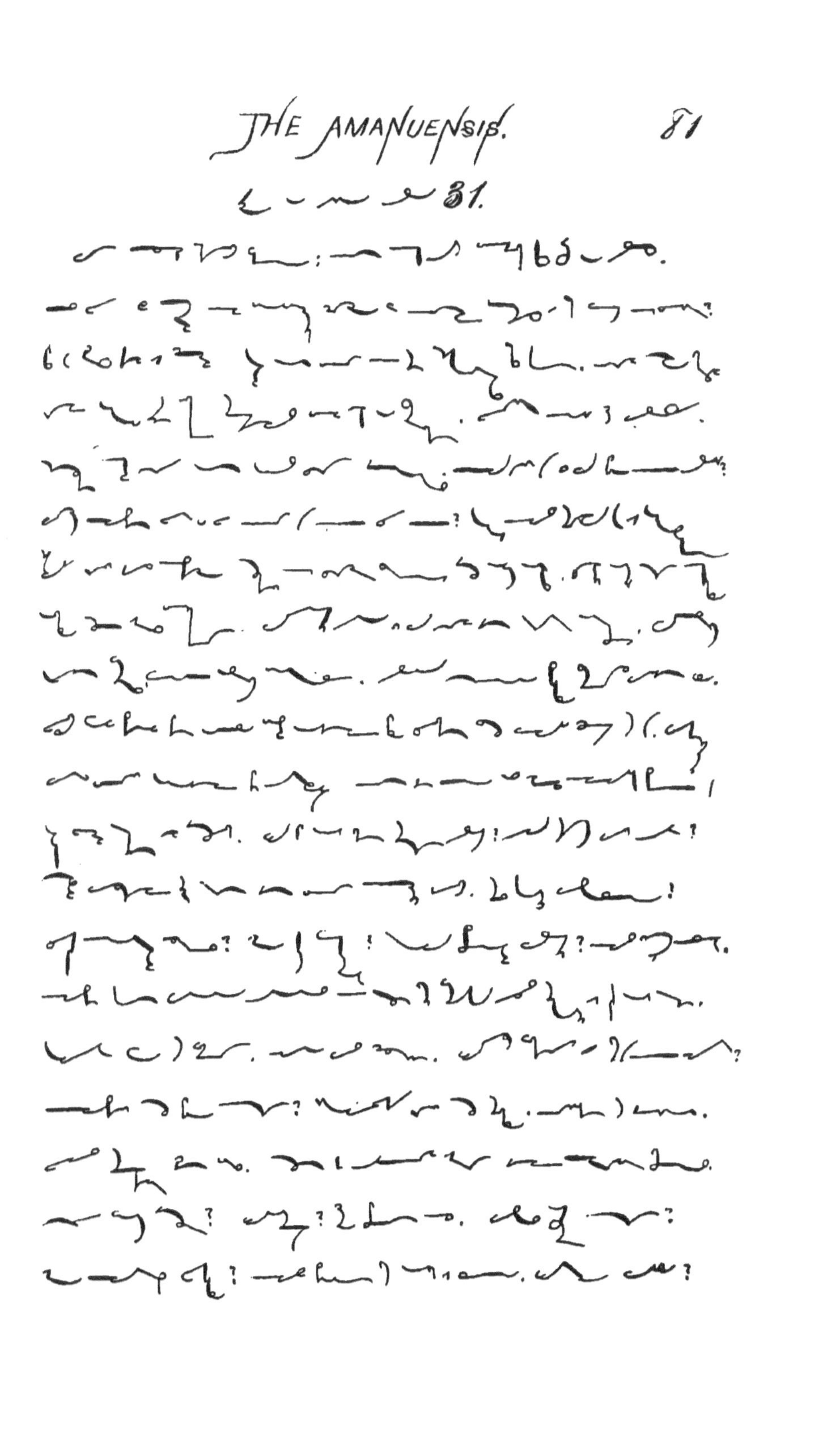

31.

82.

1.

2.

3.

4.

5.

6.

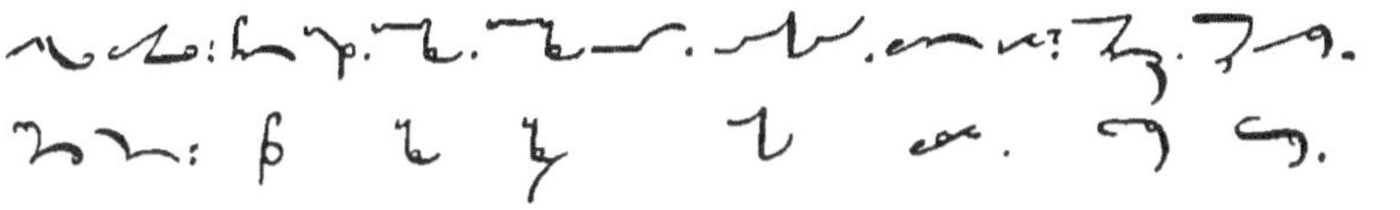

32.

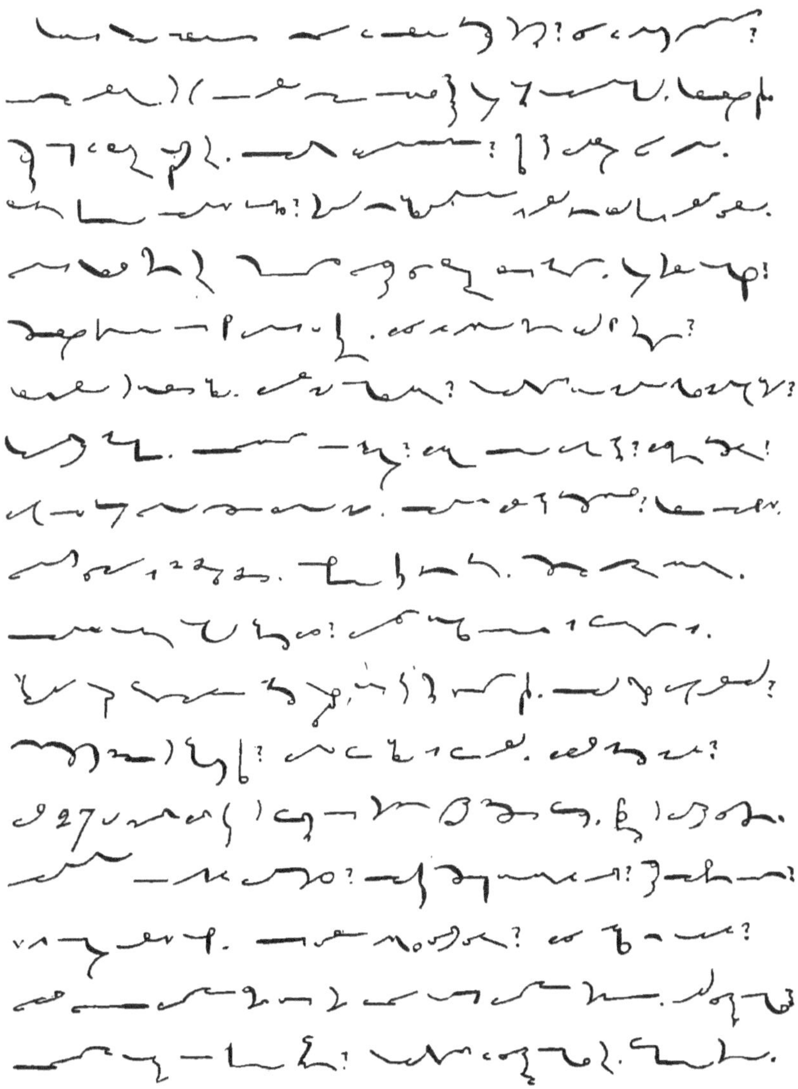

33.

1.

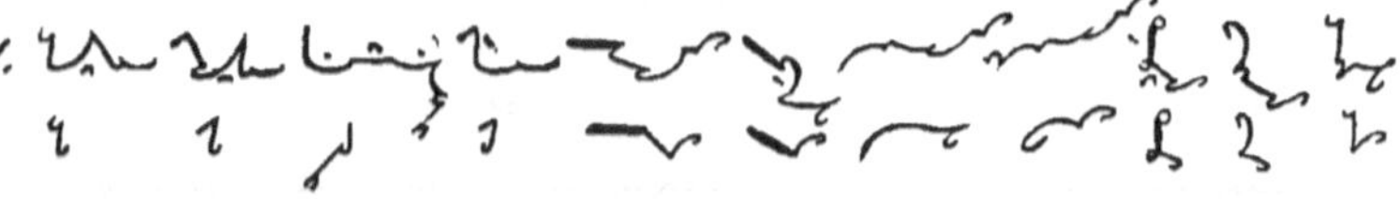

2.

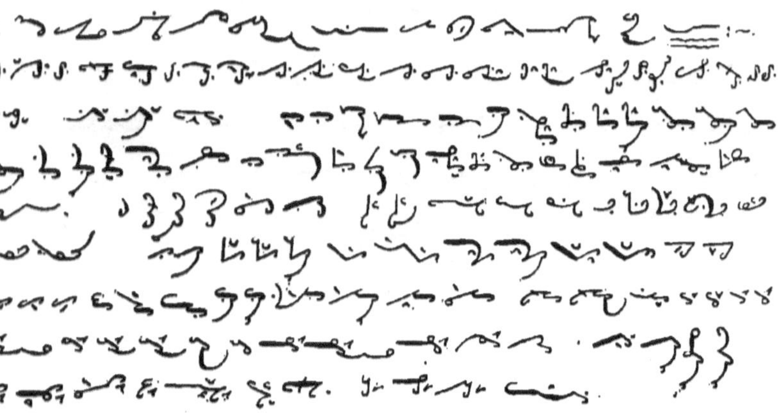

3.

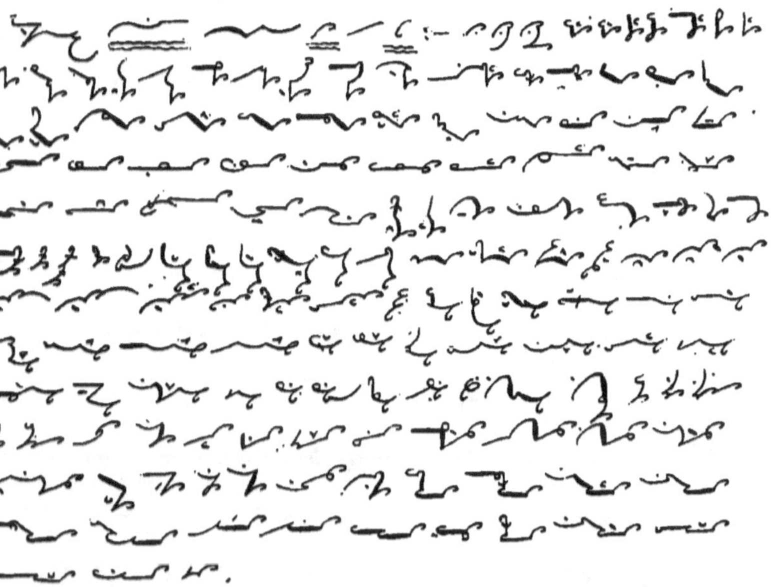

88.

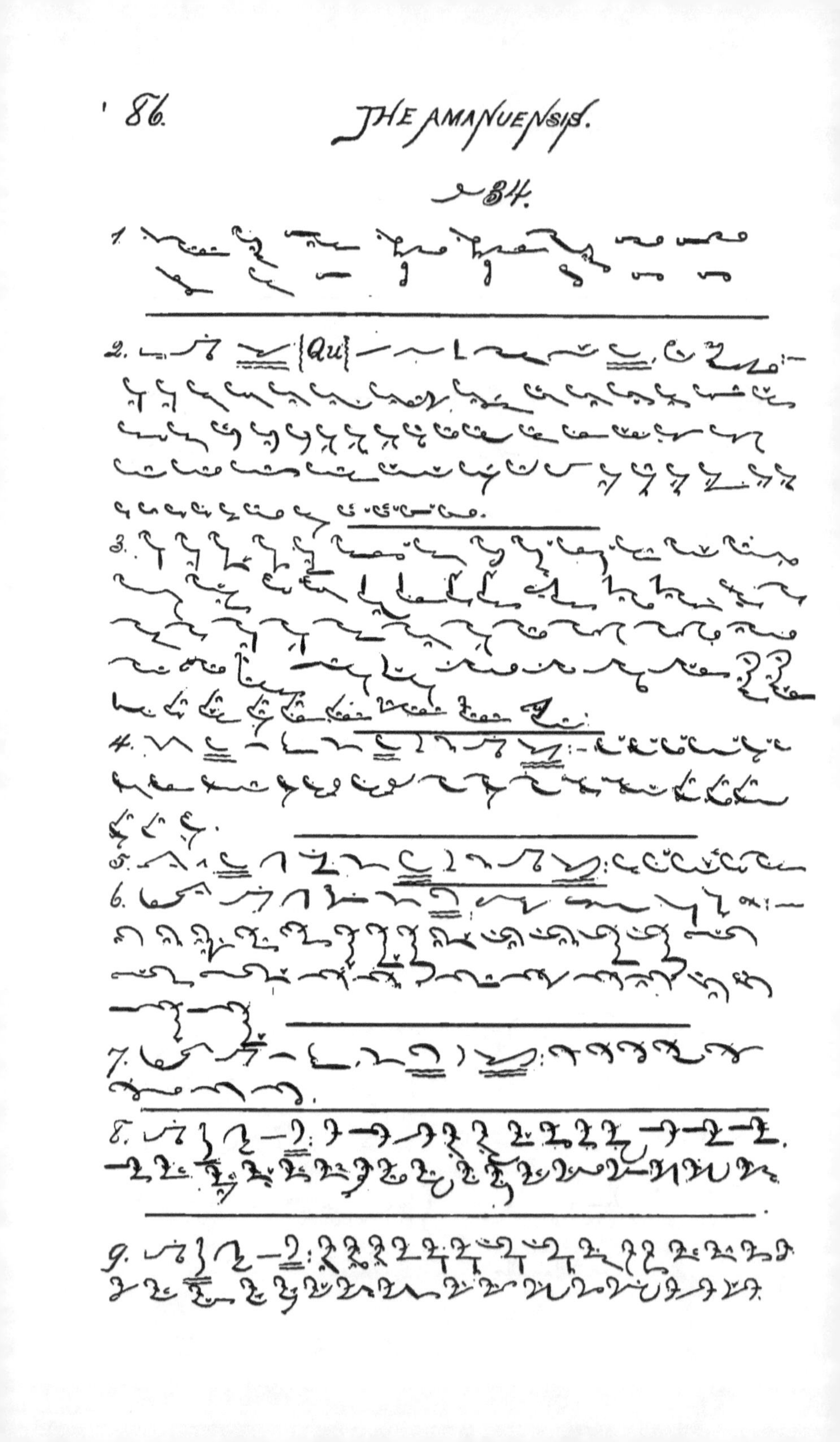

84.

1.

2. [Qu]

3.

4.

5.

6.

7.

8.

9.

34.

35.

1.
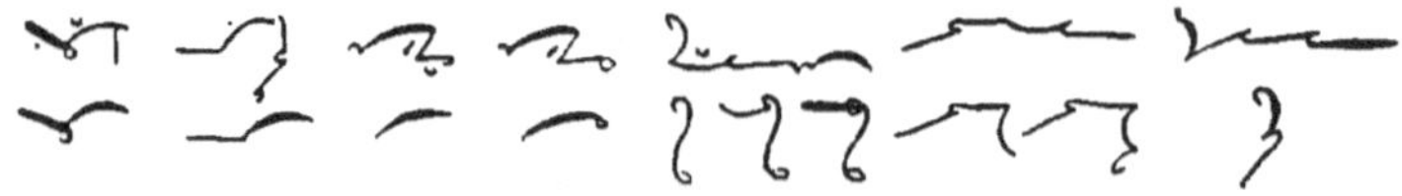

2.
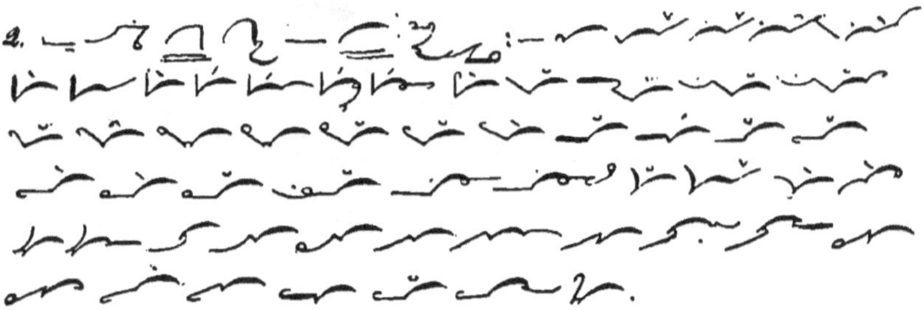

3.
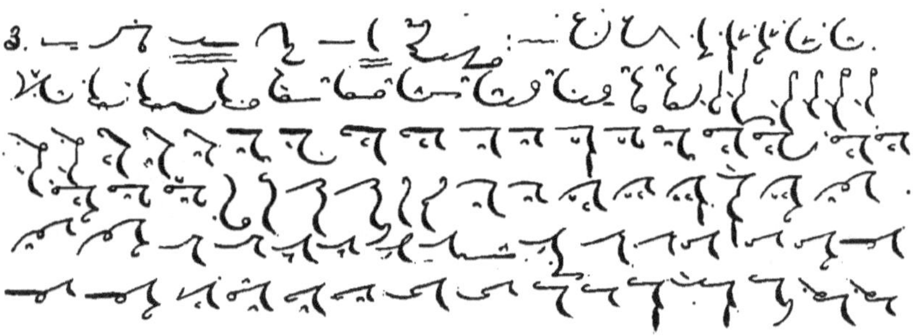

4.
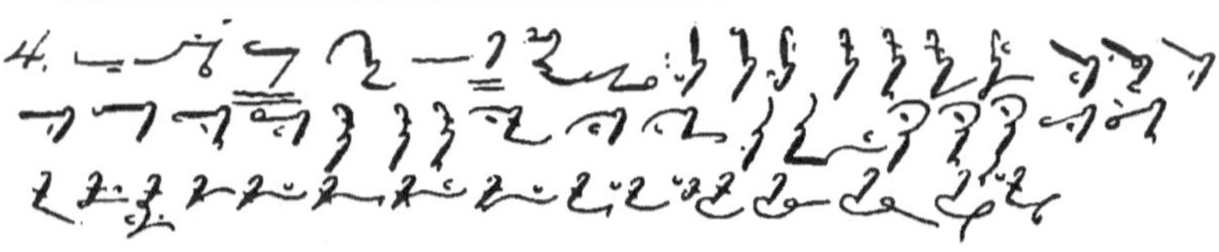

5.
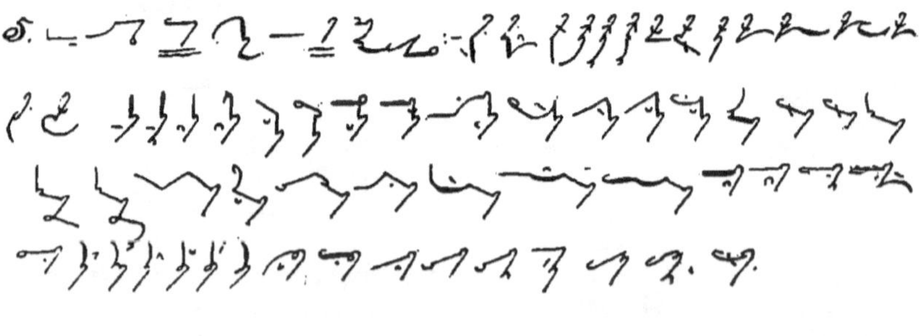

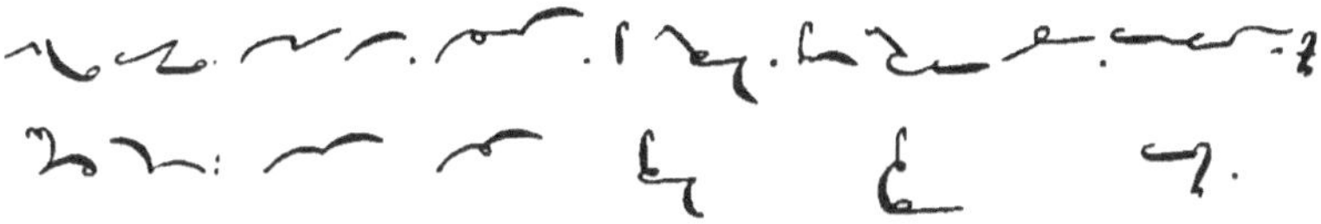

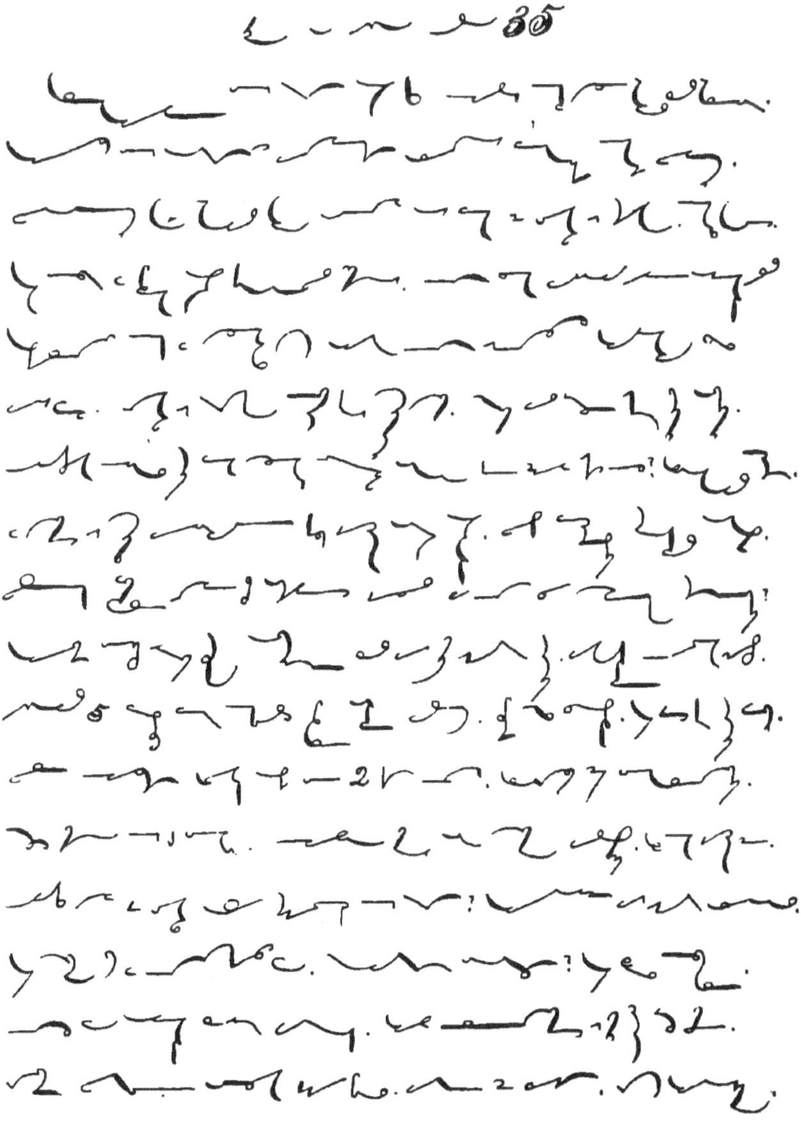
35

~ 86.

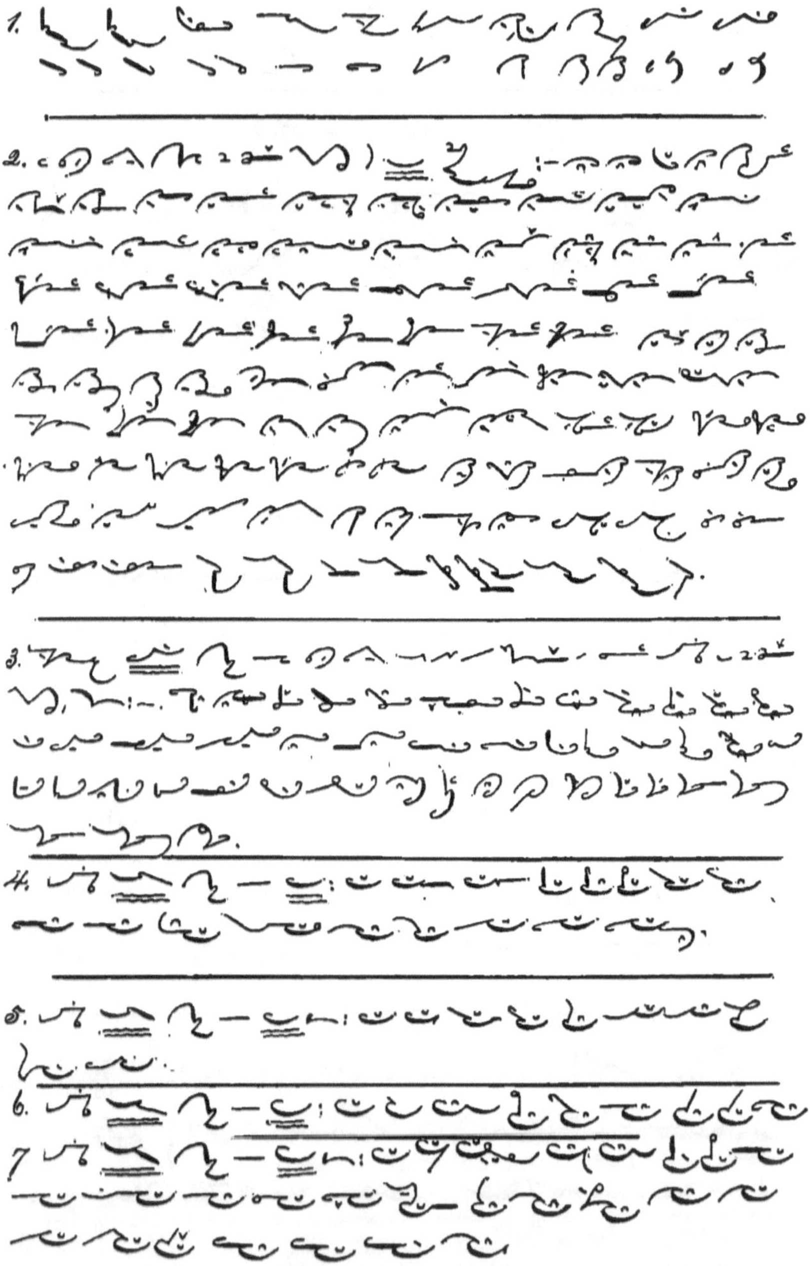

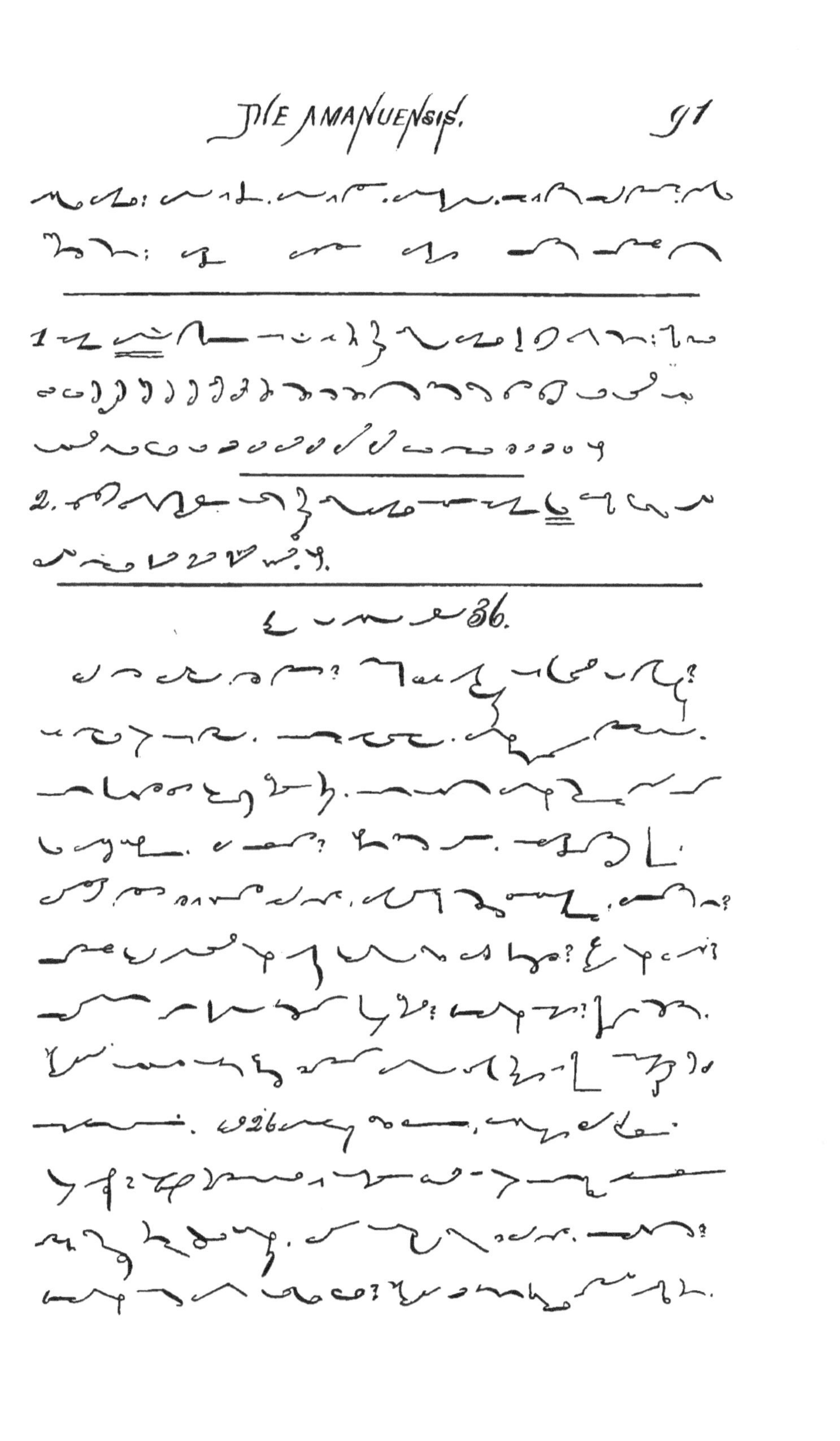

1

2.

36.

37.

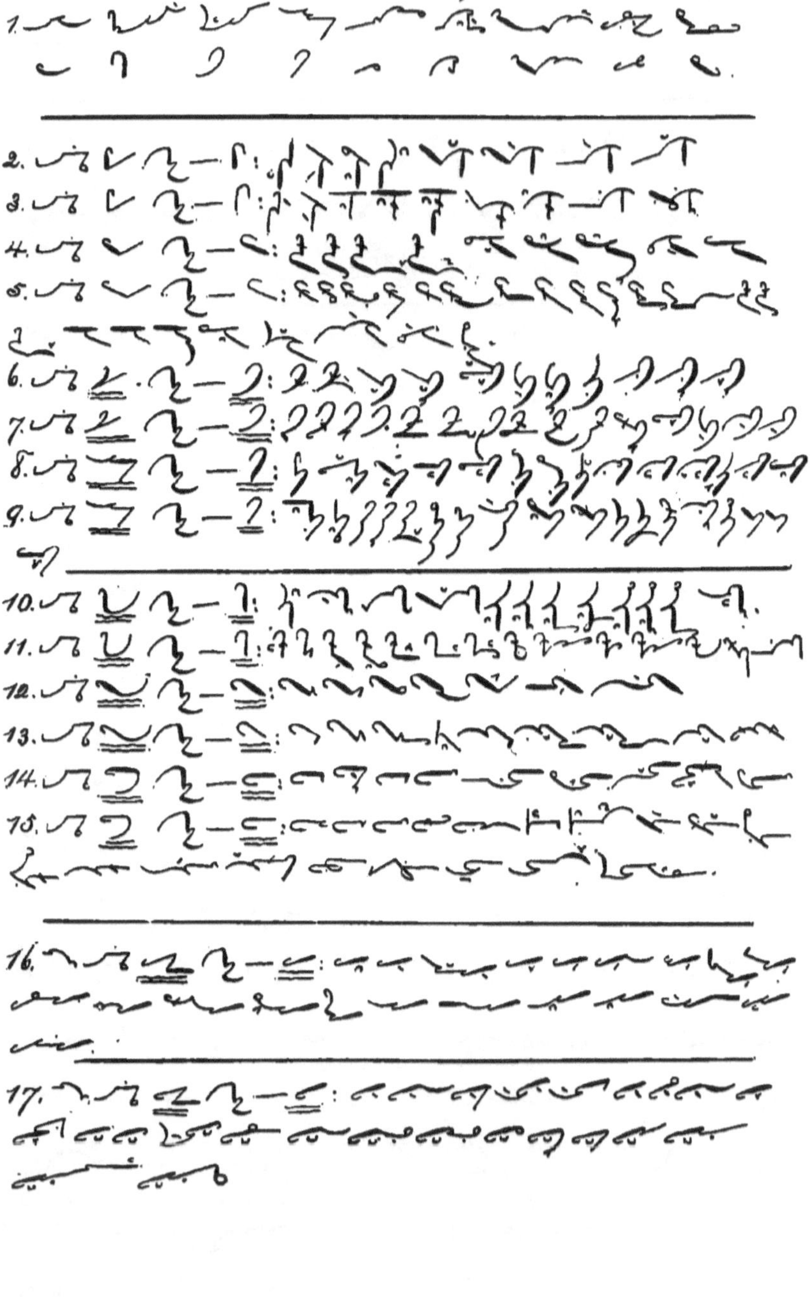

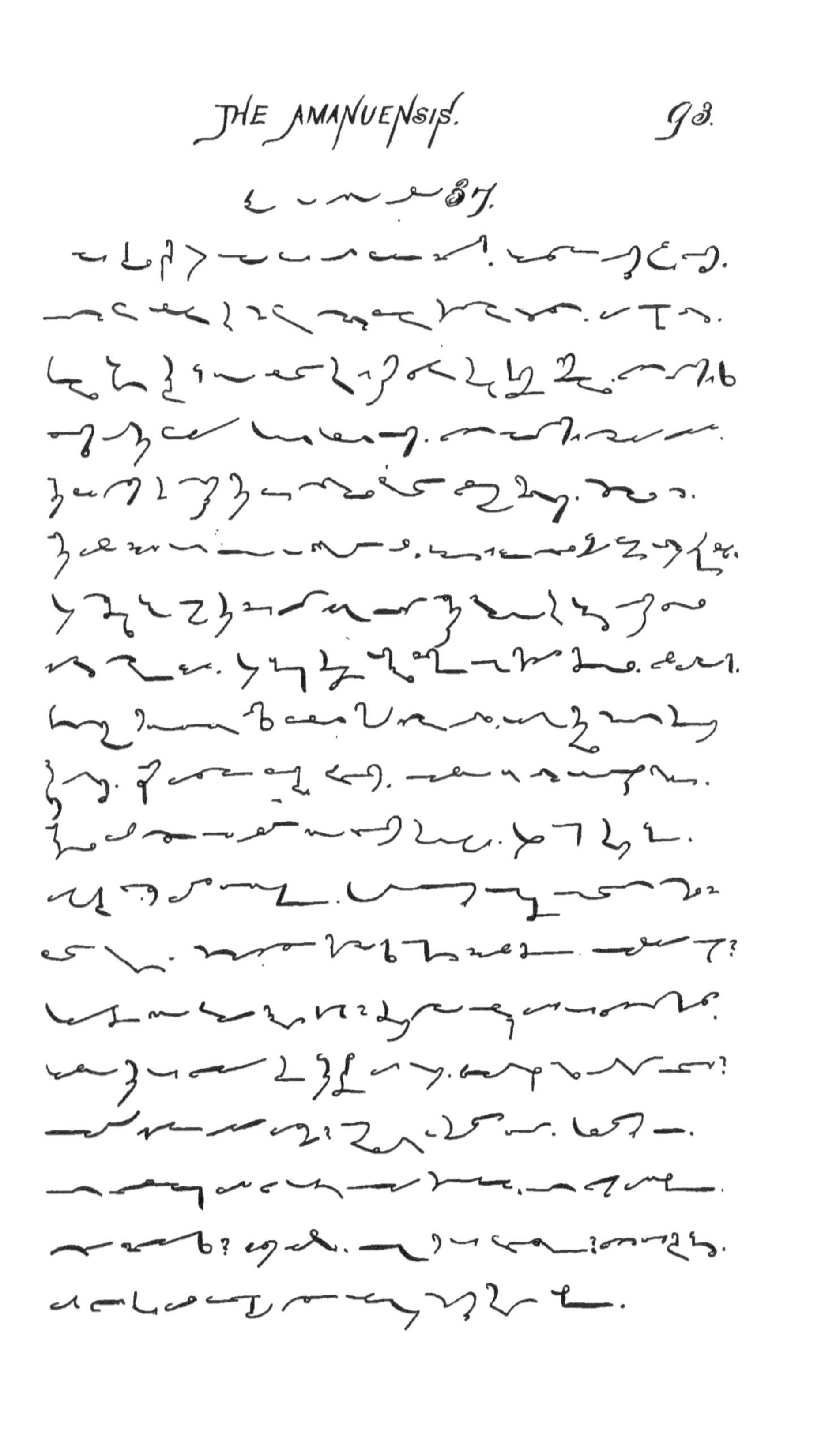

37.

38.

1. 

2. 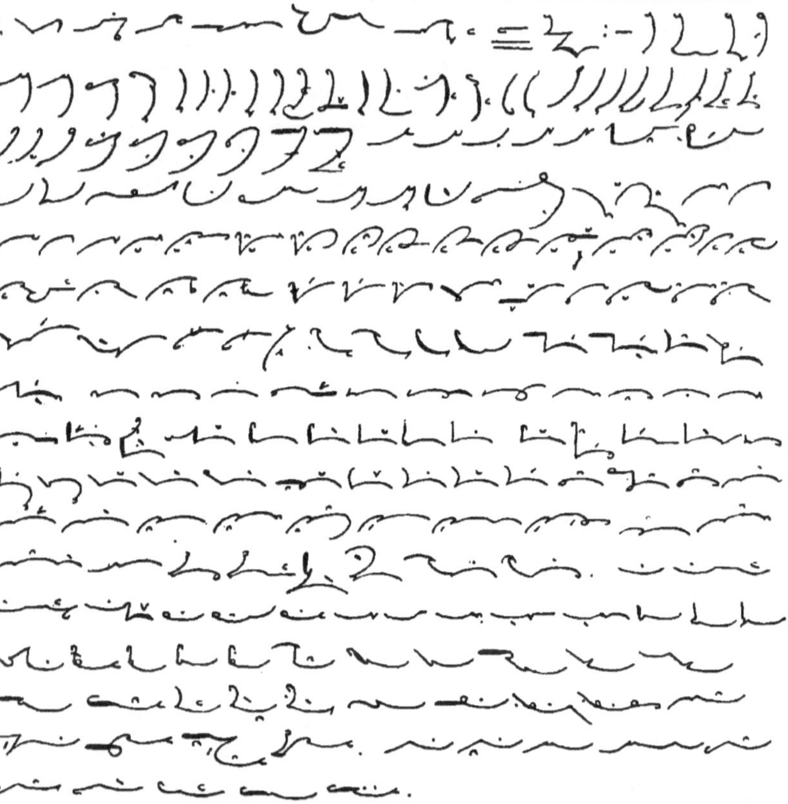

3. 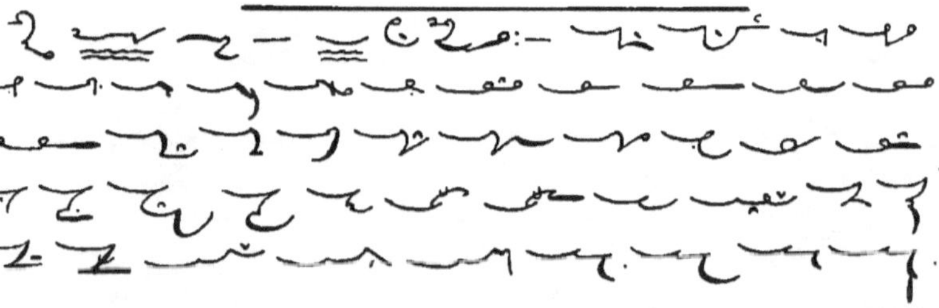

38.

— 39.

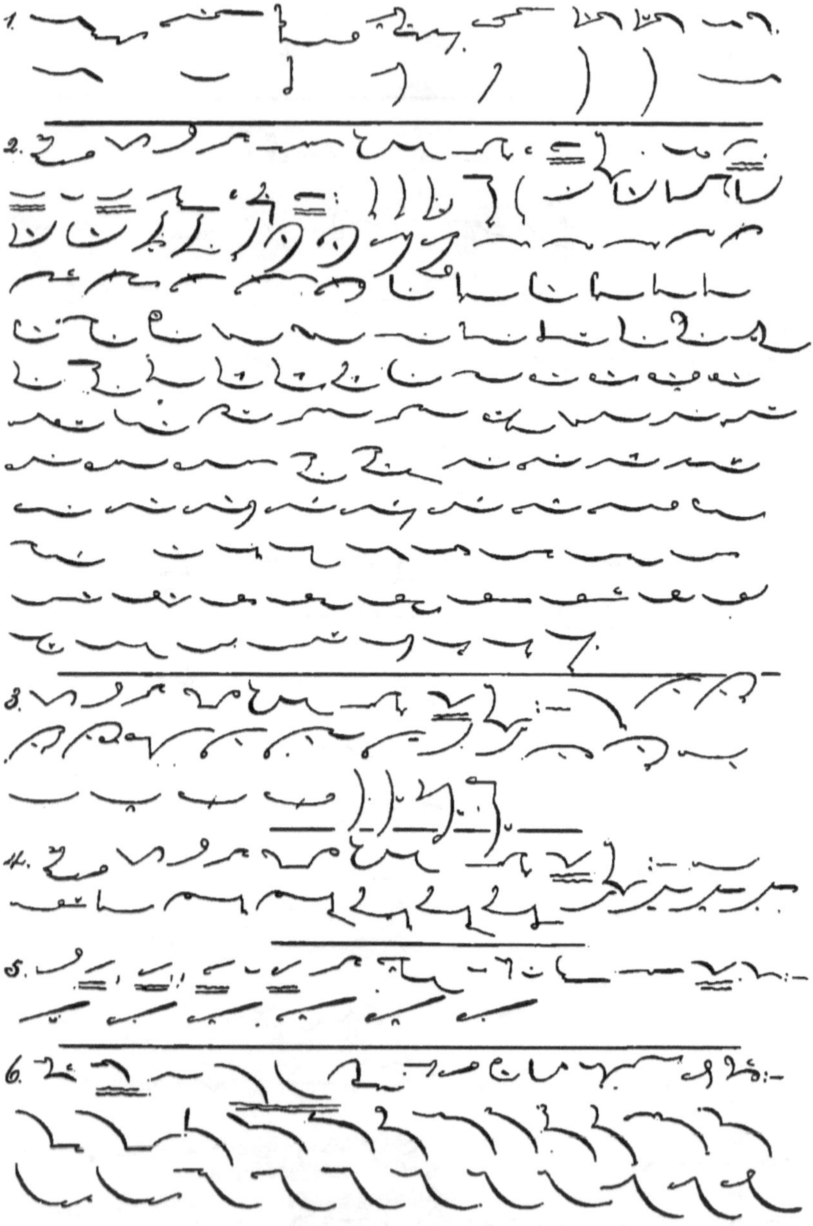

89.

there, their, or

40.

1. 

2. 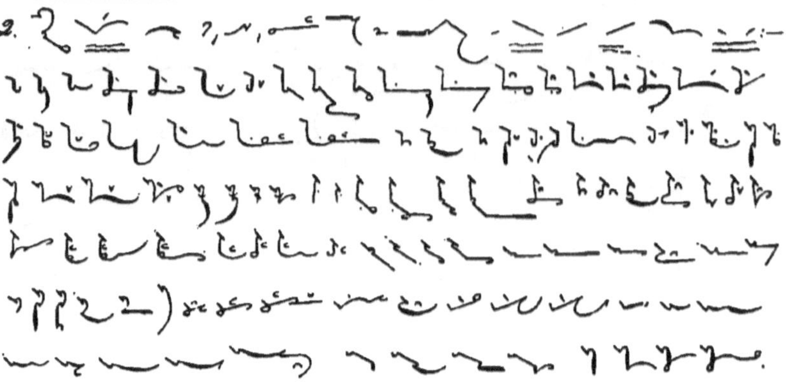

3. 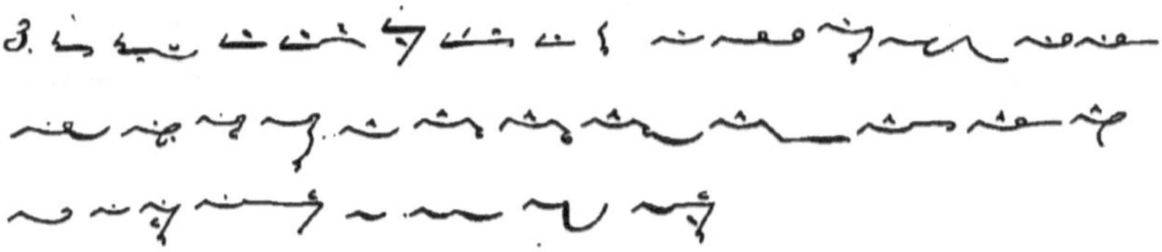

4. 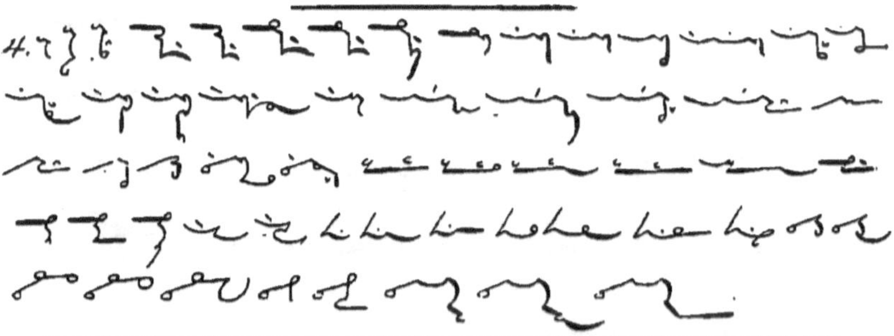

5. 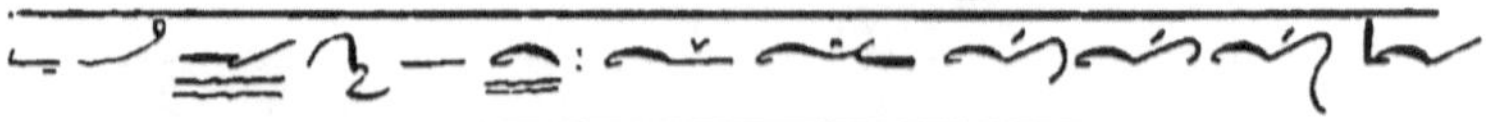

6. 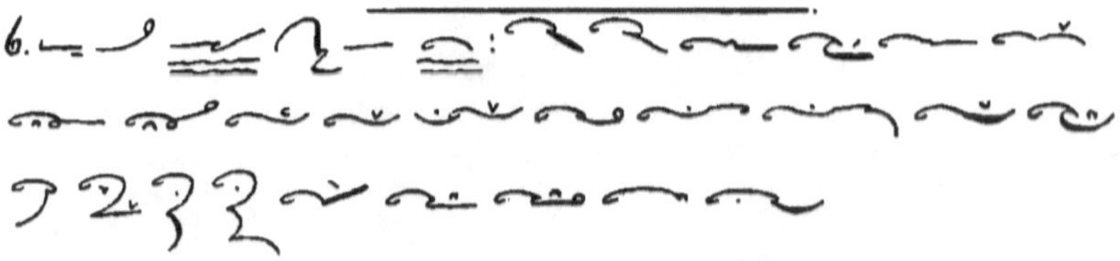

40.

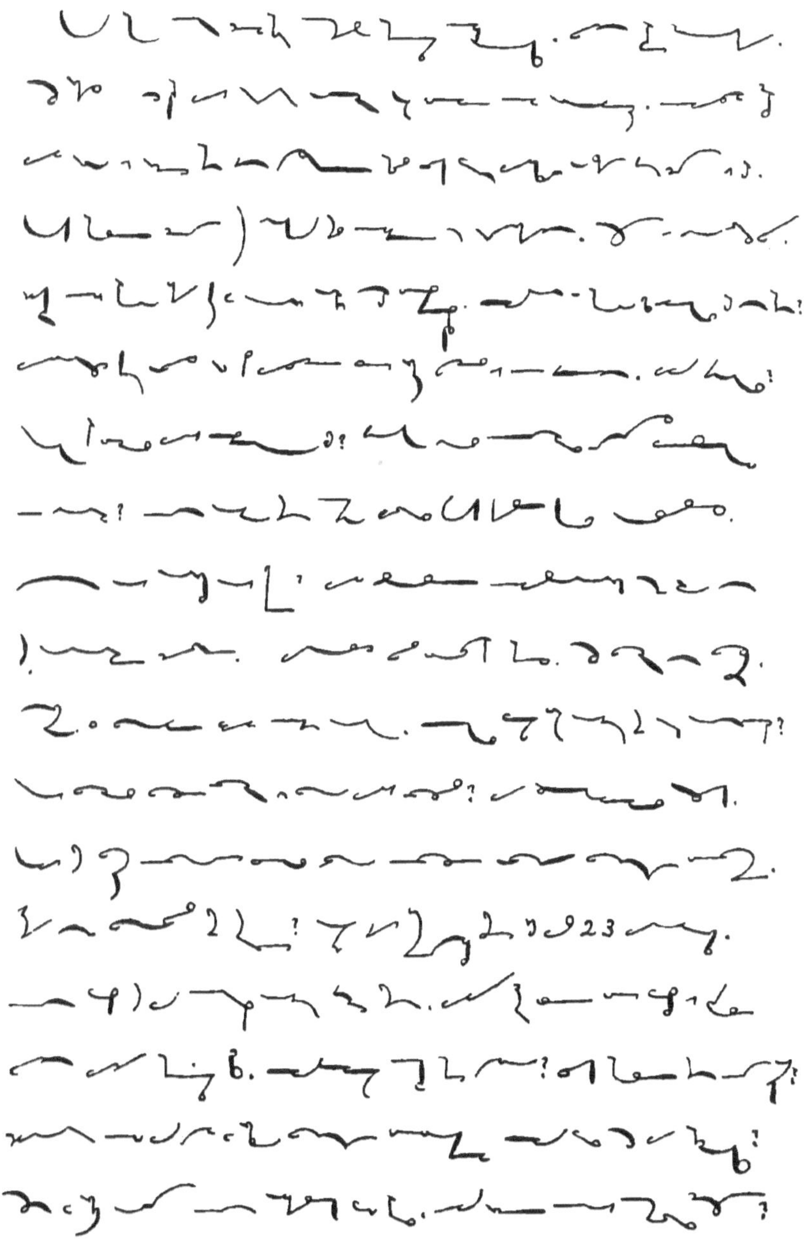

41.

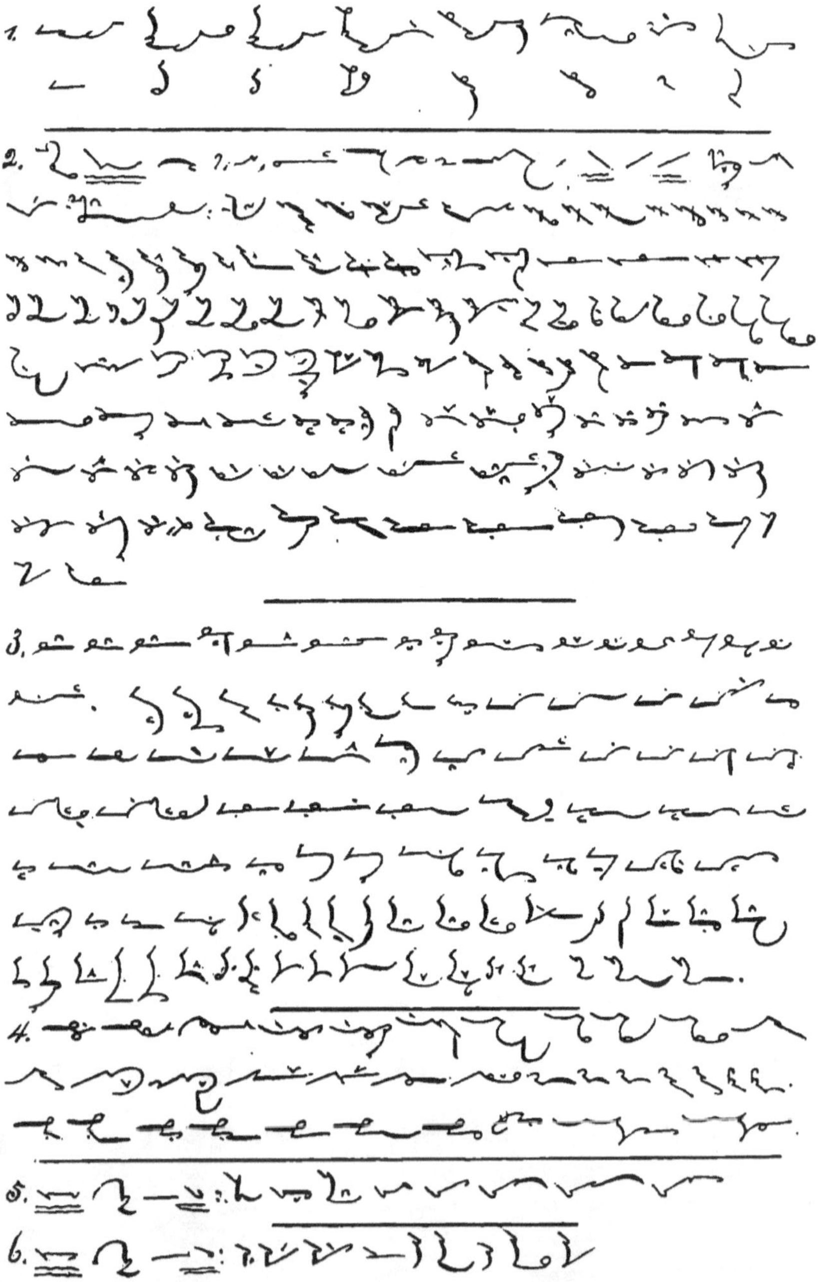

41.

42.

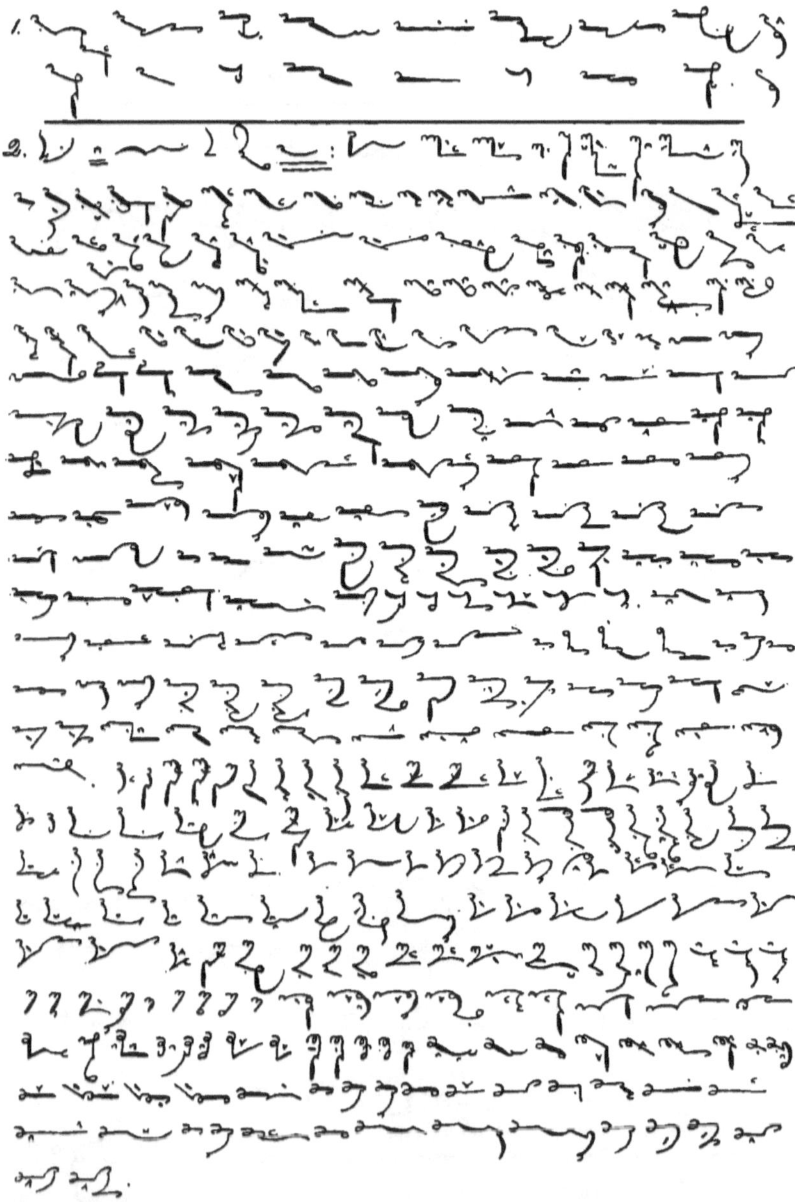

 42.

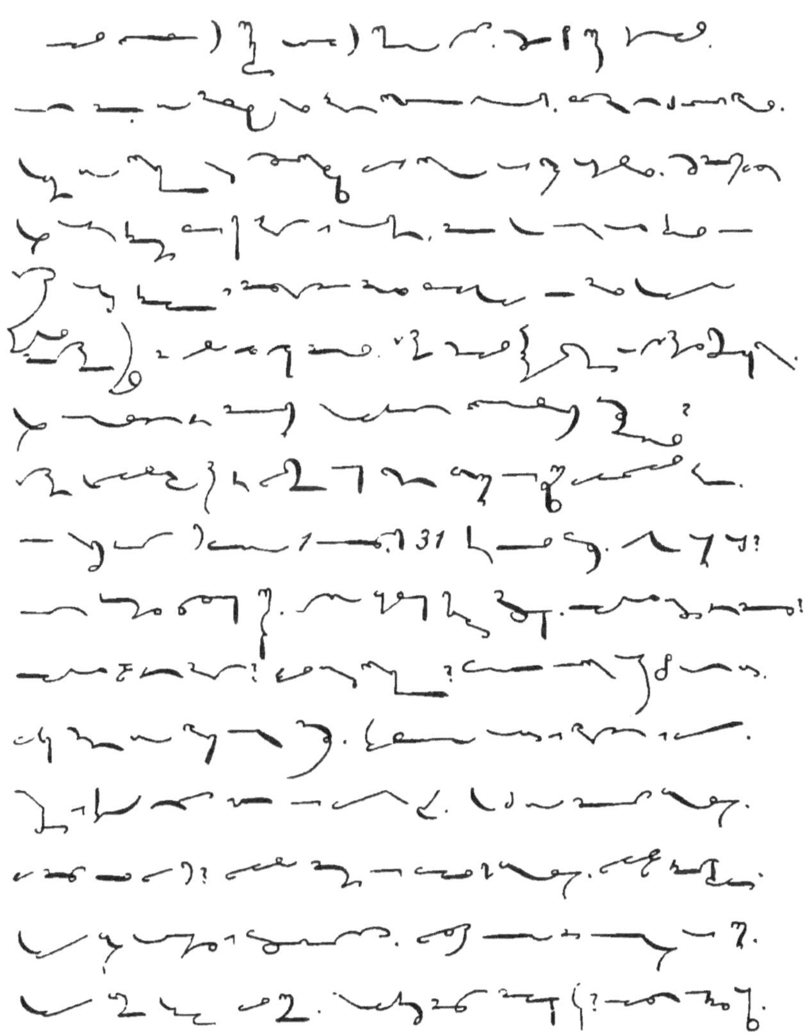

43.

1.

2.

3.

4.

5.

6.

7.

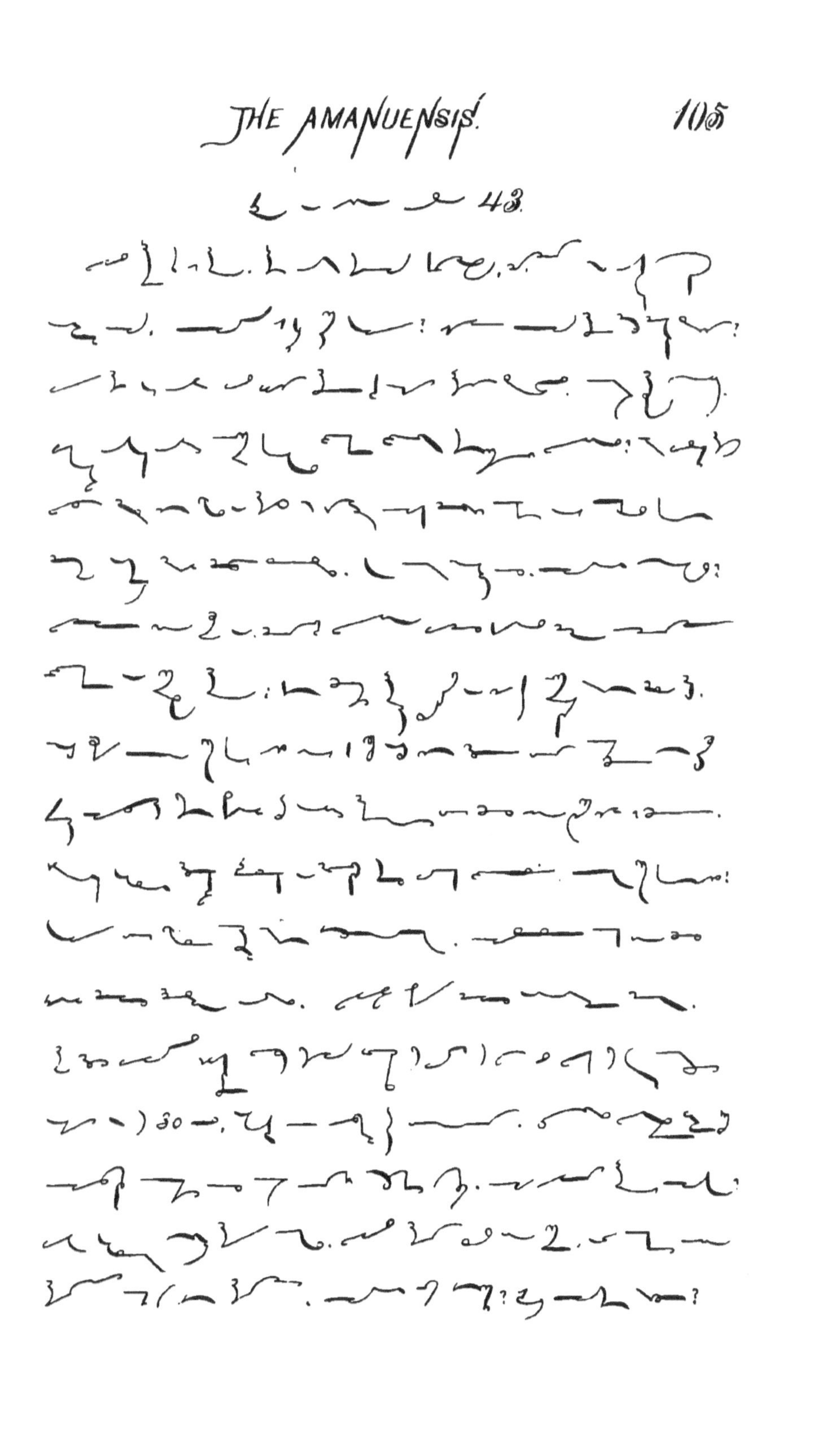

43

44

1.

2.

3.

4.

5.

6

7.

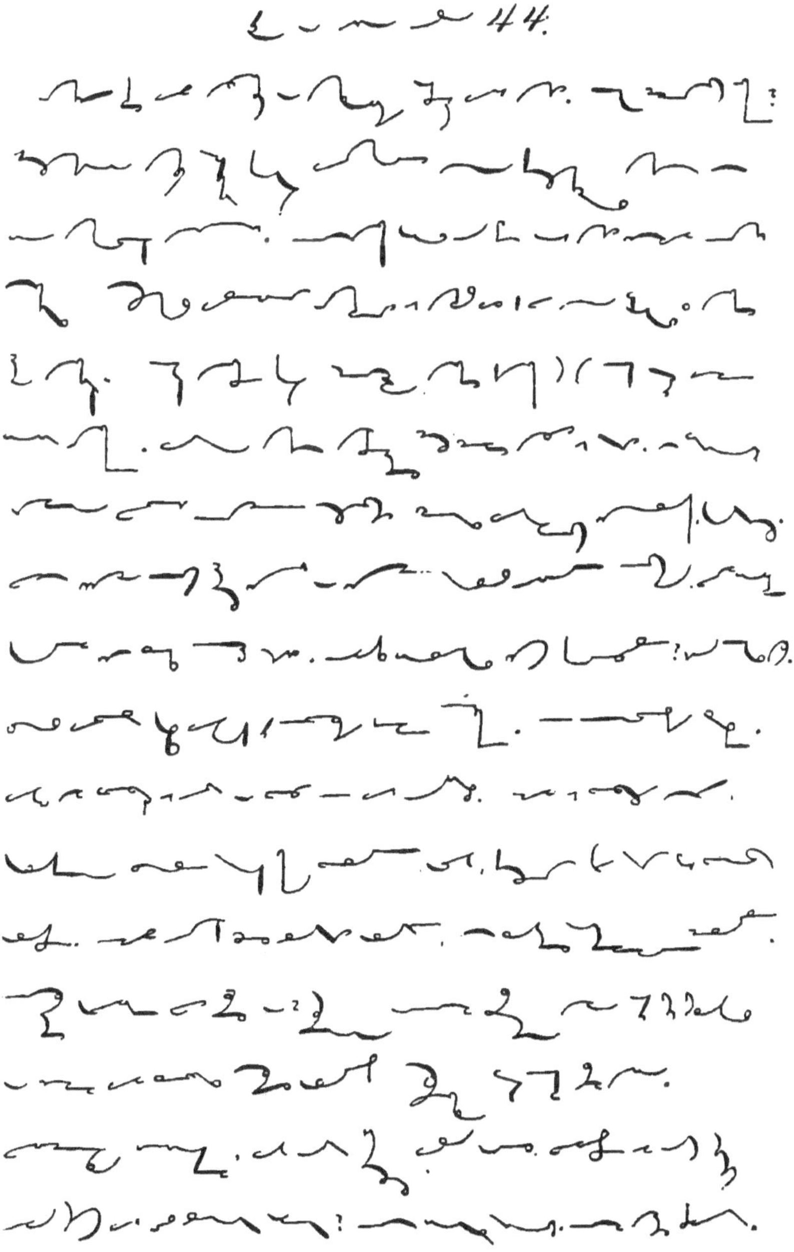

45.

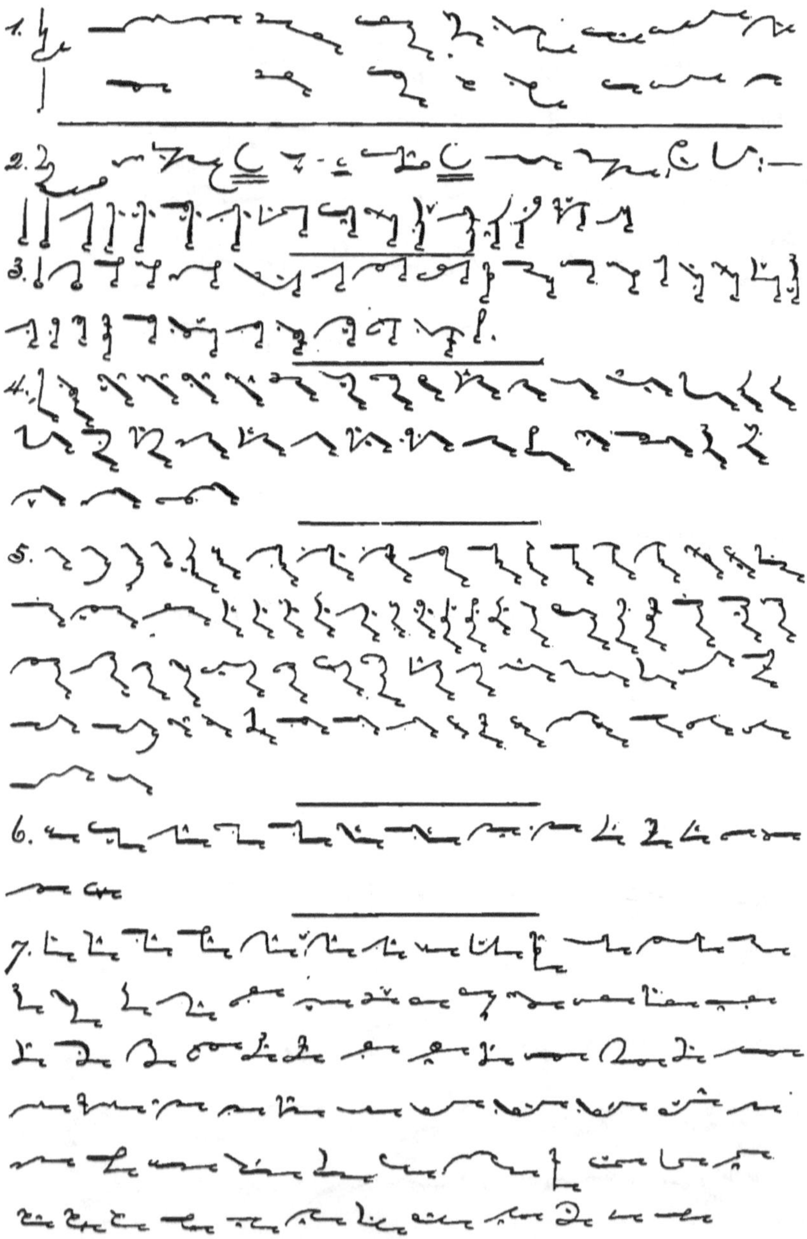

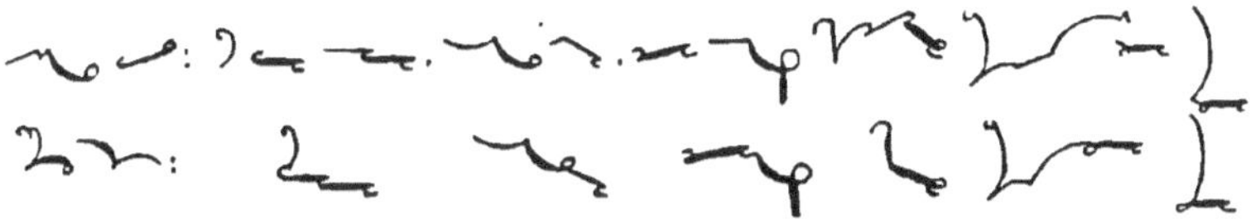

 45.

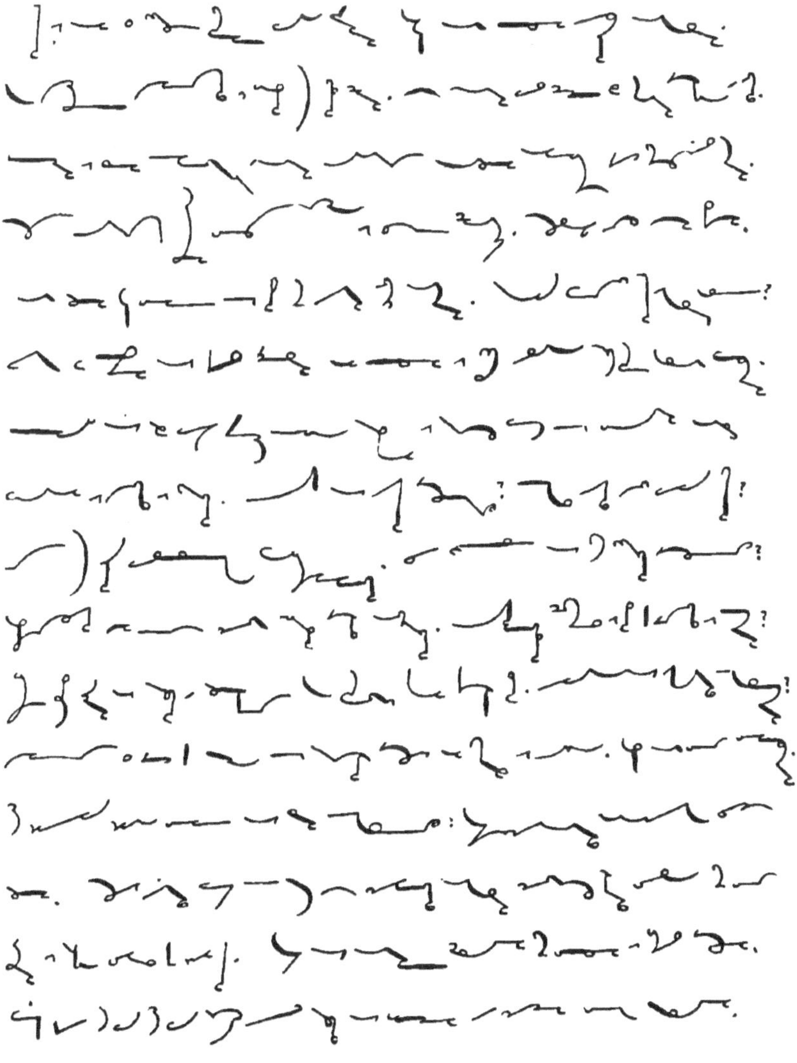

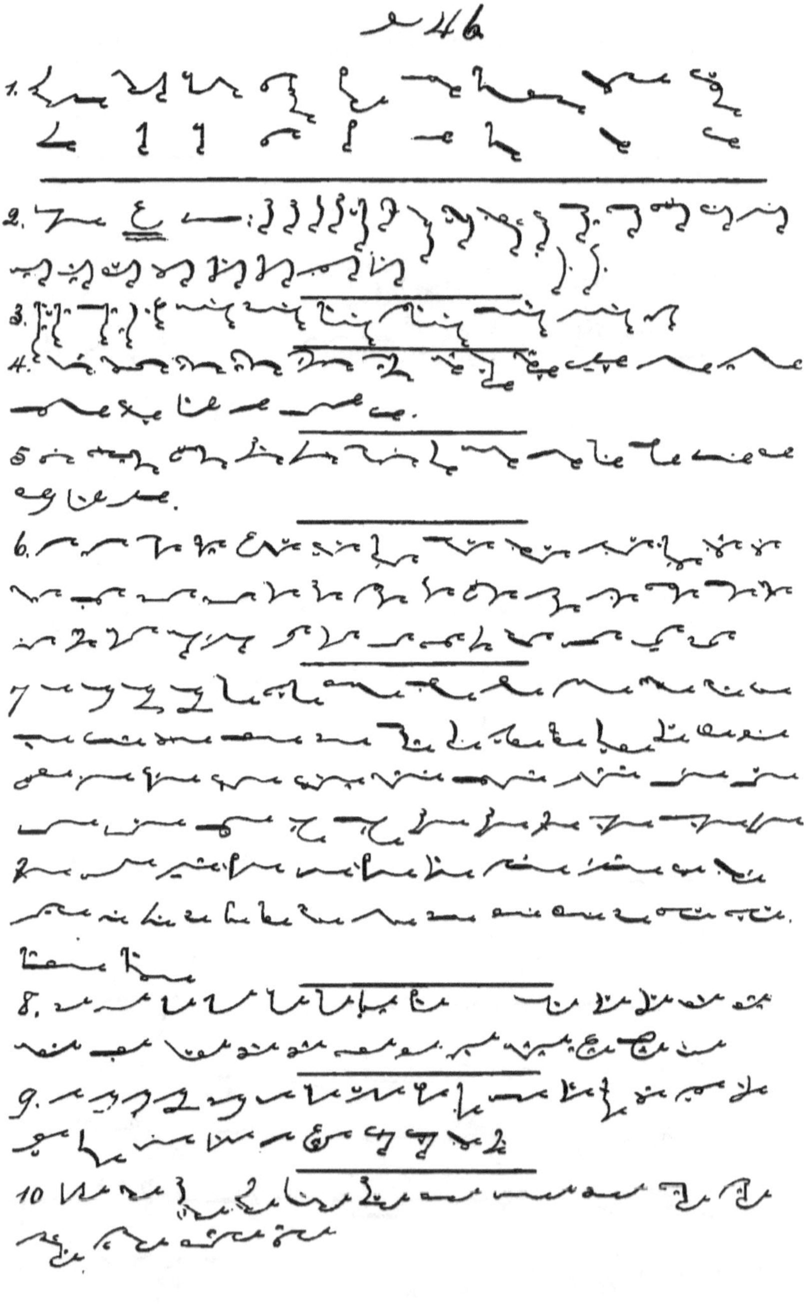

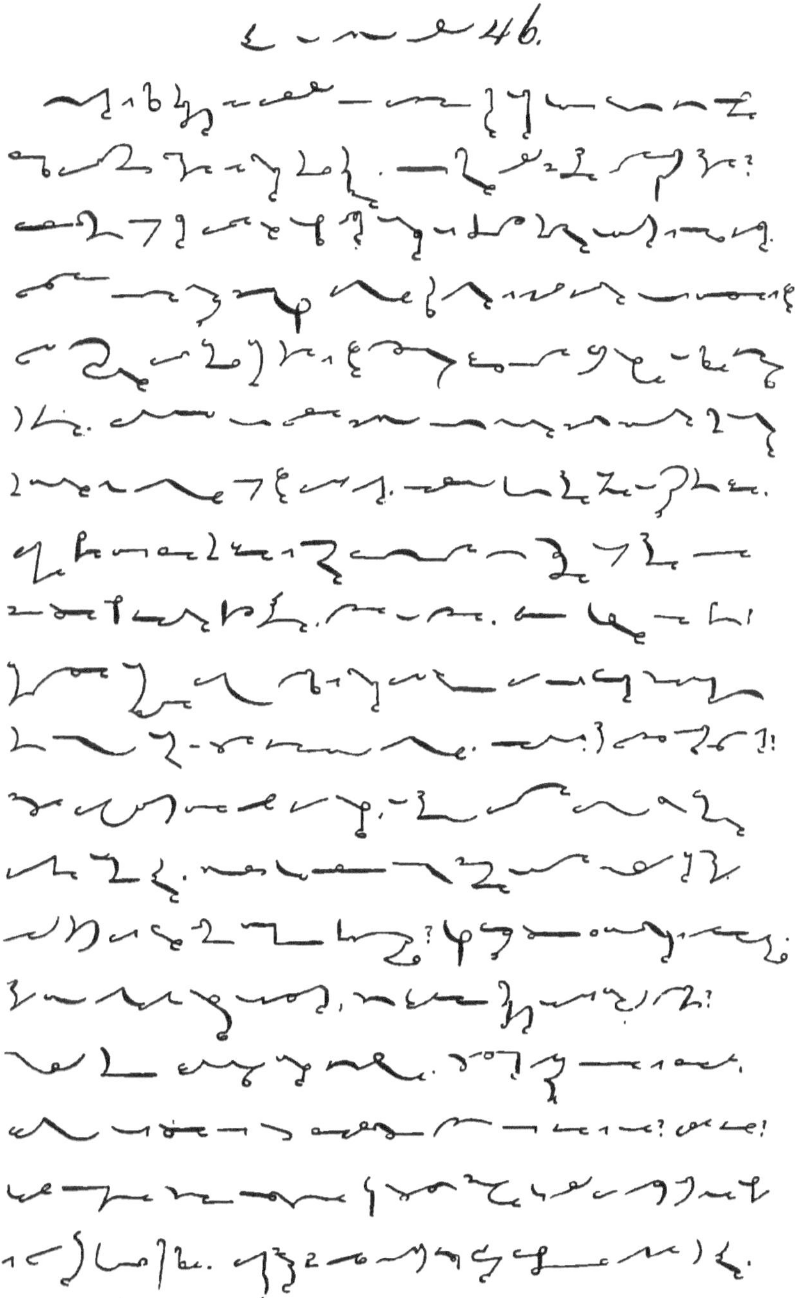
46.

47.

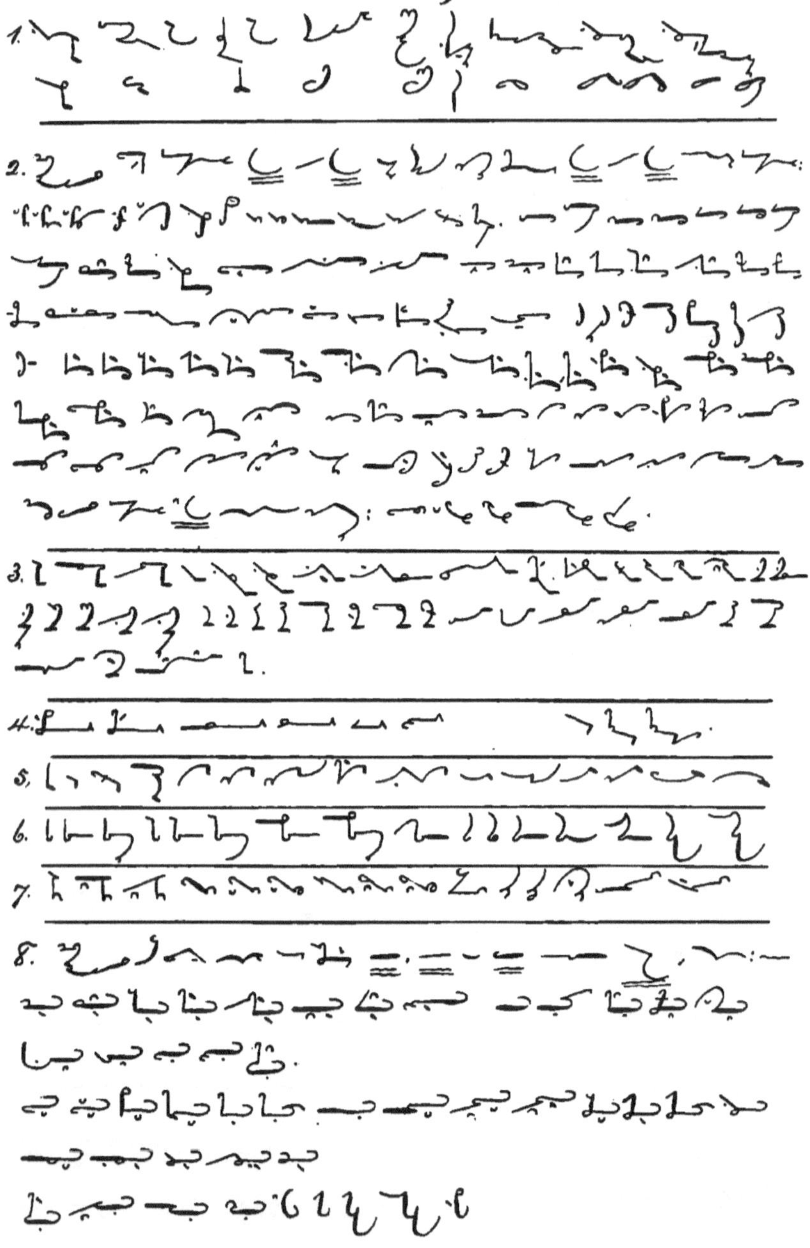

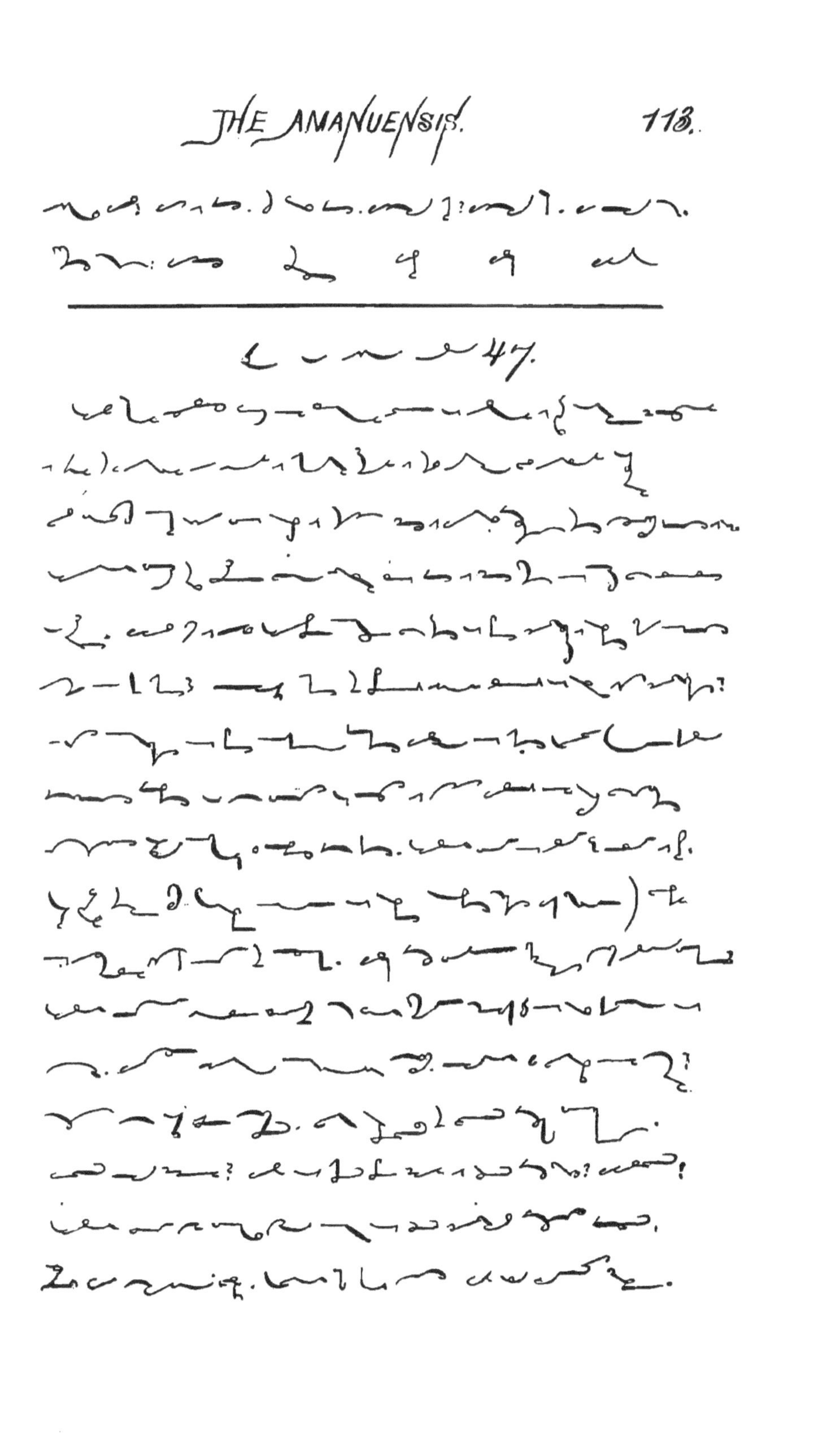

47.

§ 148.

1.
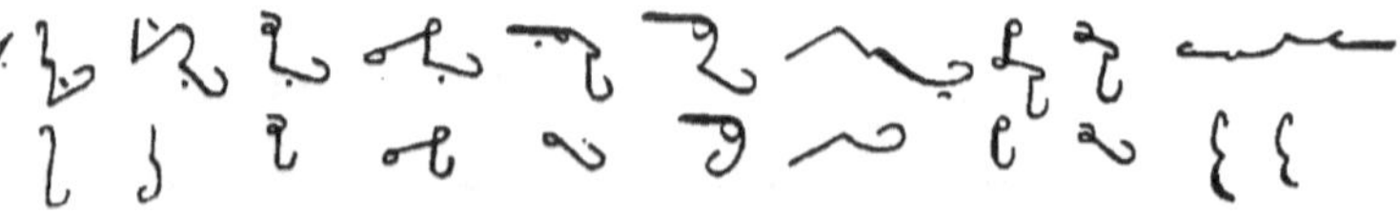

2.
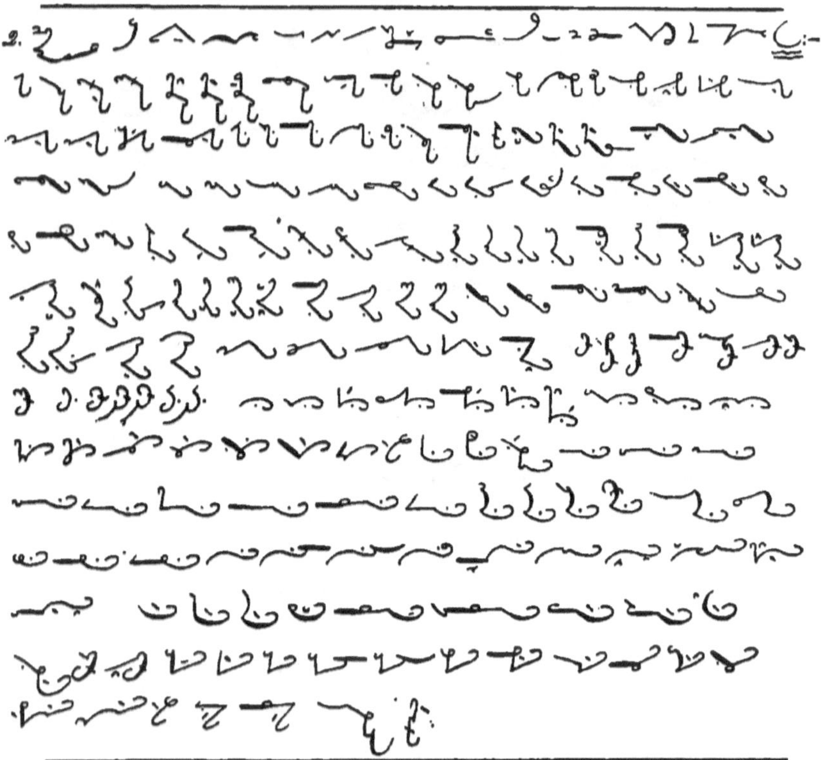

3.
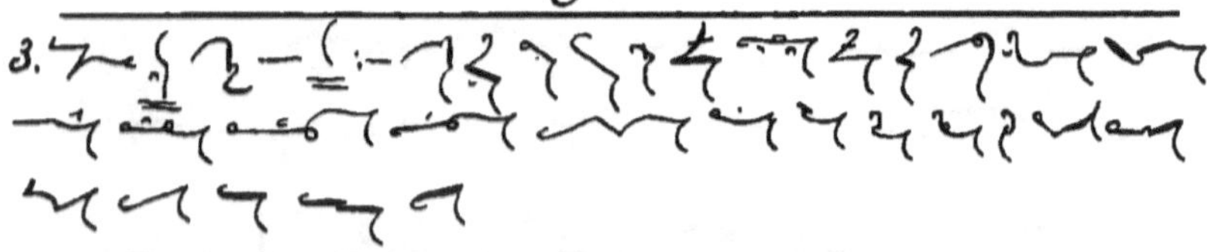

4.
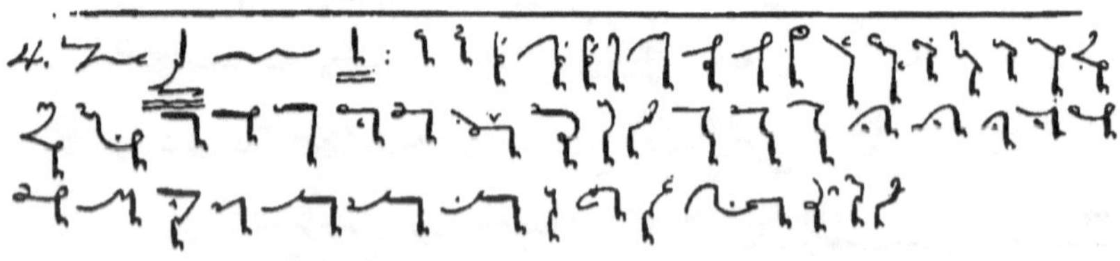

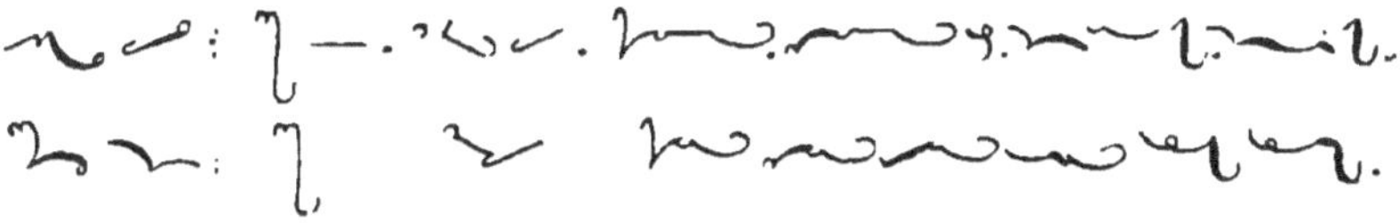

48.

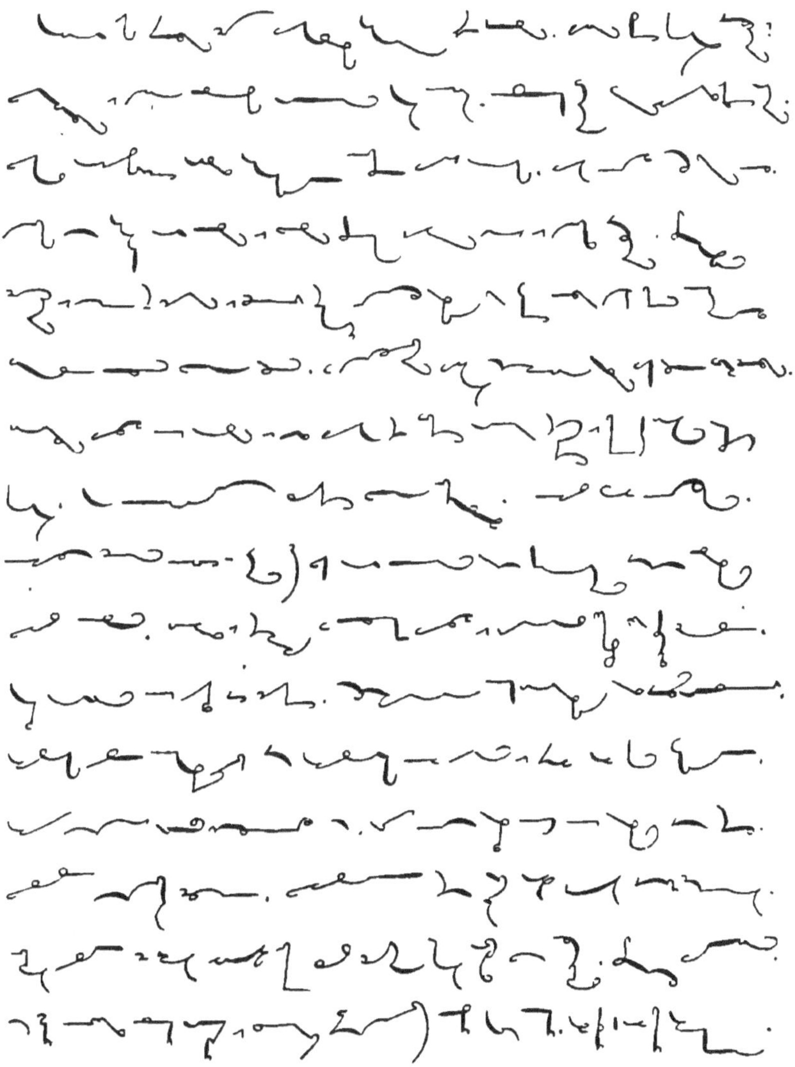

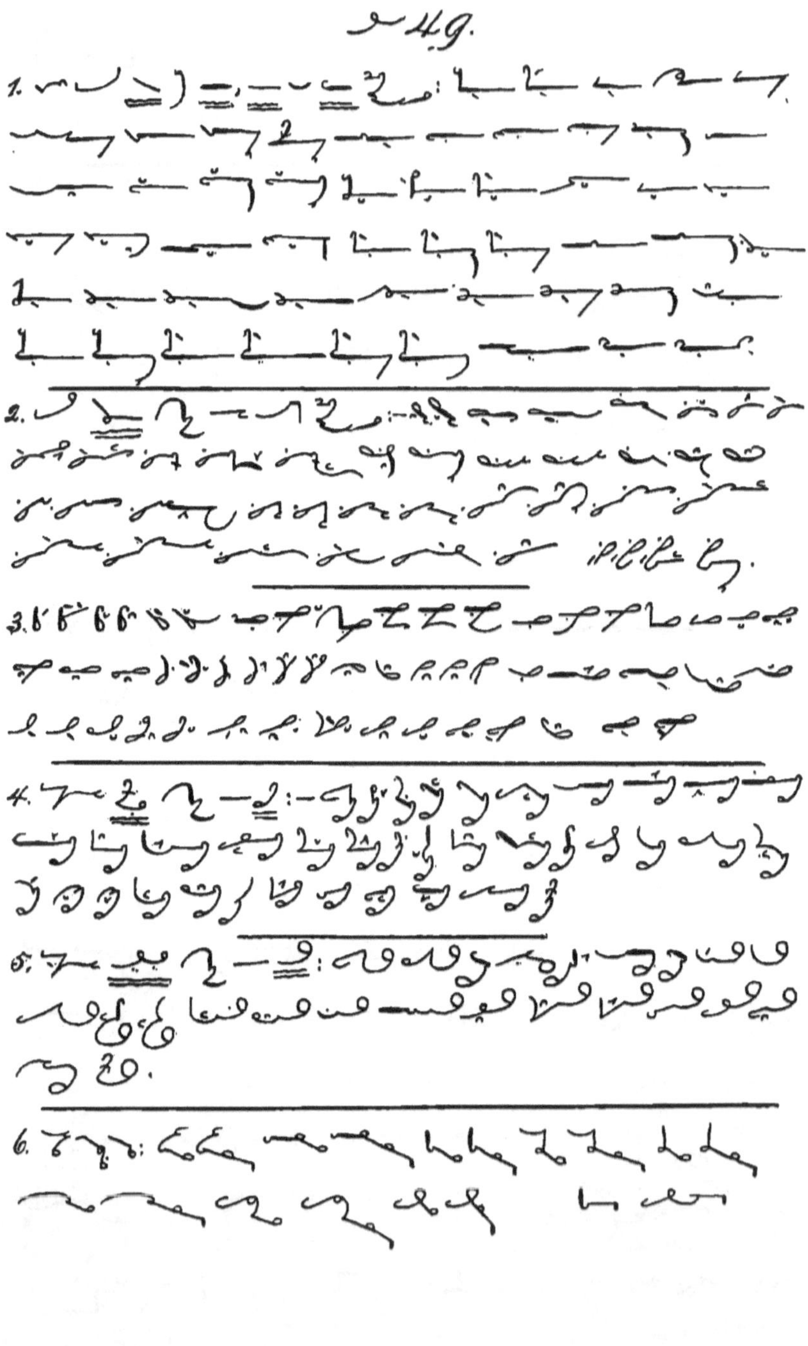

 49.

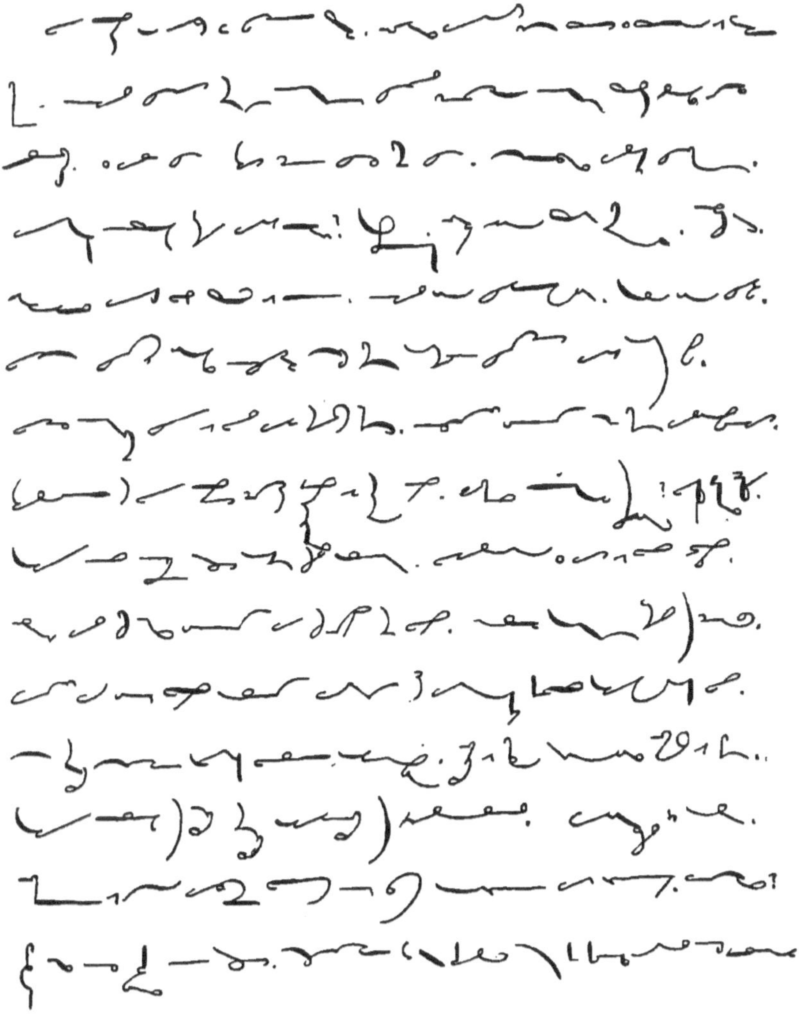

50

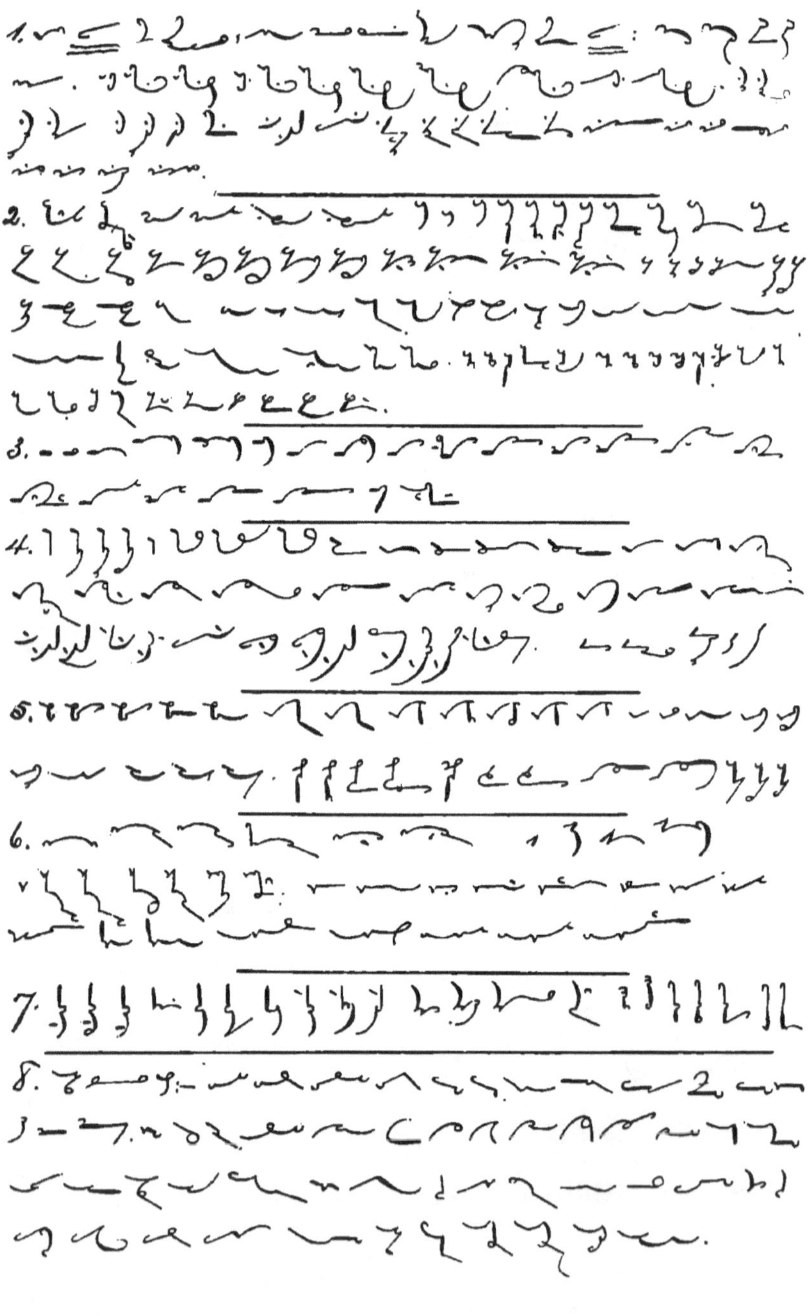

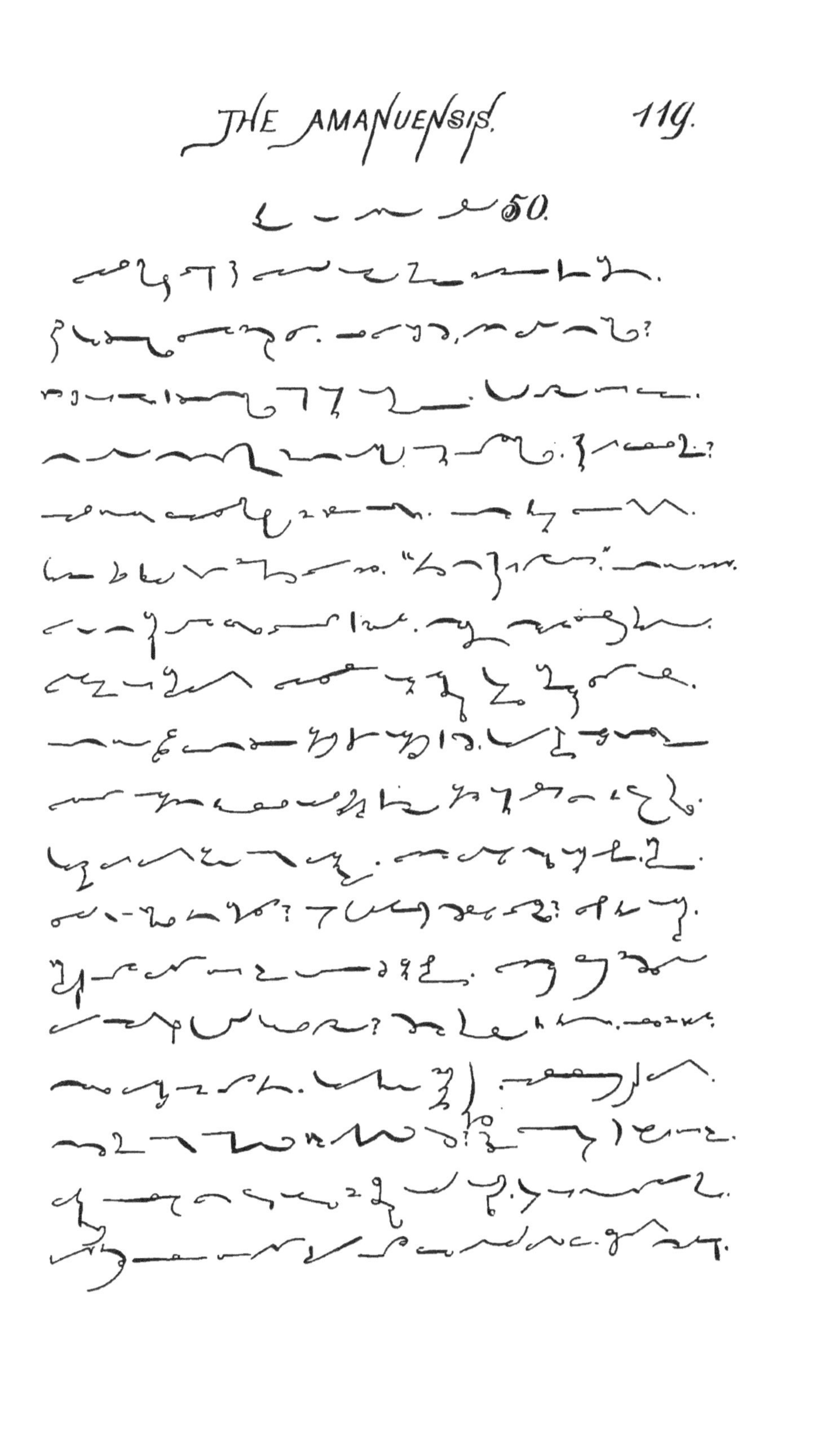

50.

51.

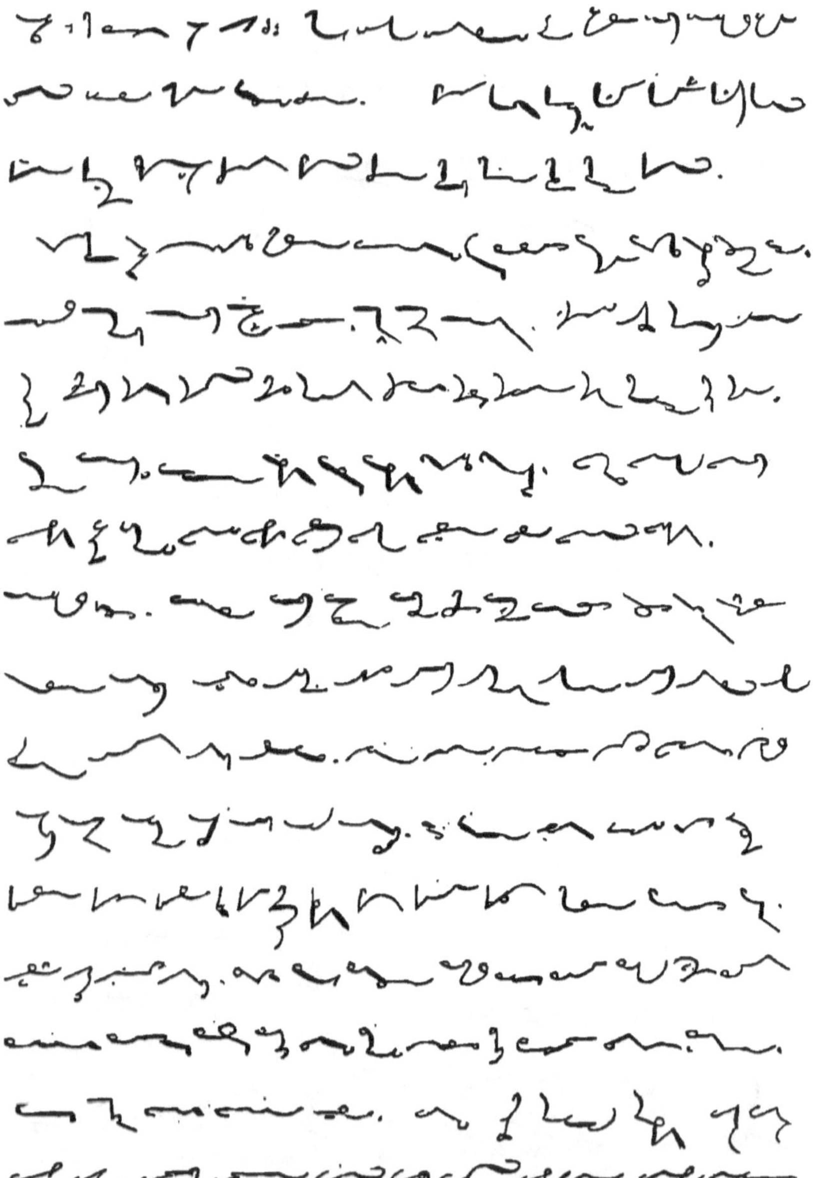

 51.

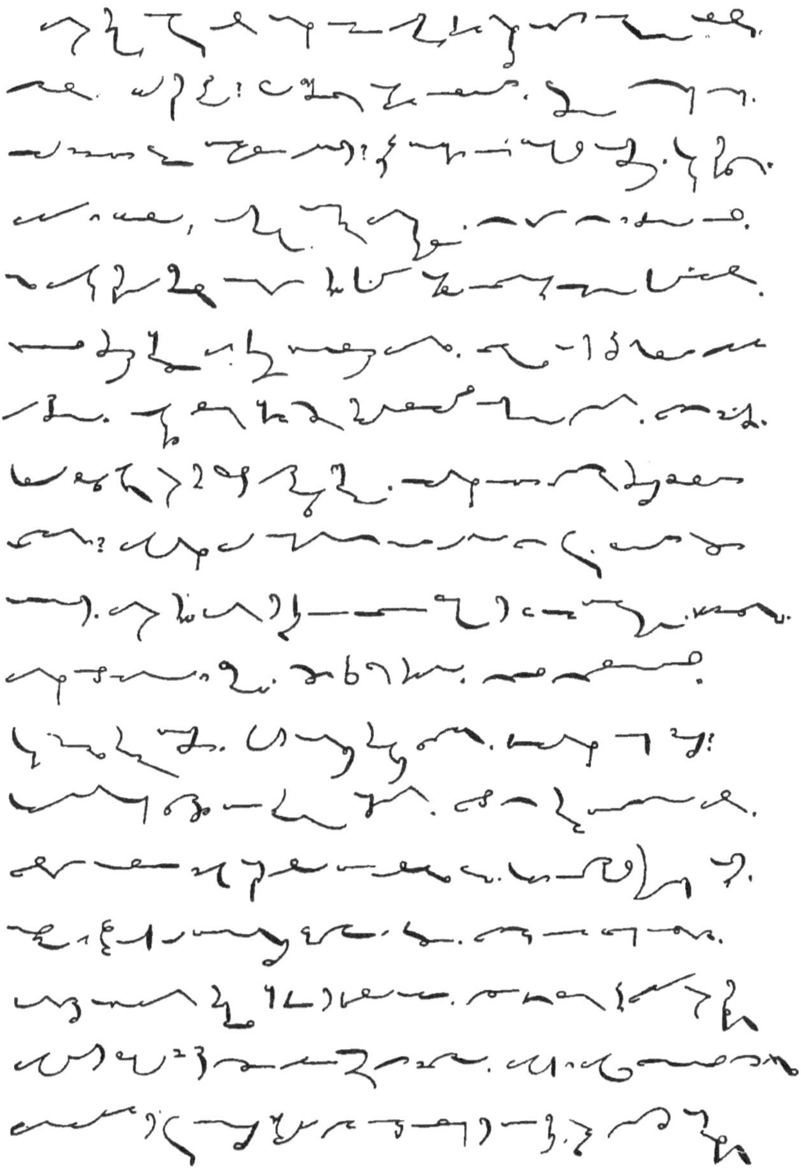

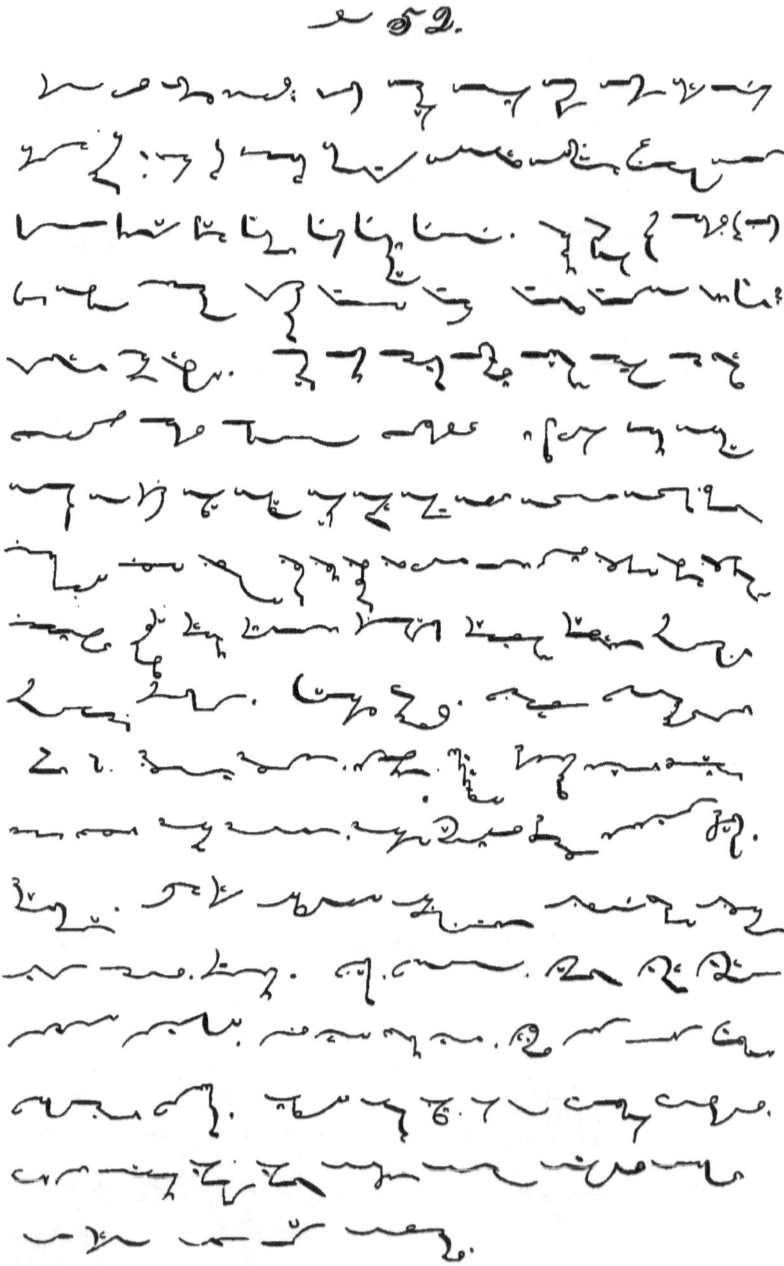

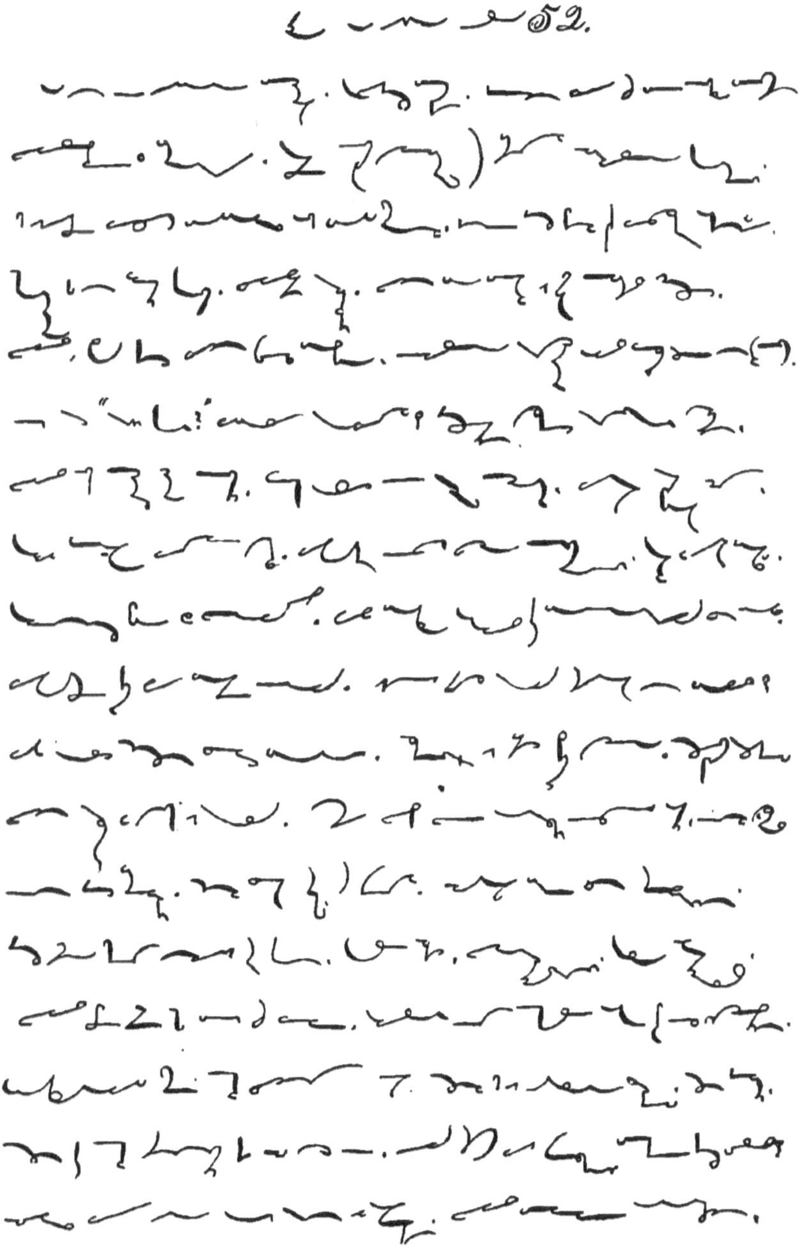

53.

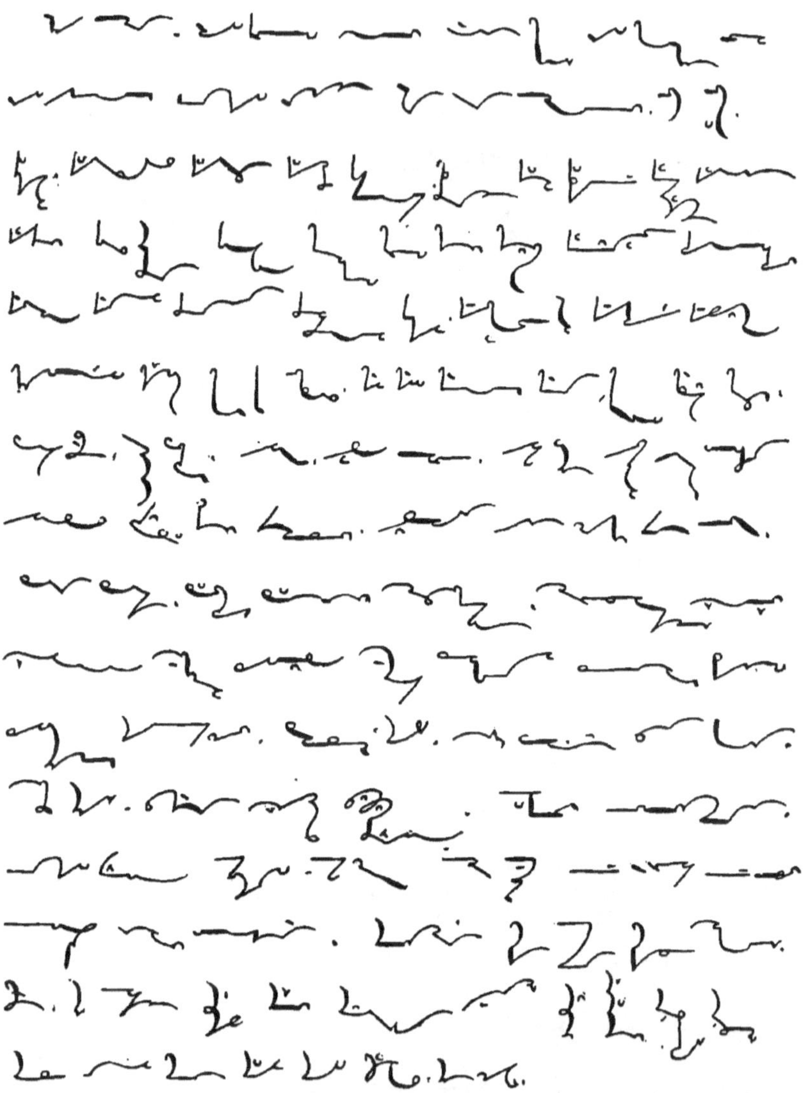

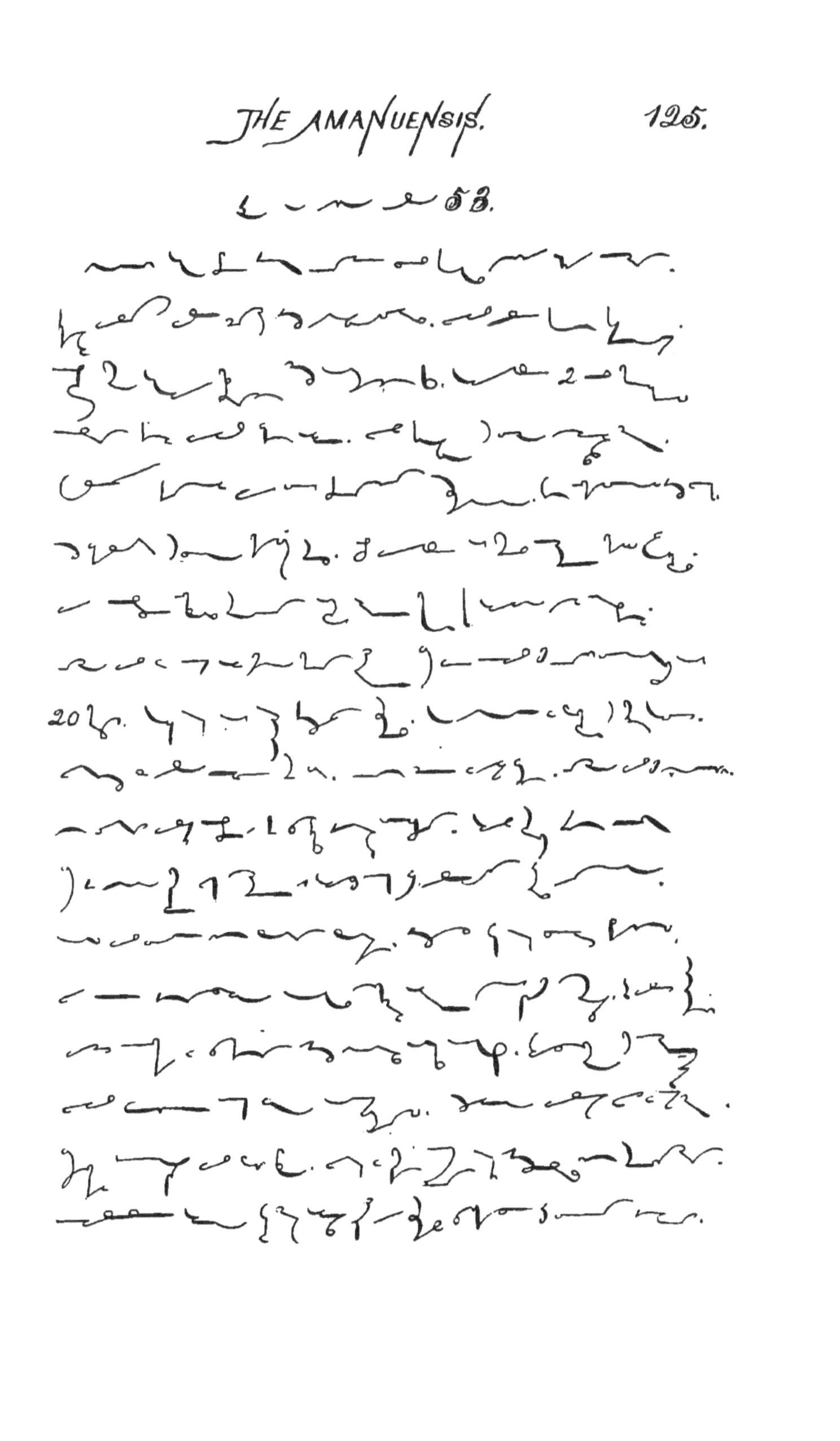

53.

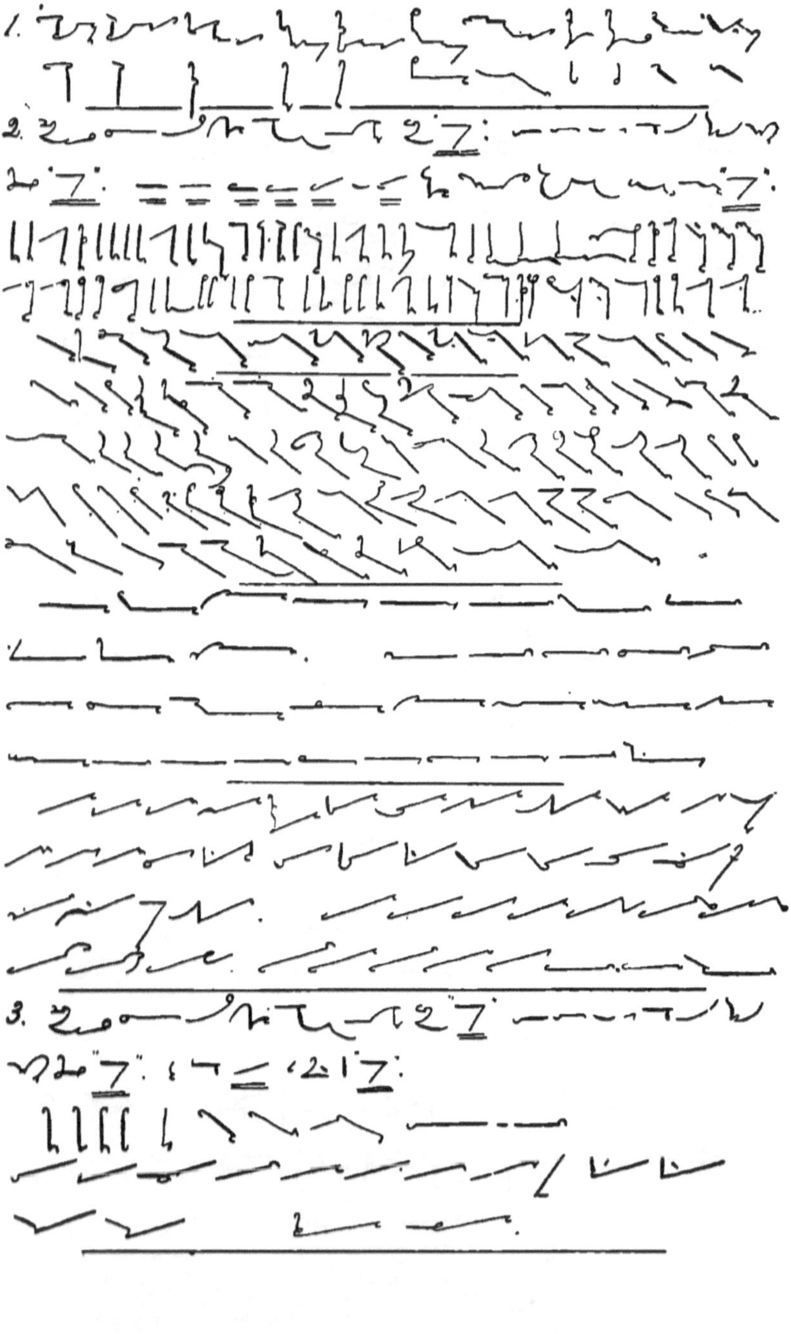
1.
2.
3.

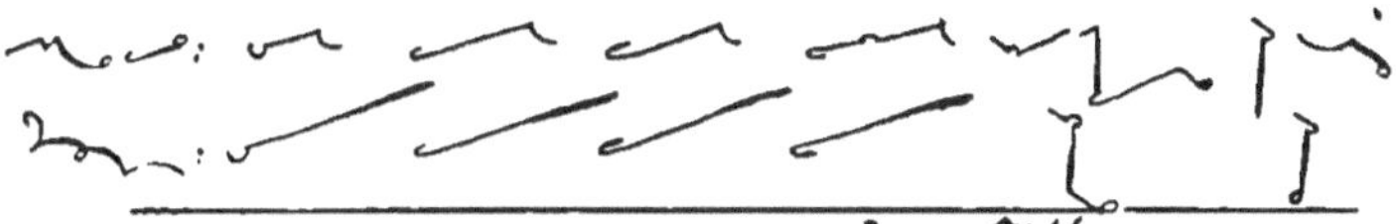

54.

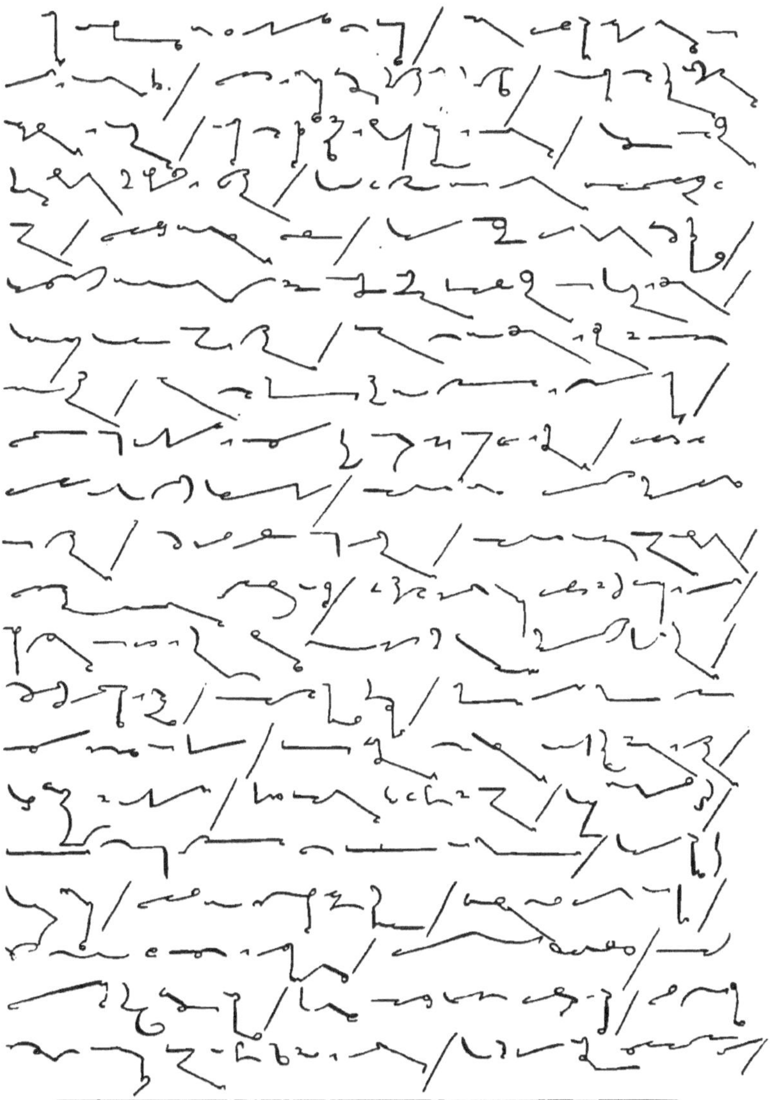

BOOKS AND SUPLIES.

Alfabet Charts, 36 x 44, large clear print, to hang on the wall for use in teaching classes, and as an aid in teaching fonetic analysis in Public and Private Scools.. $0.50

The Manual of Fonetic Analysis—givs a seris of lesns in detail for teaching the Elements of the Language from the Alfabet Chart, and in conection with that chart is the most thoro, eficient and satisfactory means of giving instruction in this important branch of study. Both Chart and Manual will be sent free of charge to teachers of private or public scools who will ask for and promise to use them in their scool-rooms. To others the price is.......................... .25

The Nutshell, a 32-page pamflet, briefly illustrating the principles of the Simple Style. Just the thing to get to examin the construction of the system. Paper.......... .10

The Manual. A profusely illustrated text-book of the Simple Style, explains the principles fuly and givs exhaustiv drils for practice. This is the only book needed from which to lern the Simple Style, which is the style adapted to general use in place of the ordinary longhand. 128 pages. Board bound, $1.00. Cloth...... 1.25

A Short Course in Business Shorthand—Mr. Lindsley's latest work teaching a moderately contracted style for Amanuensis and note taking purposes. Employs the new vowels. 96 pages. Cloth........ 1.25

The Handbook. An elaborate text-book of the Reporting Style, baset upon the old method of teaching by corection of exercises. The Simple Style must be lernd from THE MANUAL before taking up this book. 170 pages. Cloth, gilt title.... 2.00

The Amanuensis. This book embodis the most succesful method of teaching yet devised, by means of carefuly aranged and graded reading, dictation and riting lesns, which contain the corectly engraved forms for about 15,000 of the most comon words and frases from which to lern the Contracted Style for Amanuensis and Reporting purposes, together wi'h ample directions for their use. The instruction starts with the Alfabet and teaches a style suficiently brief and rapid for all ordinary amanuensis or reporting work. It contains very litl theory, rules, explanation, etc., but teaches thru the faculty of *imitation.* Students uzing this book will need no other, unless it is THE KEY, and can rely upon saving by its use fuly haf the time and labor required by the old method. 128 pages of solid work. Descriptiv circular and sample lesns sent on request.... 2.50

Key to The Amanuensis and Student's Drill Book, is a reproduction in comon type of all the shorthand part of THE AMANUENSIS, conveniently aranged for reference. It contains a chapter on the best methods of private study, especialy desined to aid those who must lern in that way. THE AMANUENSIS and KEY form the most complete self-instructor in shorthand evr isued. The admirably aranged and graded dictation lesns in this book ar "just the thing" for practice drils for students or riters of any and all systems as wel as for dictation typeriter practice. Cloth, with gilt side title........................ 1.50

Humphrey's Manual of Type-writing, contains over 180 pages of instruction and exercises for type-riter practice, including comercial, law, and legislativ frazes, tecnical terms, chapters on speling, punctuation and use of capital letrs, a large number of bisnes letrs, statements, law forms, specifications, theatrical work, etc. The most comprehensiv and valuable work on the subject we hav seen. Cloth, gilt side title.................................. 1.50

The Shorthand Writer, a Monthly Educational Jurnal devoted to the advocacy of speling reform, and of the linear, conectiv vowel, facil and rapid Educational and Bisnes Shorthand, Takigrafy, for general and profesional use. It is printed partly in comon type and partly in Takigrafy, in which is now being publisht in the Simple Style a seris of interesting skeches from favorit authors; and in the Contracted Style a colection of actual bisnes letrs, clasified under their apropriate heds, afording to Amanuenses valuabl practice in both reading and riting. It is as indespensibl to riters of Takigrafy as ar the jurnals devoted to Law, Medicin, Theology, etc., to those who folo those profesions. To keep up with the best thot and practice in Shorthand, you must subscribe for and read it. Single Nos. 20 cts. Per year (ten numbers)........................ 1.00

Suggestions in Punctuation and Capitalization .... .25

Pencils– Underwood's "Stenografic," per doz. by mail postage paid.............. .75

Notebooks For pencil, 200 pages, Manila covers. Price, purchaser paying postage (8 cents each) or expres charges, 10 cts. each; per doz........................ 1.00

Writing Machines ar not kept in stock but to acomodate those out of the city I wil aid them in the selection and purchase of such machine as they may want—new or second-hand. Say what kind and style you want and I wil giv you quotations promptly.

Copy Holders—Iron frame with screw adjustments, springs to hold notebook, plated line indicator. By expres only.............................. 2.00

Ribons for Typewriter, $1. Re-inked for. .... .50

Ribons for Caligraf, 75 cts. " " .... .40

Carbon Paper for manifolding. Legal Cap size, 5 cts. per sheet; per dozen sheets.. .50

Kimball's Shorthand and Typewriting Training Scool furnishes superior and thoro instruction by a teacher of many years' practical experience, in the branches taut, who, by reason of original, new, time and labor saving methods can guarantee rapid progres, least time and labor, satisfaction and succes to all admited. For further information, Free Sample Lesns, terms of Free Test Trial to determin probabl succes, etc., call on or adres

D. KIMBALL,
85 E. MADISON ST., CHICAGO, ILL.

www.ingramcontent.com/pod-product-compliance
Lightning Source LLC
Chambersburg PA
CBHW020754020726
47495CB00008B/2432
* 9 7 8 3 3 3 7 4 2 3 4 1 4 *